Strange Animals

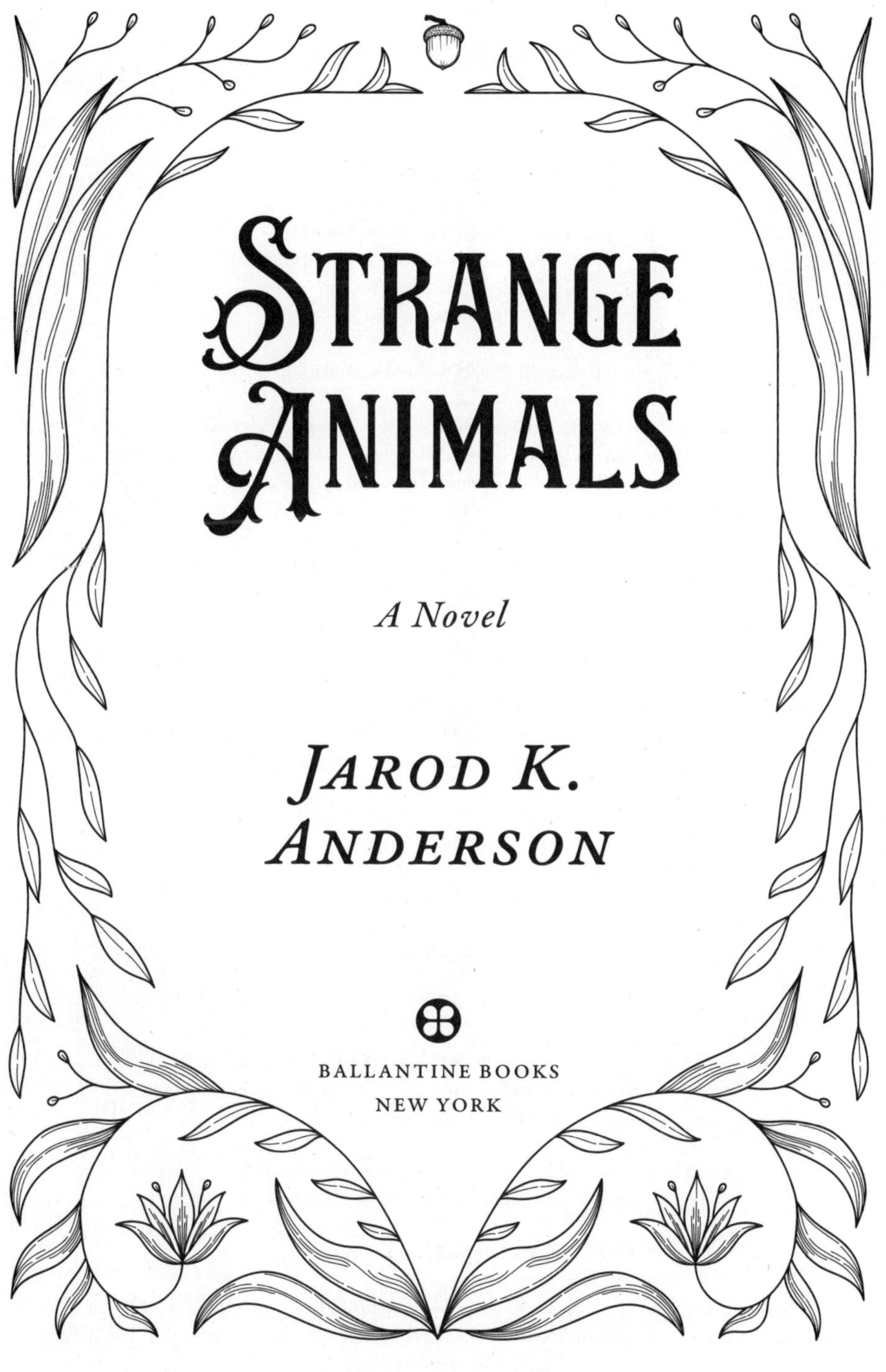

Strange Animals

A Novel

Jarod K. Anderson

BALLANTINE BOOKS
NEW YORK

Ballantine Books
An imprint of Random House
A division of Penguin Random House LLC
1745 Broadway, New York, NY 10019
randomhousebooks.com
penguinrandomhouse.com

Grateful acknowledgment is made to The Charlotte Sheedy Literary Agency as agent for the author for permission to reprint three lines from "The Poet Dreams of the Mountain" from *Swan* by Mary Oliver, copyright © 2010 by Mary Oliver. Used with permission of Bill Reichblum.

Hardcover ISBN 9798217092468
Ebook ISBN 9798217092475

Printed in the United States of America

1st Printing

First Edition

Book Team: Production editor: Christa Guild • Managing editor: Pamela Alders • Production manager: Chanler Harris • Copy editor: Sheryl Rapée-Adams • Proofreaders: Michael Burke, Megha Jain, Nicole Ramirez

Adobe Stock Illustrations: ennona (acorn) • merfin (title page and chapter-opener illustrations)

Book design by Sara Bereta

The authorized representative in the EU for product safety and compliance is Penguin Random House Ireland, Morrison Chambers, 32 Nassau Street, Dublin D02 YH68, Ireland.
https://eu-contact.penguin.ie

For everyone who feels like a strange animal.

Strange Animals

CHAPTER 0

CROW BUSINESS

GREEN DIED AND THEN HE DIDN'T.

He twisted his ankle and toppled off the curb. Pain flashed as his cheekbone hit the blacktop. Twenty feet away, the crushing mass of a city bus rolled toward him.

Cheek on the pavement, he watched the zigzag tread of a bus tire, ten, nine, eight feet off and closing.

Brakes squealed. Too late.

At the office, ad copy for a new psoriasis medication sat half written next to a wilting pothos plant. At home, a shadow box diorama of an old Model T car made from salvaged clock parts sat unfinished next to a sewing box full of tiny gears, springs, and minute hands. He was less than a breath away from the lesson that lives are not finished, they are concluded. That lesson was arriving at thirty-five miles per hour.

The black tire filled his vision. No time to scream.

One final thought.

No, this isn't how it happens.

Then, he was back, standing on the sidewalk as if someone else's life had been roughly spliced atop his own.

It was a crude edit, his death overwritten. The bus roared past, stinging his eyes with grit and a wall of warm, displaced air.

He might have wept or collapsed, but before he could a sound sucker punched him like a thunderclap. It was a caw that sent him stumbling backward, knocking a rolling suitcase from an elderly man's grasp.

Time moved sluggishly.

The man shouldered Green aside and retrieved his luggage, muttering something vicious that Green didn't catch. A bystander with graying dreadlocks looked up from his phone, then back down.

Green saw the crow.

On a nearby No Parking sign, a black bird the size of a golden retriever was croaking and chittering, punctuated by caws loud enough to rattle storefront windows. The sounds kicked over something inside Green's guts. The looming creature paused and looked at him as if waiting for an answer.

No one else stopped. No one else looked at the crow.

A final corvid cry inexplicably sent Green's hand to his pocket.

There was something new there. He pulled it out.

An acorn the color of coffee with cream sat on his open palm. It was a commonplace object that menaced him with its simple presence.

The crow was gone.

His old life was gone with it.

Not finished. Concluded.

Beyond Green's awareness, somewhere in the Catskill Mountains, a peculiar patch of woods and the things that hunted there were waiting for him. Already, the thread-thin roots of a place he had never visited were reaching for his future. New pathways sprouted from the moment like mushrooms after sunset.

In the dark soil at the edge of his perception, dangerous ideas were growing.

CHAPTER 1

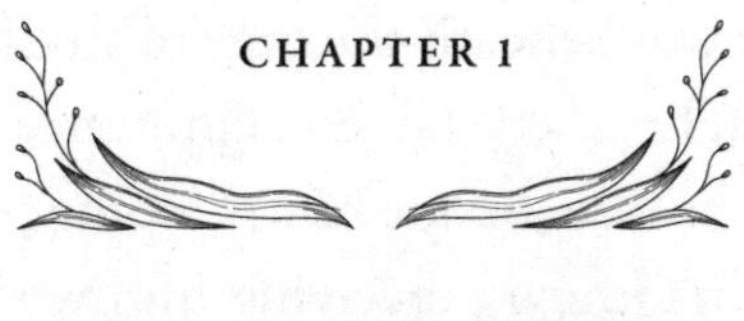

OUT AND AWAY

GREEN STEERED HIS INDIGO TOYOTA PRIUS AROUND another switchback, stitching his way into the mountains. He willed himself to stop clenching his jaw and try to enjoy the beauty of the landscape, raising his thumb to massage a knot of muscle just below his ear. It was no good. Fifty miles ago, the approaching mountainside wilderness looked beautiful. Now, as cell service became spotty and the sun sank low, beauty shifted to threat.

The one comfort of Green's drive into the wilderness was that he could not be lost because he didn't know where he was going.

The acorn rested in his pocket, its figurative weight transferring through his leg to press on the accelerator. That strange little object drove him forward. Only habits and memories drew him back.

His condo in the city was sold.

His resignation was accepted in a neutral, businesslike manner.

His uncle in Columbus didn't object to being his forwarding address while he "shopped around for a new town to call home."

Given the end of his engagement to Jess last year, everyone seemed ready to accept his sudden need for a change of scenery. They didn't ask about his motivations, and he didn't correct their assumptions.

He started his drive a day ago, passing through city, then suburbs, then soy and cornfields, then forested foothills.

The mountains had looked correct from the distance, but here, now, they felt wrong up close. They were pretty as a far-off vista, smothering once he was beneath the cage of tree branches.

The place felt watchful, as if Green's ignorance were a loping thing that raced through the trees beside him, keeping pace with his car. All the things he couldn't know perceiving him with unguessable purpose and senses. Unguessable, but real and alive all the same.

There, just beyond his windshield, the woods drank in radiation from a nearby star and used that energy to create oxygen, to reproduce, to send chemical messages in a language older than humanity, older than the warm blood of mammals.

The trees lived among practically immortal fungi and spiders that remained largely unchanged since before the dinosaurs came and went. The place knew the constant ebb and flow of species and wonders for which it needed no spoken names.

He knew none of this, but it surrounded him anyway. It tickled the back of his neck until he checked the rearview mirror again and again. That inescapable pressure of the woods defied his social-media-hiking-boot-ad understanding of nature. This wasn't a bright portrait of inviting mountainsides or families canoeing crystalline lakes dappled with autumn leaves. This was a dark corridor of trees that leaned down to scowl at you. This was a winding little road through perpetual twilight where help was always too far away to arrive in time to matter.

In the narrow line of sky above the road, he could see the dark silhouettes of three turkey vultures tracing a wheel in the hazy blue as they descended to find their roosts. He swallowed, thinking of coming to *this* place to rest, then realizing he was on the same errand.

Earlier that morning, waking in his car, stiff in a litter-strewn parking lot, avoiding busier roads had seemed a pleasant plan. Now, his plan soured as the sun sank low in the west and the once-distinct tree shadows swelled into a unified darkness.

He poked the console to silence the podcast that was dying a slow death, starved for cell service. As real dark arrived, the sound seemed like a liability. He should be listening, alert to . . . what? He imagined the click of a key in a lock, the final time he stepped away from his condo less than forty-eight hours earlier. A sound like a lit fuse.

In the month following his not-quite-death, he had become preoccupied with moss. And ferns. And a certain mental image of a low fire in the twilight, the way the sparks floated up toward black branches stark against a painter's sunset. Each morning, he awoke to the feeling that he had just stepped away from that fire and the smell of it clung to his pillow.

As the weeks had passed, a growing part of him remained in that forested elsewhere, with the moss and the ferns and the sparks. To Green, these things became symbols. Talismans. Magic that quieted the constant, silent demands of the absurd acorn that rarely left his pocket.

That acorn was, somehow, his salvation. It was also killing him. Not grinding him into the roadway like a speeding bus, but sending the essential machinery of his inner life off into an unknown wilderness until he felt as hollow and brittle as a cicada shell, a cast-off molt scraping along a city sidewalk. It had driven him here to the mountains to try to become whole again.

He'd thought it would be easy to find a campground when he reached the Catskills. He'd also thought he would find it before dark. His predictions began failing more frequently the farther he got from the city.

Up the road, electric lights striped the pavement with branching shadows.

Green let out a breath.

Civilization.

His headlights illuminated a weather-faded sign with pink block letters reading THE COUNT AND COUNTESS. Beyond, a squat pink storefront stood behind a row of three gas pumps. The station was an outlandish pink-on-pink oasis amid the dark woods.

He pulled into the lot and took in the ambiance of the place, the ten-dollar firewood bundles and chicken wire cages of stacked propane tanks, the analog gas pumps, the running-mascara rust stains on the pink rain canopy supports, and the way the darkness was absolute just beyond the humming halo of the station's lights.

"*Pay inside first*" was written in Sharpie on a "Hello, my name is . . ." tag stuck on the pump.

The lot was abandoned except for a pickup with a plywood tailgate. It had a bumper sticker with no text and a drawing of a vivid yellow banana. He checked his phone. Eight P.M. on a Tuesday in September. No service.

As he walked past his back window, he glanced at the camping equipment piled on the seat. The gear was all new, tags gleaming white. It smelled of rubber and the chemical tang of nylon and preservatives. He had only the most basic knowledge of how any of the equipment was used, but he also had a kind of stubborn, tight-smiled optimism that he would figure it all out in due time.

The gas station storefront looked like an unfinished mosaic built from moths instead of tiles. Green watched the fluttering shapes and thought, *My first glimpse of wildlife outside the city.* He tapped his thumb against the acorn.

"Happy now?" he asked the lump in his pocket.

It didn't answer.

Most of the moths were motionless, but occasionally one would blur in a flurry of wings and skitter in a vertical circle before coming to rest again. Leaning in to study them, he couldn't believe the variety. Shades from ashy gray to violet with a pattern of heavy-lidded human eyes staring back from the papery wings. Several of the moths had perfectly round mirrored spheres for heads, like droplets of shining mercury. Others gave off heat distortion like the mirages that sway above the surface of summer highways.

Green swallowed and stepped back.

He forced a smile as he turned and reached for the door.

"Nature," he said to nobody. "Real nature."

He entered with a sleigh bell jingle, colliding with a warm, damp wall of hot dog–scented air. There were other smells. Dirt. Popcorn. Artificial pine. Motor oil.

Two teenagers beneath a sign that advertised LOTTERY AND LIVE BAIT turned to look at him. One was working the register and the other, a tall young man wearing a banana-yellow hoodie, seemed to be there just to keep the other company.

"Evening," the Banana said. "Need something?"

His friend behind the register gave Green a deadpan stare while his hands mechanically shuffled a deck of playing cards.

"Some interesting moths out there," Green said. He winced internally. Somehow, in the twenty-four hours since he had last spoken to a person, he had forgotten the trick of it.

The Banana frowned, looked toward the storefront, then tapped the counter just above a taped-up handwritten sign that read "*Please No Moth Talk Inside The Station.*"

"Oh . . . um . . . sorry."

The Banana shrugged.

"We got a complicated history with entomology here. Plus, ya know, the tax implications. Don't worry about it. You couldn't have known."

"Right. Sorry again."

Green hesitated.

"Alright, man. Do-over. What can we help you with?"

"I need thirty dollars on pump three."

The quiet one tapped his deck on the counter with a sharp *click, click,* and the Banana looked at him.

"Oh, yeah, fine. He wants you to think of a card, man," the Banana said.

"Think of a card?"

"Yeah, just think of one. Got the picture in your head?"

Green nodded.

King of clubs.

The quiet one flipped a two of clubs out of the deck and displayed it.

"That it?" the Banana asked.

"Uh, no," Green said.

The quiet one sighed and went back to shuffling. The Banana patted his shoulder.

"It'll work one of these times. Got to. Law of chance. The universe owes you one."

The Banana leaned toward Green and spoke in confidential tones.

"He really wants to show off other card tricks, but says he can't until he pulls off that one at least once. I don't know why. Do you?"

Green shook his head.

"Yeah. Thought not. The ways of gas station magicians are not for us to understand."

Green laid his cash on the counter and watched as the quiet one switched to a one-handed shuffle, cutting and recutting the deck while working the register.

"Alright, thirty dollars on three. You're golden."

Green faltered, then surrendered to the relief he felt from electric lights and human company.

"Something else, brother?"

"I could use some advice," Green said.

The Banana pressed his lips into a line, then pulled a spiral notebook from his hoodie pocket. He flipped to a blank page like he was about to take notes, but he didn't have a pen.

"Okay, man. Shoot."

Green dipped into his pocket to clutch his acorn.

"Well, I'm looking for a campground."

"Like, the state park? Bro, you're on the wrong road for that."

Green frowned. Why hadn't he gone to the state park?

Because that's a place people go for a visit. I'm not a visitor. I'm something else.

"Not exactly. I want to find somewhere that's a little more long-term. I'm looking to stay awhile."

"Yeah? Maybe you should be visiting a realtor instead of a campground."

"Fair, but I'm not looking to own property. I'm looking for a camp that's friendly to the idea of semi-permanent residents. If there is such a thing."

"Yeah, bro, ain't we all semi-permanent residents?"

The Banana looked out the window. Green followed his gaze, but he could barely see anything beyond the moths he wasn't allowed to mention.

"You gonna live in that car?"

"I've got camping gear. And I'll figure out the rest when I get there."

"Uh-huh. Alright. Respect."

The Banana exchanged an unreadable look with his friend behind the counter.

"We got a brochure rack of attractions and parks. Boy Scout camps and boat rentals. Cabins. That kinda shit."

He shrugged toward a wire carousel rack near an out-of-order ATM.

"But that rack is for tourists. The for-real one is in the back. Go through the door by the beer cooler. We'll hit the button that unlocks it."

The Banana nodded at his silent friend, who paused his card shuffling to pantomime extending his button-pushing finger and sending it through a wide, slow arc until it touched the featureless counter. There was no button.

The Banana said, "Click," then grinned like a fox.

Green suspected he was being mocked, but his nerves told him to swallow his annoyance and play along.

"Thanks. I'll check it out."

He headed to the back, expecting to find nothing. Instead, he spotted the door by the beer cooler. It was only two feet wide and covered with yellow wallpaper depicting looping knotwork and swans with pronounced, angry eyebrows slanting down over black pits for eyes. It was unlocked and Green slid through the narrow opening into a perfectly round room the size of a bathroom stall.

A naked lightbulb hung from the ceiling. He could feel its heat on his scalp. An intense, artificial coconut smell with no visible source filled the space. The brochure rack stood in the center.

Green spun the rack and read the titles.

Ghost Stone: See the Most Haunted Rock on Earth
Harker's Black Bear Sanctuary and Massage Therapy Center
Knife Ridge Tooth Museum
12 Jeffs' Pizza and Ice Cream
Candle-Fly Camp: Choose Your Own Payment
Sara's Garden of Tomorrow
Experimental RV Dealership and Service Center
Honest Cal's Turtle Pond Aquatic Bed and Breakfast
Hike to the Hole in Nothing
Jake Peatmoss: Financial Combat and Unconventional Investments

None of them looked professionally printed.

There were also a few oddities jammed into the rack that weren't brochures. A taxidermized frog on a wooden plaque with a small label reading ASK ME ABOUT SKITTERSHINE SWAMP. A can of black beans with red pen corrections all over the label. A single flip-flop.

The teens were absolutely mocking him.

A cold feeling flooded into Green's stomach. He had imagined the gas station as a doorway back to civilization, a break from the heavy presence of the tree-crowded road. But civilization meant shared cultural reference points. It meant mutually agreed-upon social norms and a familiar context. Whatever this was, it did not feel like civilization.

He noticed his hand was trembling, so he stuffed it in his pocket and focused on taking deep, slow breaths. He took inventory of his goals.

He was here because his old life stopped working for him.

He was here because an inscrutable nut bullied him into being here.

"I'm here because I've lost my mind."

Breathe. Just breathe. Try to rationalize.

Change was always uncomfortable at first.

Change could be frightening.

Familiarity could be cultivated with time and patience.

He couldn't judge his current path until he actually walked it.

Green plucked up the one and only brochure for Candle-Fly Camp. It advertised "real wilderness" and "a quick hike to each and every point of interest relevant to you" and "stay as long as you like" and "pay what you feel you owe."

Well, it makes as much sense as anything else about what I'm doing.

Much of the flyer was handwritten, which deepened Green's uneasy feeling, but the substance of the text matched his needs. There was an address. It was good enough.

The station door jingled and Green heard new voices.

He squeezed out of the brochure room and saw two college kids shopping the snack aisle. A third, a young blond woman wearing a puffy mint green jacket, hefted a bag of ice onto her shoulder and made for the register.

"Grab me some peanut M&M's," Mint Jacket called to the others.

"On it," said a boy in a gray Ohio University hoodie. Green thought he looked twelve and was probably twenty-two.

Standing at the periphery, Green felt a pang of jealousy for the group's confidence and comradery. They were probably on fall break, taking a little camping trip before their next semester started. His fearful wilderness was just a fun trip for a trio of twentysomethings.

They paid and jingled back out the door.

He stepped to the counter and raised the Candle-Fly Camp flyer.

"Thanks for your help. I'll try this one."

The Banana lifted his chin.

"It's nothing, brother. Withholding help in a world like this? That's almost the same as doing evil on purpose, ya feel me?"

Green wasn't sure how to answer.

"Do you think those others are going to Candle-Fly too?"

"Nah, man. Kinkaid Cabins. Cheap, but still a tourist place. Not like where you're going."

Green's core temperature dropped.

"Where I'm going? So . . . what's Candle-Fly like then?"

The Banana smirked.

"Chill. I'm not sending you anyplace I wouldn't want to go myself. It's like you, bro. Different. That's what you were asking me for, right?"

"Maybe."

"Well, you tell Dancer that Alf says 'hey.' "

Alf hooked a thumb at his wordless friend.

"Jerome too."

"Okay. I will. Thanks, Alf."

Alf handed Green a banana from a basket on the counter and then leaned in close.

"It's got potassium. You might need that."

He laughed a genuine laugh. Behind him, Jerome's expression cracked for the first time, shifting to a cringe of embarrassment. He shook his head and gave Green an apologetic shrug, then returned to his mask of indifference.

Green took the fruit and turned to leave.

"Hey, what's your name, bro?" Alf asked.

"It's Green."

"Alright, Green. If you end up staying at Candle-Fly, we're gonna be neighbors. Me and Jerome live down the road in Hickory, but we spend most of our time here. We'll see you around."

He turned to go, then paused.

"Hey, why didn't you ask that last group to pick a card?"

Jerome's eyes smiled a fraction and he gave another ghost of a shrug.

"Life's a mysterious thing, ain't it?" Alf said.

Green managed half a wave as he departed, but already his thoughts were back out in the darkness.

Outside, Green watched the college kids climb into a boxy van and pull out onto the dark road. A gravel-dust specter rose up as they departed and flew away on the breeze. He pumped his gas and tried to keep his eyes off the storefront moths.

The numbers on the pump clicked up to thirty dollars, then stopped.

Movement at eye level drew his gaze to a spiderweb strung between the pump and a support column. A spider that looked very much like a human molar was tracing the outer edge of its web, crawling in slow circles. It made a faint chiming sound as it moved. Green felt a nervous laugh bubbling up. He looked away.

His eyes traveled to his reflection in the driver's side window. A tired man with a five-o'clock shadow. He was a little wild-eyed, but that was fair. He'd slept in his car instead of a bed last night, parked in the yellow glow of a Waffle House by a busy interstate. That was a first. He had spent the last two days driving away from every familiar touchstone in his life.

"I look like I'm unraveling."

He'd seen other things unravel. He knew the look. His ninety-year-old neighbor, Mr. Reynard, who taught him the hobby of making art from old clock parts. His relationship with Jess. The effortless grasp he once held on his own goals and identity. An underpinning of sanity he'd taken for granted.

He thoughtlessly pulled the acorn from his pocket.

There it was, resting on his palm again without his conscious choice to put it there. He studied it. Smooth, polished sides. That rough cap. The way it unnerved him then made him feel ashamed for being intimidated by such an ordinary thing.

He sighed.

The crow might have been a hallucination. Falling in front of the bus, a vivid daydream, a momentary slip of his hold on reality. But neither hallucinations nor temporary madness could put an acorn in your pocket in a place with no oak trees. It was the tangible, enduring anchor for all the strangeness that had pushed aside his old life. He could almost hear it whispering, *You can't pretend me away.*

A tapping sound made Green turn back to the station.

Alf was at the window. He gave Green a thumbs-up and a questioning look. There were words in that look.

You okay, bro?

How long had he been standing there? If possible, the night beyond the station lights seemed even darker than it had a moment earlier.

Green waved at Alf, pocketed the acorn, and climbed into the car.

Nothing to see here. Normal guy. Doing normal guy stuff.

He started the engine and drove to the edge of the lot, just to mitigate the threat of Alf coming out to talk to him. He parked and entered the address for Candle-Fly into the GPS.

"Proceed to the highlighted route," said a reasonable voice from the dashboard.

He hesitated.

Here in the dark woods, his plan to live somewhere wild and remote felt more like self-harm than it had while shopping for camping gear under bright store lights. He brought out the scales of his reason and loaded his current plan on one balance and the life he left behind on the other. The result was the same as it had been for weeks.

Along with fear, the acorn brought a suspicious clarity.

He had been checking off all his "supposed to" boxes for many years and they had brought him neither purpose nor satisfaction. His life had been on the defensive, not so much taking actions to build something he wanted as constantly fending off imagined threats and criticism. Something changed on the day he arrived home, drunk on survival, and sat the acorn on his kitchen counter.

The bizarre yet incontrovertible fact of its presence created a space outside his plans, his reasonable decisions, a space where he could stand and judge his life's path in a new way. All his careful choices still landed him beneath that bus, so how reasonable could they be? Hadn't he been compromising in the name of safety? If safety wasn't really on the table, then . . . what?

Death crowded out all the voices that had been prodding him along. In that quiet aftermath, he listened to a new and perfect internal silence, waiting for the small voice that was his actual desire, divorced from practicality and social expectation. When that voice finally came, soft and distant, raspy with disuse, it spoke of childhood memories of the woods and the wild things that called it home.

Green heard that faint voice, amplified by the acorn, and did the unthinkable. He listened to it.

"Proceed to the highlighted route," the GPS repeated.

This time, he went.

The dark woods rose up around him and the gas station lights were swallowed by a bend in the road.

Don't think. Just drive.

After five minutes of winding up the wooded slope, he noticed that the image of his car on the GPS console screen was now off the road, hovering in the green space to the right. A blocky blue question mark blinked above the vehicle icon. Either the satellite connection was weak or the maps were out of date.

"Turn left on Lost Creek Road," the GPS said.

There was no road.

The thin line near his displaced car on the GPS was called 32, but zooming out on the digital map didn't show any other roads nearby, just an endless expanse of green.

He eased off the gas and looked around, scolding himself.

"What exactly are you going to see?"

The road was the same narrow slash through dark trees, sloping up into another blind curve. He felt his heart begin to pound in his ears. There was nowhere to stop. Nowhere to regroup. Not even a place to turn around.

It hit him how alone he really was. What if he had a tire blowout or hit a deer? Would his phone work? Even if it did, could he describe where he was? Back in the city, there was a constant unspoken safety net of goods and services a button press away.

"It's just a road. It's just a road. Quit overthinking this."

Around the next bend, he saw a pickup truck parked along the narrow berm.

A man with a floppy hat and a red beard was loading fishing tackle into the back. The truck's taillights made his shadow a dark giant on the nearby ruddy tree line. A rod leaned against the tailgate.

Green slowed and lowered his window. He clicked on his hazard lights.

This feels like a great way to get shot.

"Excuse me."

The man stepped toward the Prius and hunched down, his hands on his knees.

"Yeah. What's up?"

"I'm trying to find Candle-Fly Camp? Uh, it's on Lost Creek Road, I think."

"I don't know the camp, but I've seen the road. You're almost there. Around the next bend. Tiny little gravel turnoff to the right. Go slow and you'll see the sign."

"Thank you. I was starting to feel really lost out here."

The man shook his head.

"Not from around here?"

"No. Just arrived."

"Well, bud, you can't get too lost out here. Not on the roads. A lot of these roads are loops. When in doubt, keep going. If you get dumped out in a logging camp or the way turns into somebody's gravel driveway, turn around. Don't run out of gas and don't take the curves too fast. You'll be fine."

"Thanks again."

"Not a problem. Drive safe."

Green drove on and the man, Kyle Cartwright, watched him go.

Kyle had driven an hour to spend the day at an old fishing spot his father showed him thirty years earlier. He didn't reach into holes in the bank to try and coax a catfish bite anymore. He didn't peel up flat stones to catch crayfish in fast-food cups anymore. He couldn't convince his daughter to take a break from the computer and keep her dad company anymore. But he came anyway. The fish weren't biting this trip, but that wasn't the point.

He loaded his rods into the truck bed along with his cooler and camp chair.

Something glinted in the trees.

Kyle stopped to look.

Cellphone camera?

The lost man's headlights had trashed his night vision. He couldn't see anything up the slope. He closed his eyes and listened. Not hikers. Hikers wouldn't be that quiet unless they were standing still just to watch him. That was horseshit. There was nobody out there.

He needed to piss, but his truck cab was suddenly very inviting.

Kyle wrinkled his nose at the idea. Had suburban life softened him so much? He hadn't been afraid of these woods as a nine-year-old. He wasn't going to start today.

He pulled out a compact flashlight, hard and heavy as a roll of quarters. Its beam lit up the woods, dropping a circle of noon into the trees. There was nothing.

Maybe it was a leftover from the stranger's high beams. Maybe it was fox fire. Maybe it was aging eyes.

He pocketed the light and stepped up to a honeysuckle bush, unzipping his fly.

When his chest started to hurt, he assumed it was the fear running its course.

He coughed and it felt like it knocked over some furniture inside his rib cage.

His lungs caught fire and his vision wavered. He spun for his truck. His phone was in the cup holder, where it had been all afternoon. *No phones while fishing.* Calling 911 was a crapshoot out there, but if it was his heart . . .

Gravity did something and the roadside rushed him.

Gravel and twigs pressed against his lips like they wanted in. He turned his cheek and puffed out a plume like white smoke. He wanted to follow that pale vapor up and out, into the warm glow of his brake lights, but something took hold of his thoughts and shook them like a hound with a rabbit.

The world shattered into fractals against a cream-colored backdrop of pain and panic.

The thing that had robbed Kyle's fourteen-year-old daughter of her father was already moving away. It was unchanged, there and gone like a moon shadow blotted out by a passing cloud.

Kyle Cartwright never saw what killed him.

Green would see it. Green would see it before daybreak.

CHAPTER 2

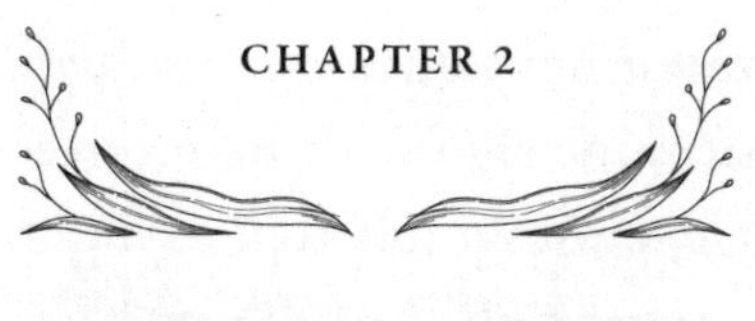

MAKING CAMP

THE ENTRANCE TO CANDLE-FLY CAMP WAS A GRAVEL driveway with a single signpost illuminated by a dim solar-powered landscaping light. There was a bulky black mailbox and a wooden sign the size of a paperback. Dark letters were burned into the wood along with a stylized moth.

CANDLE-FLY CAMP.

A haze of insects orbited the LED glow.

Surrounded by unbroken night in every direction, suspended in a globe of arthropod movement, the camp's logo looked like a magic sigil inscribed by a storybook witch. A warning. Or the kind of invitation that smiles with sharp teeth.

Beyond the sign was an uneven, rutted drive barely wide enough for one car sloping up a steep incline and rounding into utter darkness. The place looked like the private driveway of a hermit, a paranoid hermit who collected shotguns and named them after his favorite B-movie heroines. *"Meet my girl Sonya!"* It did not look like a commercial enterprise.

Green pulled in next to the mailbox and put the car in park. The way ahead didn't look meant for hybrid vehicles with impressive fuel efficiency.

He glanced down at the GPS. It showed his car icon on a blank green space with no roads at all. As far as technology was concerned, he was off the edge of the map.

He poked an interior light on and consulted his brochure. There was a picture of that same sign with its moth logo. It seemed a lot friendlier on the page, photographed in daylight. He swallowed and flicked off the light, turned off the GPS, and coaxed his car into the lightless woods.

Green was used to places where headlights were more about being seen than lighting your way. There was no real night in the city, just an aesthetic shift. This was different. If not for the two blue-white cones of illumination ahead, the darkness was as complete as any deep-sea trench or subterranean lake beneath a hollow hill.

The gravel drive wound up and up. Green cracked his window to see if he could hear any camp sounds, whatever those might be, but instead he found a monochromatic wall of insect chirps that were part of the living darkness. The only human sounds were the purr of his heater and the stony growl of his tires struggling up the drive.

Some automatic instinct of self-preservation kicked in and he threw the car into reverse, craning his neck to look over his shoulder and begin his retreat.

No.

"This is what I came here to do."

Speaking was harder here. The woods didn't like his voice.

A tree branch off to the left fell with a crack like a gunshot and Green flinched.

"This is the plan. This is the plan."

He summoned the will to overrule his reflexive need to escape and put the car back into drive.

Nothing leapt from the trees to clamp jaws around his throat and he forced himself onward through the inhuman din and the alien dark.

Once, Green drove his old neighbor, Mr. Reynard, to an antique shop called Honeywell Treasures forty minutes outside the city. It was a repurposed barn in the middle of farmland. The vast cornfields made him feel alone and exposed. There was something deeply haunted about all those rows of green hissing in the breeze. There were words in that sound. It wasn't a wild space. It wasn't a human space. It was something in between, where the stink of manure and hay dust tapped him on the shoulder and asked, *Are you lost?*

This was so much worse.

He finally reached level ground and saw a double-wide trailer sitting on blocks, tucked back with a couple muddy parking spots carved out in front. There was another lit sign with the stylized moth logo above the word OFFICE. Below the sign, a hunk of obsidian hung on a chain. The volcanic glass was wrapped in rainbow-colored Christmas lights that made the stone's surface shine like an oil slick in the dark.

He didn't have a chance to park. Someone was approaching his window. He shrank away from the movement, felt rude, and wrestled a smile onto his face. As soon as the window hummed down, a large woman with a shapeless hat like a brown paper lunch bag planted her elbows on the car door and leaned in uncomfortably close. He felt the car tilt in her direction.

"Hi, Mack. I'm Dancer. Like the reindeer. I see you admiring my hat. Sad news. It's one of a kind and I don't sell them anymore. Don't ask why."

Green's heart pounded in his throat.

"Fair enough. I'm Green. Looking for a place to camp. For a while."

"Smart you coming to a campground then. Sound plan. I was just joking, by the way. About the hat, I mean. I do sell them."

He did his best not to let his anxiety show on his face. Dancer was very close and so was her hat. She appeared to be in her mid-fifties and smelled faintly of maple syrup.

"So, um, how do I sign up for a campsite? I'm planning to stay awhile."

"Yes, you mentioned that. You want me to build the price of the hat in or do you fancy a separate bit of haggling for that discrete piece of commerce?"

"Maybe just the campsite for now."

"Shrewd. I like it. Well, you pay what you think you owe here. How much would you like to pay up front?"

Green fished in his wallet and pulled out three twenty-dollar bills.

"Would sixty dollars be alright to start?"

"It would sorta violate the premise of you choosing the amount for me to weigh in at this juncture, but I think we can confidently say that I do not feel taken advantage of at this stage in our business dealings. Hell, you've earned yourself a hat. Here, take mine. I warmed it up for you."

Dancer pulled the formless felt thing off her head and deposited it snugly on Green's scalp. It was warm and a little itchy.

"Now then, I expect you wanna meet the patch of dirt that you plan to call home, yes?"

"Yes. If possible, I'd like something next to the woods with a little privacy."

Dancer laughed like a clogged pipe and dramatically scratched her chin while scanning her surroundings.

"You don't say? Yes, we'll see if we can't find something next to the woods. As for privacy, most days you could walk around out here buck naked and have a very good chance of not sullying the eyes of another human being, though frostbite may well exact some form of retribution for your audacity."

Green felt a grin tug up the corner of his lips. Dancer was not what he had expected.

"Great. Should I just park here or . . ."

"Nah, just unlock for me."

She rounded the car and got in the passenger seat. She must have pulled another hat from a pocket, because she was wearing one again by the time she got seated. Green was six feet tall himself, but was certain that Dancer was taller. She filled the car and the glow of the dash lights made her eyes look as black as old coffee.

She thumped the dash affectionately.

"Good car. I like this car. Personable. Drive on."

He did as he was told and followed Dancer's directions down increasingly narrow lanes.

"Turn right at the moss man," she said.

"The what?"

Dancer pointed.

"That big old stump that looks like a man. The one with the moss. You really couldn't pick that up from context clues, fella?"

"I'm new here. I'm not at my best tonight."

"Well, such things may be forgiven in the fullness of time."

Green turned and entered a road so narrow that twigs squealed against his mirrors.

"Just a little love tap from your new neighborhood," Dancer said.

The interlaced branches overhead and the darkness beyond made the way feel very much like a tunnel.

"Is there a place to turn around somewhere in here?" Green asked.

"Sure, with the correct application of motoring skills. You thinking of leaving already? Having second thoughts about your privacy request?"

He was, but he wasn't about to admit it.

"No, I'm just wondering how I'll get my car out again."

He was also wondering how many victims of serial murderers

thought their killers were charming moments before they realized their mistake.

"Don't worry. Your site has a parking spot right off the road here. Easy as a mosquito's lunch."

Green nodded, not terribly satisfied with the answer.

Maybe she'll say something folksy while she orders me to dig my own grave at gunpoint.

"Now, this is your road. You and Valentina are the only ones up this way. 'Course she mostly keeps to herself and her studies or whatnot, so I wouldn't worry about your privacy and all that. We call this Moss Man's Row and I have the utmost faith that you can figure out the etymology of that particular moniker."

"I think so, yes."

"Now, you'll have plenty of space, a fire ring, a tent pad, and if the mood takes you, there is room for a more permanent domicile. Of course, if you plan on any construction of a serious nature, I would ask that you keep me informed. Can't have people building things willy-nilly around here. That's how towns happen and between you, me, and the katydids, I do not have mayoral ambitions."

"Understood."

"Green, I like you. I hope you will not think it too forward of me to consider you an acquaintance."

"Uh, no, that seems like the right word."

"Well, that's alright then. Ope, here we are."

Dancer poked a finger at her window and Green pulled onto a small gravel patch just off the right side of the road. If there were other campsites, he hadn't seen them.

"That path there leads to your place."

She pointed to a gap in the wall of brush a foot from his bumper.

"It opens up. Just fifty feet or so into the trees. Valentina is up another half mile on the left, just before the road ends. Couldn't miss it if you tried. 'Course, I'm not suggesting you bother her this evening, just good policy out here to know where your closest neighbor is, get what I mean? I'm told cell service around here is a coin flip most days. Not that I would care to know."

"Okay, thanks."

Green eyed the dark path leading from the parking spot into the inky tangle ahead. Continuing this adventure meant clicking off the headlights and exiting the car. Taking a flashlight into . . . *that*. Dancer's cheerful confidence was infectious, but she was a stranger and her comfort was fleeting.

"Alrighty, I'll see myself back to the office. If you need anything, Valentina should be your first stop. We look out for neighbors out here. That's how it's gotta be. Stickin' together whether we like it or not is pretty much our only advantage over the other more capable animals of this world, huh?"

"Thank you," Green said. His voice shook. His adrenaline was starting to flow at the simple prospect of being alone in the dark woods.

He didn't want her to go. He fumbled for something to say.

"Oh, Alf and Jerome say hi."

"Them those kids from the gas station?"

"Yeah. I just met them."

"Huh. I'm a little surprised they remembered me out here. Folks will surprise you, won't they?"

Green didn't answer. He was distracted, staring out the windshield at the formidable patch of night meant to be his new home. His fingers crept to the acorn in his pocket.

Dancer smiled and clapped a hand on his shoulder.

"You'll settle in. The most dangerous thing in the world is people and there are blessedly few of them around here. All the other things in these woods will mostly just be curious about you. Can't much fault them for that. Well, have a good night. Welcome. I'll expect your next payment when you deem the time to be appropriate. I'll let you know when we're having our next camp community meal. Come see me anytime, but I gotta warn you up front . . ."

Dancer paused for emphasis and Green's eyes widened.

Serial killer. Serial killer. Serial killer.

"One hat per customer."

With that, Dancer hopped out of the car, quick as a cat, and was swallowed up by the darkness. He imagined he would hear her footsteps trudging back down the road. He imagined wrong.

CHAPTER 3

MONSTERS IN THE WOODS

He gathered the courage to step out of his car soon after Dancer left and he stood in the dark trying to acclimate himself to his new surroundings.

A memory surfaced.

Years ago, while working a temp job at a call center, Green had a supervisor named Dylan who said he had been in the U.S. Navy SEALs. Dylan was a thoughtful, quiet type. One day, on a lunch break, Dylan broke the customary silence and told a story of his time in the Navy. He had been called on to do dive work at night, removing communications cables. It wasn't far from shore, but still the kind of deep that meant you couldn't ascend too quickly without inviting decompression sickness. While working, slicing wiring, Dylan had cut himself badly.

"I nearly lost my thumb to that cut," he said. "Thankfully, surgeons saved it."

He showed off the puckered scar at the base of his thumb. It looked like a wad of chewed bubble gum.

"And that wasn't the worst part of it," he said. "There I was. Deep underwater. Pitch-black. Trying to hold pressure on the cut. Shit, trying to hold my thumb on for all I knew. I was bleeding out into the open water. And I had to take my time surfacing. Wouldn't do me much good to rush up and die of the bends. And, all the while, I could just imagine how far my blood was traveling into the water, billowing out into the blackness. I could imagine what might be smelling my blood, tasting it, tasting me. How far would the blood travel before I surfaced? It was a breadcrumb trail leading straight to me, wounded, helpless, and blind. An easy meal. What was nearby? What was hungry? Most of all, if something did come for me, I knew I wouldn't even see it before I felt its teeth. Sure, I knew there were sharks. Even a small shark can take you apart. I also had absolute faith that there were things worse than sharks. Things that have never been photographed, never described by science. And I knew, just knew, that they were looking at me. I can't explain it, but they were there, watching me. Things I couldn't comprehend were deciding if I would ever make it back up to the open air. And their decision, their risk-to-reward analysis, was gonna be based on stranger things than just hunger."

At the time, Green just thought Dylan was pulling his leg. He only half believed the man was in the SEALs. After that conversation, Green started taking his lunch break in his car.

Now, he wasn't so sure.

He stood in the cold air, holding his flashlight in both hands, looking at the little footpath that led to his campsite.

Just fifty feet that way.

A puff of breeze tumbled the dry leaves at his feet.

Something that might have been an owl called in the distance.

He licked his lips and got back in the car.

Tomorrow. I'll set up camp tomorrow.

He wasn't going to learn the ins and outs of his new camping equipment in the middle of lightless woods surrounded by unknown creatures with unknown business. It was reasonable to sleep in his car. Perfectly reasonable.

Dylan smirked from the past and took a bite of his vending machine sandwich.

Green rested a hand on the steering wheel. He thought about hard metal doors and nice predictable locks. He thought about engineers and safety tests. Stamped metal and molded plastics, all built by human tech with human purposes. His car was a tiny embassy of the known world amid the nations of wild things.

He reclined his seat, hoping to rest his body while staying alert.

Dylan spoke as he chewed. "Keep pressure on that wound."

Sleep crept into the car unobserved.

He sat with Mr. Reynard in his hospice room.

Jess hadn't wanted him to go. She called his visits to the old man *morbid*. He went anyway.

His past was unraveling at the edges.

Green's little card table by Mr. Reynard's bed held a clockwork picture of a moth with a perfectly spherical head shining like a mirror, a work in progress.

His elderly neighbor looked at him through a haze of pain and medication.

"Do you think you'll ever get back together with that fiancée of yours? Jess?"

It was a strange question. They were still together.

"No, I don't think so."

He was answering with the future's voice. The speed of his answer startled him.

Mr. Reynard coughed and took five slow breaths to recover.

"Why not?"

Green thought about it.

"You know, I don't think she actually liked me very much. She would talk about me like I was work, like a second job."

He waited out another rasping cough and recovery.

"Honestly, I once caught myself daydreaming about her just . . . disappearing. Moving out while I was at the office. Even having a car accident. Just, I don't know, going away without me having to make any hard choices or be the bad guy. Not my proudest moment."

Mr. Reynard watched him from the bed with wet eyes the color of old paper. His white stubble was becoming a snowy thicket in the hollows of his sunken cheeks. Green wasn't sure if he was actually listening. He went on speaking with a future self's voice.

"Kinda pathetic. I know. I was just so tired of selling her on the idea of me."

Mr. Reynard looked at the ceiling and Green thought his mind had left the conversation and drifted elsewhere. That was fine. He just wanted to be near his friend.

"You're right," Mr. Reynard said. "Good for you. Marriage is hard, but it was never hard to love my Andi. Even when I was furious with her. A good partner makes you feel strong. Better to be alone than with someone who treats you like a chore."

He shut his eyes. Green watched his pulse flutter beneath the thin skin at his temple.

"You deserve better," he said in a whisper.

When he looked back at his art project, the moth was gone. The new picture had long copper minute-hand teeth.

Green woke shivering and started up the engine to run the heater, aware it wasn't the first time he'd woken to do so.

2:55 A.M.

He looked at himself in the rearview. In the dashboard glow, he felt conspicuous and vulnerable. Folded in the absolute dark of those woods, he was a solitary light, a beckoning glimmer in the permanent midnight of the ocean floor, bleeding out a shining summons into the dark, calling to unseen fish of unknowable size and appetites.

This time, he would keep watch until dawn. He could sleep when the sun was up. He could set up his tent and start camping the way it was meant to be.

Sleep returned.

He was back in his condo.

Jess was gone. Mr. Reynard was gone too.

The acorn sat on his kitchen counter.

The days began ticking away faster and faster. The sun leapt and fell outside his windows in time with his breathing. Day. Night. Day. Night.

The acorn grew more and more vibrant as the colors of his home dulled and faded to a photograph in an old newspaper. It was absorbing the vitality of the place, becoming more real as the life Green spent his best years building withered.

How can such a small thing take so much?

The acorn shuddered once and began beating like a heart, filling the room with a pounding rhythm.

Lub-dub. Lub-dub. Lub-dub.

Day-night. Day-night. Day-night.

The condo walls flitted away like ash. Crickets chirped. Old trees stretched their branches and cracked their knuckles like fighters preparing to brawl. Mushrooms split his tiled floor with their passing, soft and unstoppable.

He started awake. This time, the car was too warm. He was sweating. He'd fallen asleep again before turning off the engine. He ran a dry tongue over chapped lips.

Sipping warm, flat soda, he cracked the window. The air was cool and smelled like autumn. It smelled utterly unlike the city.

3:32 A.M.

The night wore on in fits of sleep and fear.

Green bobbed up and down in rolling tides of contrasting sensation, exhaustion, and tense alertness, until that, too, became familiar. He slept in twenty-minute chunks chained together by moments of confusion as he struggled to remember where he was and why he was cold and uncomfortable.

He walked through a dream of grocery shopping, the store shelves packed with items he didn't recognize, but he felt immense pressure to buy.

One of these things is the thing that's been missing.

One of these things will fix me.

One of these things will tell me who I am in a way I can finally trust.

Something tugged him back to wakefulness.

He was shivering again.

A press of a button and the engine was warming.

4:59 A.M.

Nearly dawn.

A light moved in the trees beside the lane. Green looked up to see a luminescent figure stitching its way through the woods forty feet from his window. It was a deer, though it didn't look like any deer he had ever seen. Its skin was translucent and shone with a pale glow akin to bioluminescent fungi. Within, its dark organs were visible as shapes pulsing with rhythmic life. It looked like an anatomy illustration escaped from the pages of a zoology text.

The deer paused and looked at Green, stepping toward him. Its dark eyes found his. There was something inexplicable inside its head. It was too distant to see, but he could feel it. A shape.

The creature took another step closer.

Green's breath fogged the glass and the deer became a patch of moonlight through smoke. He raised his sleeve to rub away the crystallizing condensation.

The glow sprang off into the darkness, though its legs weren't participating in the movement.

"Heads up," Dylan said from a memory.

He was starting to reach for the acorn when a nightmare thing the size of a pinball machine slammed onto the hood of the Prius.

The car rocked. The steering wheel sucker punched Green in the face, cracking the bridge of his nose. Phantom lights exploded into his vision with the impact. He struggled for breath as tears blurred the world.

The car swayed with the weight of the animal as it swung its muzzle toward the windshield and the cowering man within.

Metal groaned.

Green let out a choked cry as he fought for air and thought. He tasted blood. Something was on the hood, but he couldn't make sense of it. There was black, oil-smooth motion and a flash of pale rigidity like weathered concrete.

He clutched his nose with one hand and reached to turn on the headlights with the other.

The sudden flood of light dazzled Green, but the creature on the hood didn't react at all.

It was lupine and liquid, like a thick-limbed timber wolf with soft, undulating edges that gleamed wet. It had waves of moving flesh, black and midnight blue in constant, senseless motion. Its inky musculature traveled with viscous grace, but there was never enough of it to fully hide the creature's skeleton.

Here, a glimpse of bleached skull. There, a rib. Two vertebrae. The sharp blade of a scapula. The orchid-white curve of a pelvis.

Green froze, terror pinning him to his seat.

He couldn't scream.

The creature tilted its broad head and the inky flesh retreated fully, leaving a skull with living eyes peering into the dark car. It was a wolf's skull, but too big. A monster from a comic book. Thoughts of wolves died as Green noticed the S-curved horn rising from the canid snout, a weapon of sharp bone.

He locked eyes with the thing. A mental pit opened and he was falling deep beneath the earth. Around him the air pulsed with perfect, shared understanding. He was locked in hateful connection to the intelligence behind the bone-rimmed eyes. There was nowhere to run, not even within his own thoughts.

Yes, I see you cowering there, the eyes said. *No, glass is neither a mystery nor an obstacle to me. We both know this.*

He wanted to look away. He couldn't.

But my business is not with you. Unless . . .

The monster was still, a ten-ton boulder balanced on a pinnacle, a thing of terrible potential energy, a snarling chain saw poised above something soft and breathing.

Leaning in with deliberate slowness, it pressed its horned muzzle through the windshield. The surface whined and shattered. The tempered safety glass divided into a topographical map of cracks and fell away in blunt cuboid chunks. The huge predator's head didn't slow as it moved toward Green.

Black flesh flowed over the skull until an oil slick that was half grizzly and half dire wolf filled his vision.

His arms shot forward, trying to push away from that terrible head. He fought for inches, straining against the steering wheel, trying to force his seat backward. The car horn screamed a sustained note, breaking the unnatural silence left in the thing's wake.

The flesh of the wolf's skull receded again, flowing away like a tide. The digital display lights gave the skull a green undersea glow. Teeth longer than his fingers, teeth that should only exist in a museum display of megafauna hunting megafauna, hung inches from his eyes.

The wolf sniffed deeply. Again and again. Closer and closer, a tide of stygian muscle ebbing and flowing over the skull. The sharp edge of its nasal cavity caught on Green's chin and opened a gash. Blood ran down his throat, soaking his shirt collar.

He was there in the dark water with Dylan, but the hungry thing was no longer hypothetical. It wasn't mercifully "out there."

It was here. It was right here.

All the while, he could still feel that alien understanding speaking directly into his mind. He could hear the thing's thoughts as words, but the words made no sense.

No, you're not a clay-walker. Not changed by the Knothole Man or riddle kissed. Not one of the motherless. Not one of the Duke's people or one of the twilight movers breaking your own laws. But not a man.

A tongue as hard and dark as wet asphalt touched Green's chin, tasting his blood. The creature's breath smelled so strongly of pine it made Green's eyes water.

Frustrating. Unwise to leave it alive? Unwise to simply eat it? No time for this.

Green couldn't answer.

He couldn't think.

An ancient part of his hardware screamed *run* again and again.

The wolf paused. Its mind silent.

With a sound like tearing cardboard, it extracted itself from the destroyed windshield. Glass clinked on the hood like hailstones.

It stared through the ragged hole. The lower half of Green's face was bearded with smeared blood. His death grip on the steering wheel still goaded the horn's ceaseless scream.

Black flesh rippled, ears sprouting up like mushrooms, and the wolf cocked its head.

My prey is gaining distance. There will be other nights for whatever you are. We will meet again, not-man. Be silent.

Green's hands fell to his sides and the horn died.

The wolf's spine rose into view like a sea serpent and sank again beneath the rolling darkness. It raised its nose skyward, sniffing the air, then leapt off in the direction of the glowing deer. The car rocked so hard two of its tires left the ground.

The creature was gone, lost from sight three feet from the vehicle.

There was no sound of snapping twigs or shifting leaf litter.

The Prius was still.

A moment later, the few insects still braving the late night's chill returned to their song. One of their final performances as real autumn cold came to the mountains. They were so much louder with a shattered windshield.

The cool air flooded in.

Green jabbed a shaking finger at the door locks. They were already locked.

He was trembling.

A laugh-sob bubbled out of him and he snapped his teeth shut to end it, fearing if he didn't he might never stop.

He rubbed his face and his hand came away sticky with blood from his battered nose and cut chin. Fishing out a wad of fast-food napkins from the console to stanch the bleeding, he pressed the radio button and found a weak, staticky version of Merle Haggard's "Mama Tried" whispering from the speakers, distant as the ice age.

The singing felt like a threat, so he turned off the ignition to stop all sound.

How long had he blasted the car horn? It struck him that no one had come to investigate and, with a confidence as certain as gravity, he knew no one would come.

He brushed pebbles of safety glass off his lap.

I'll just drive away. I'll make it back to a town. Any town. A hospital. Rent an apartment. Drop the acorn down a storm drain.

In his mind, he was already reaching for the ignition.

He was backing out of his campsite.

He was moving down that ridiculous woven tunnel of a road, a blood cell in a dark capillary.

Gravel crunched. Headlights cut down the dark.

Dancer loomed up, watching him leave with her raven-black eyes.

He was already passing that odd pink gas station.

Alf and Jerome watched him go.

He was back on a real highway, back on his way to a place where people were supposed to be.

Consciousness betrayed him and snuck out the back without warning, leaving him slumped and bleeding with only the dream of escape to protect him in the last hour before light.

CHAPTER 4

FRESH WOUNDS

DAWN WAS STILL A PALE GLOW IN THE EAST WHEN GREEN shivered himself awake.

He had never been so happy to see sunlight.

He pushed the ignition button and curled his whole body around the dash vents, willing the heater to sprint up to temperature.

"Shit. Shit. Shit."

The words felt clumsy.

He brought fingers to his mouth, worried what he might find.

His lips felt intact. There was a bloody napkin stuck to his face. He peeled it away with a Velcro tearing sound.

The birds were so loud. Too loud. Movie-pterodactyl loud. Had birds always been so loud at dawn?

He stayed huddled close to the dash for five full minutes. His bladder screamed at him. There was a dull fire burning in his face. His hands and feet ached with cold.

He blew his nose and gagged at the brown and red globs on the napkin.

He coughed and spit and worked to clear his airways, praying he didn't start the bleeding again.

A hundred things screamed for his attention, but he just wanted to be warm. Warmth meant some control over his environment.

He shivered and rocked and cupped hands over his frozen ears, feeling the air from his broken windshield duking it out with the heater for control of the space.

Dancer's voice startled a gasp from him.

"Yikes. On. Bikes," she said.

Green looked up to see the woman, perfectly framed by the hole in his windshield. She was carrying a huge red plaid thermos and staring with unmasked shock.

"Green! You alive in there?"

He couldn't bring himself to chat through the shattered glass. He nodded. His nose throbbed with the motion. He took a deep breath and steeled himself as he pushed open the door.

"Green? Talk to me, bud."

His body felt terrible, like a hangover on a cellular level. The bridge of his nose pulsed with electric shocks in time with his heartbeat. A little avalanche of glass rolled off his clothes and tinkled on the gravel as he stood. He needed to pee so badly that standing was a kick in the gut.

He winced.

"Morning, Dancer."

Any chance you're more of a morning-type serial killer?

He tried to sound composed, but the words felt insane.

"Good morning, Dancer? Are you funnin' me? What's good about your morning? You look like crime scene photos come to life. You're shivering like a Chihuahua. Your face is honestly disturbing and it looks like you sailed your car into an eighteenth-century naval battle."

"Yeah," Green said.

"Yeah? What did this? Don't tell me a black bear did . . . this."

Green shook his head.

A wave of nausea hit him and he slumped against the car until it passed.

She leaned forward and made an exasperated *go on* gesture.

"I . . . I'll tell you . . . just. I forgot to ask last night . . . bathrooms?"

Dancer pointed at Green. Then lifted her hands in supplication. Then swatted the air. She turned in a circle. Her face ran through a dozen expressions.

He winced. It was a stupid question.

"Wha? How? You don't actually . . . Green. You can't be this . . . Stitches. You're gonna need stitches and . . . I gotta get somebody to call a squad, don't I? Hell."

She pressed a fist against her temple like she was trying to physically still her thoughts. She shut her eyes tight before speaking again.

"It's the woods. Go relieve yourself over by that big hickory and report back here. Don't do *anything* else."

She looked him over again.

"Good God, you make it hard to know where to begin. Triage. We need triage."

Green did as he was told and if it had been hard for him to pee near strangers in the past, it wasn't that morning.

When he returned, Dancer had opened her thermos and had two steaming cups set out on the hood of the Prius.

"Come here. Let me see you."

She took his head in her hands and turned it left and right.

"Probably a broken nose. Nasty cut on your chin. Superficial, I guess. You got a concussion, Green? Headache? Vision okay?"

Green pulled his head away.

"Ow. No, I don't think it's a concussion."

He had no idea what a concussion felt like.

"Okay, then. Was it a bear? Is there an axe murderer on the loose? Tell me if I need to be checking over my shoulder at least."

"No. Nothing like that. Not exactly."

Green looked hard at Dancer. He didn't know this woman. The acorn in his pocket called for a hand and got it.

"I don't know what it was. I don't think I want to know. And . . . if I try to describe it, I don't know if you'll believe me anyway."

Dancer shook her head.

"Not another one of you."

"What?"

Dancer waved off the question.

"Forget it. Just . . . let's get you rearranged a bit before we do anything else."

She nodded to the hot drinks on the hood.

"Here, fella. You look like your mortal coil is fixin' to shuffle off this moment, so let's bribe it to stick around."

He met her eyes.

She was one of the weirder people he had ever encountered, but he had a bone-deep instinct that he could trust her. Whatever else she might be, whatever threats his imagination could summon, he sensed no guile in her. As odd as she was, Dancer brought a staggering normalcy with her. He was dizzied by the relief of that normalcy and it made his eyes fill with tears.

Dancer noticed.

"Yeah," she said in a softer voice. "Let 'em go. We have those waterworks for a reason."

Green looked away.

She clapped a big hand on his shoulder and squeezed once. Then, to his surprise, she pulled him into a tight hug. There was no resisting.

She released him and slapped him on the back.

"There we go. Morning is here. Your favorite camp owner is here too."

There was a brown smear on the shoulder of Dancer's Carhartt coat from his wounded face.

"I got blood on your coat."

"It'll wipe off. Or add character. Whichever. Now, drink your tea. You're safe. You're on your feet and, heck, have you even been to your site yet?"

Green picked up the metal mug. It was almost too hot to hold, which made it just perfect.

Dancer motioned for him to follow and moved down the narrow path from his parking spot.

It wasn't a tunnel through endless brush. It was an archway leading to an open hall with living tree pillars.

The rear of Green's campsite sloped down and away into a river valley. The view was like something out of a fantasy, a painting of idyllic mountain solitude. Not the stone and snow of the Rockies. These were the Appalachian Mountains. The Catskills. Far older than the Rockies. Blunt and thick with trees.

Whereas images of the Rockies made Green think of the barren austerity of lunar landscapes, these were living mountains, a place where the rolling lands were less an obstacle to life and more a showplace for it. Raked seats in an auditorium. A colossal curio cabinet lovingly displaying treasures of flora and fauna.

He realized what he couldn't have known the night before. His campsite was stunning. Dancer had given him a gift wrapped in night.

It was the worst morning of his life and, somehow, it made him feel present and alive within himself in an entirely new way. He felt drunk on contradiction. He was living a nightmare and a dream come true.

Green clutched his steaming mug and looked into the distance. Dancer let him. She sipped her own tea and didn't say a word.

"What kind of tea is this?"

"It's sassafras. Good for a spiteful tummy. Probably won't fix a broken face."

He smiled. It hurt.

"There he is. There's my new acquaintance starting to feel like himself again, based on the fifteen minutes I've known you and wild speculation about your character."

"Last night—" Green began, but Dancer interrupted.

"Hang on, bud. Maslow's hierarchy of needs prompts me to ask where's your GD coat?"

Green looked down at his coat. It was from Macy's. Windproof. Rain resistant. Stylized pine tree logo. He hooked a thumb at the garment.

"Yeah, no. That's a jacket at best. I mean a coat. A real coat. Coat. Noun. An ugly, knobby thing, like a couch you can wear. A windowless dungeon for body heat. The ancient technology that allowed any of us hairless apes to follow our foolish whims and wander away from the caring bosom of our sweet mother Africa. A REAL COAT."

"This is what I have."

Dancer frowned and walked back to the car. He followed. She looked in the windows, then she started opening doors and pawing through Green's gear.

She commented on each item as she took inventory.

"No. Wrong. Weird. Wrong again. Weird some more. Good for a different season. Good for a different part of the world. Cute, but wrong. Weird again. Don't know what this is. Survivalist BS. Expensive and wrong."

She emerged long enough to throw Green the hat she had given him the night before. He had abandoned it on the passenger seat.

"Cover your head."

Green caught the hat. He'd forgotten about it. He put it on and felt instantly warmer and idiotic. Why hadn't he thought to sleep in it?

Dancer grumbled and returned to her investigation. She shouted from the back seat.

"Fella, there's a new sleeping bag back here. Why is it unopened?"

She reemerged and gave Green a level look. She pulled off her own matching hat and ran a hand through short salt-and-pepper hair.

"I figured you were from a city. Was I wrong to assume it was a city on this planet?"

He raised his palms in surrender.

"Green, I don't want you to leave. I just met you, but you're making me feel like it would be a literal crime to let you stay here. One of the real crimes too. Like manslaughter. Look at you. It's gotta be illegal just talking to somebody who looks like you. I'm an accessory to something right now."

"I can get the right equipment. I have money. I just need . . . advice."

He was floundering.

"Remind me. Did you declare that you were here for camping lessons? Camping 101? No, scratch that, not just camping. Camping in the path of oncoming winter in the Appalachian Mountains. More of a 201 or 301 sorta course, wouldn't you say?"

Green shook his head.

Dancer frowned.

"You know the term 'emotional labor,' Green? You understand that it's more than a little inconsiderate to go someplace semi-dangerous, requiring specialized knowledge, and just sorta expect that it will all work out. Who exactly do you expect to make it all work out? My mama used to say, 'Be mindful of the work you leave for others.' Are you following my train of thought here?"

"I get it. I'm sorry. Just coming here frightened me so much, I guess I was too focused on getting here, you know? That was the big problem to solve. And I really assumed . . . I don't know . . . I could get away with a few simple nights without knowing much."

Dancer's expression softened.

"Well, most times you might have been correct. Pal, if you were so afraid, why *did* you come out here?"

"That's hard to explain. I'm still trying to put that together myself."

"I guess a morning like this will help you figure it out. One way or another."

She snorted. Retrieved her tea. Took a sip and drummed a fingernail against the cup.

"Okay. That's enough scolding the injured, shivering newcomer. Man, but you are a horror. That face should come with a content warning."

She opened the back door again and pulled out a roll of paper towels.

"Here. Dip a corner in your tea. Do me a kindness and get some of that gore off your face before I'm forever changed."

He did. Using his cellphone camera as a mirror, he mopped at the blood. The no-service indicator winked at him as he worked. His chin ached and it hurt to touch anywhere near his nose, but the heat felt wholesome.

Dancer appraised his work.

"Still terrible and also much better. You got two black eyes ripening nicely. You're gonna be a raccoon for a fortnight."

"Thank you. And sorry again."

"Well, being the 'apologizing when wrong' type might get you some points back on the scoreboard. And I guess I own the place, so maybe I share a bit of the blame. Now. I have had the stoic patience of the patron saint of bedrock, but if you don't tell me more of that story you doubt I'll believe, I am going to catch fire."

Green looked Dancer in the eye, then took stock of what he had to lose by telling the full truth. He decided the answer was very little. So, he told her all of it.

"So?" he asked when he finished. "Do I sound crazy? Glowing deer and monster wolves. Do you know about that wolf thing? Will it come back?"

Dancer pursed her lips.

Green held his breath.

"Bud, I have no idea what you saw and I honestly can't guess."

He let his breath go and closed his eyes.

"But you live out here. You *live* here. You've never seen something like that? Even heard about it?" he asked.

"Happily, no. Not exactly."

"You think I made them up?"

Dancer chuckled and kicked at a chunk of broken windshield.

"No. No, not at all. I'm sure such things exist. I've heard weirder stuff than that from more established sources than you. Like you said, I live here. As I understand it, some people see things like that pretty regularly, I'm just not one of those people. Knock on wood, I never will be."

Green gestured at his car.

"That wasn't done by my imagination."

"You're misunderstanding me, fella. I'm not being patronizing here. I mean it. I believe creatures like what you described exist. I believe you. It's just that such things are a part of some people's worlds and not a part of others'. You get me?"

"No. Not really."

She hooked her hands into her coat collar and looked up into the branches.

"I'm not the right person to explain this," she said.

"Well, who is?"

Dancer smirked.

"Funny you should ask that. The best expert I know on such things is your very own neighbor."

"Valerie?"

"It's Valentina. Valentina Blackwood. A'yup."

"That's quite a name."

"Heh. A'yup again."

"So? What? I should tell her about the monsters?"

Dancer wobbled her head in a way that meant *Yes, you could do that, but . . .*

"Is there something else I should do first?"

"Green, let's return to the lesson of being mindful of the work you leave for others. Most people out here have some healthy boundaries. I'm one of them. Incidentally, Valentina is another. I need you to assure me of a few things."

"I'll try."

Dancer nodded.

"If you decide to stay, I'm concerned with simple, everyday things of a less scintillating nature than demon dogs and incandescent critters. Mundane things like you starving or freezing to death or dying of infection or dehydration. Now, this day, like most, is gonna come and go. It's probably gonna go pretty quickly from your rattled standpoint. You aren't planning to leave those problems for me to solve, right?"

"Right."

"Make me believe it, Green. I'm trying to determine if I'm talking to a man who made an honest mistake and has been generously corrected by his most patient new acquaintance *or* if I've just found an unaccompanied toddler wandering on a highway and a moral obligation to take control of the situation is settling heavily on my shoulders."

"No, I've got this. I'll fix this or I'll leave and regroup. Honestly, I'm not sure what's best yet, but I won't make it your problem."

Green looked toward the valley and the mountains beyond.

The acorn in his pocket seemed to have its own opinion.

You couldn't leave this. Not now. Not after you finally made it here.

The thought made his fists clench.

Yes, I absolutely can leave this. I'm not giving that monster another chance to decide if I should live.

Dancer watched the debate dance across Green's face and raised an eyebrow.

"Alright, bud. Well. Stop in the office when you decide what you're doing."

"Yeah. Thanks. I will."

She sighed.

"I hesitate to tell ya this, but if you do head out this morning, you might pass some police. A man died a little ways down the mountain last night. Right on the side of 32."

Green felt his pulse quicken.

"What? How? The wolf?"

She shook her head.

"No, no. It's a tragedy, no question, but I heard they think it was heart failure. Just died next to his pickup on the roadside. His family sent the police looking for him when he didn't come home. I heard it on the scanner while I was eating my cornflakes."

"Truck on the roadside? I think I met that man. I asked him for directions here."

Dancer frowned.

"Lotta pickups around here, but I guess it's possible. Look, just go talk to her before you make other plans today. Alright? Normally, I wouldn't suggest such a thing, especially with Val, but this feels like an unusual circumstance. Tell her I sent you."

Dancer looked Green up and down.

"Tell her I sent you before you say anything else."

She poked her chin toward his campsite.

"And I wouldn't waste that view of the morning if I were you. It's medicinal."

She retrieved her thermos and turned to leave.

"Hey, you want your cup back?"

"Bring it to me later," she said over her shoulder.

Her brown coat and broad shoulders made her look like a refrigerator box striding away into the trees.

He walked back to his empty camp and turned his eyes to the dawn coloring the mountains across the valley. The part of him that treasured the acorn in his pocket, that believed magic was waiting for him in nature, cherished that view. Yet, that part had been conspicuously quiet hours earlier when a nightmare arrived to tear out his throat.

"It's pretty here. And I am absolutely not going to stay another night."

CHAPTER 5

JOB INTERVIEW

GREEN WALKED TO VALENTINA'S CAMP FEELING THE LACK of cell service like a pebble in his shoe. He wanted a map. He wanted a distraction. He wanted to search for Valentina Blackwood on social media and find pictures of her playing with her basset hounds or holding up a chunky knitting project. All the while, Dancer's reminder that the day would pass quickly felt like a burning fuse racing toward another deadly night.

He kept touching his pockets to make sure that his phone, his keys, his wallet were all there, then remembering that none of those objects meant much in the way of utility or safety on his current errand. He imagined that giant ink stain of a wolf bursting out of the trees. Which relic of his old life would he reach for to save him? His Global Fitness card? His weather app?

Yes, in lieu of devouring me, would you accept this Starbucks loyalty program card? That's correct, Starbucks is my ally and if you harm me there will be hazelnut-flavored reprisals.

Only a day earlier he had been interested in actively courting the unknown.

It's easy to be on good terms with the unknown when it keeps its distance. Explorers in a history book. A probe visiting a far-off world. That tingle when we think about the deepest parts of the ocean or the unpeopled forests of the far past. It's different, much different, when the unknown becomes a prominent part of your daily life, there on your pillow, stirred into your morning coffee.

Dancer was right. One mercy about Valentina's place was that you really couldn't miss it.

Her site was littered with half a dozen sheds, two old campers, a small log cabin, and an honest-to-god tree house the size of a small apartment. A lopsided spiderweb of black wires and orange extension cords hung about the place, stitching together the mismatched structures. Tidy rows of solar panels protruded above several of the roofs. There were no vehicles in sight. A ribbon of white smoke rose from the cabin and hung in a haze.

Even with all its eccentricities, Green's first thought upon seeing the place was that it looked like a real home, something lived-in, especially in comparison to his own camp, which looked like a crashed car abandoned in the woods. An unexpected sorrow welled up. He felt the acute lack of such a place in his own life. Maybe ever. White couches and rooms he wasn't allowed to track mud into. A condo he hired someone else to decorate. He stood on the narrow road unsure of what to do next. There was no obvious front door. No doorbell. No signs.

"Hello?"

No answer.

"Valentina?"

A door latch clicked, and Valentina emerged from the log cabin. She was a small woman, precise, dressed practically in mostly gray. Her silver hair was pulled back and the two turquoise studs in her ears stood out like twin patches of sky glimpsed through a cloud bank. She stood just outside the cabin and studied Green.

"Yes?"

"Good morning. I'm Green. I'm your new neighbor. Sort of."

"Ah. Hello."

"Oh, um, Dancer sent me."

"Yes, I noticed your hat. Good to meet you, Mr. Green."

She spoke with an accent that Green couldn't quite place. Part Eastern European. Part something else.

She turned to reenter her cabin.

"Hang on a minute."

She looked over her shoulder.

"Yes?"

Green suddenly couldn't remember what a normal person did with their arms while talking, so he glued them to his sides.

"I was hoping we could talk. I mean, I need to speak with you."

"Mr. Green, I have time-sensitive work this morning. Not a good time for social calls. Pleasure to meet you."

She began to turn away again.

"It's just that Dancer thought you could help me. I was attacked by a thing and she said you were an expert on the subject of . . . things."

"A thing?"

"A giant wolf with a horn and not enough skin. Last night. Just down the road."

He hated the words he was saying.

She paused.

"Well. Business then. That is different. Come in if you can."

She reentered her cabin, leaving the door slightly ajar.

Green frowned at the place she'd been standing, then followed.

He pushed open the door and stumbled over the high log sill to enter.

The interior was warm and smelled like earth, smoke, and burnt coffee.

The floor was packed dirt. One wall was all wire shelves filled with storage containers of every description. A broad hearth dominated the rear wall, smoldering with dying embers.

A cast iron stove flickered in the corner and a caged lightbulb hung low over a wide wooden table.

On the table a moth the size of a bathrobe was splayed out for study beneath a huge gooseneck magnifying glass. Valentina stooped over the moth, apparently returning to the work Green had interrupted.

The massive insect was a tattered thing. It was obviously dead. At first glance, it looked like a model made from burlap and old cardboard. But it wasn't. It couldn't be. A closer look confirmed it.

The folded legs were too perfect for it to be a fake. The byzantine pattern of hairs on the abdomen. The dull inner light of the faceted eyes. The broad antennae like drought-parched ferns. It couldn't be real, but it was.

It was real and, like the wolf and the deer, it was impossible.

"Do you study . . . monsters?" Green said.

Valentina repositioned her magnifying glass. She didn't look up.

"That is a child's word. Too simple and too subjective to be useful."

Green felt his cheeks grow warm. It surprised him. For the second time that morning, he had walked into the role of scolded student. He was getting tired of it.

Sure, he had been more concerned with ad copy and SEO in the past few years, but he had a master's degree in literature. Maybe he didn't know anything about camping or wildlife, but he could talk about words. This wasn't like Dancer criticizing his camping ignorance. He decided to hold on to this one area where he could claim expertise.

"Monster seems like an appropriate idiomatic term in this instance."

She still didn't look up.

"Mr. Green, idioms are useful insofar as they transmit meaning within the communities that share them. Yes? Tell me what 'monster' means in this instance."

He had a sudden sinking feeling that he had just picked a fight above his weight class. Again. It was too late. He had to try.

"Strange or frightening creatures of unknown origin. Like . . . this moth."

Valentina spared Green a strange look.

"So, it is a subjective qualifier. Strange to you. Frightening to you. Akin to 'cute.' Or 'favorite.' "

Valentina continued to scrutinize some structure on the moth's wing.

"Might it be fair to suggest, within the context of biological study and taxonomy, that categorizing organisms by purely subjective terms such as 'cute' or 'favorite' or 'monstrous' is overly broad? Even childish?"

Green swallowed.

"Yeah. I suppose that's fair."

Valentina nodded the tiniest of nods.

She pulled two long, red glass chopsticks from a pouch and used them to pluck a feathery scale from the moth's wing and deposit it in a glass vial. She held it up to the light and the scrap of fluff sprouted black legs that wriggled before the object righted itself and began crawling up the glass.

"What is that thing?"

Valentina cocked her head and held up the vial.

"You can see this?"

"Yes, and it looks like it's going to escape."

She put a stopper in the vial just before the crawling thing reached the top and rose to deposit it on a shelf beside a dozen identical vials.

"Parasite. The last of them, I believe."

She took her seat again and met his eyes.

"Are you alright, Mr. Green? You appear injured. Your shirt is soaked with dried blood. You mentioned a wolf of some kind?"

Something about Valentina's attention felt weighty, like he was being billed by the minute, though the cost and currency were unspecified.

"No. I'm not alright. Something like a wolf attacked me. Only it was huge and it had a horn. And it spoke. But not with words. It was a monster. I mean . . . subjectively."

Valentina's eyes smiled, but it didn't quite reach her lips.

Anger flashed in Green's mind like distant lightning. She wasn't taking him seriously.

"I almost died last night. A man a little way down the road *did* die. Yes, I get why you don't like the word 'monster,' but you weren't there. You didn't see it."

"I heard about the man. Kyle Cartwright was his name."

She looked back at the moth, then at her guest. She appeared to make a decision.

"Come, Mr. Green."

She retrieved two camp chairs and unfolded them near the stove. She gestured for Green to sit. It was too warm so close to the hot iron, but Valentina held her hand toward the heat and closed her eyes, relishing the warmth.

She turned and took a narrow cup from the floor and pulled a long-handled brass vessel from the edge of the stove using a pot holder. She poured a very dark drink into her cup. She didn't offer any to Green.

Noticing his attention, she said, "Coffee, Mr. Green. Turkish style. I'm afraid I only have the one cup. I wasn't prepared to entertain. Please, proceed."

He told her everything he could remember about his first night. Valentina didn't look particularly surprised or sympathetic, but she watched him with the steady focus of a kestrel studying a meadow for movement. When he finished, she looked up at the low roof, as if gazing into the attic of her memory.

"The deer you saw is known. Some call it the glass fawn. Others name it the ghost deer or the fairy deer. Its discovery and place in oral and folk histories is a bit muddled, but your description is consistent with what I recall. The pale light. The transparent body. The half dozen other recorded encounters more or less match yours, I believe. You'll notice the article 'the' in each of the common names. Most assume it to be a singular creature. One of a kind. If memory serves, it has been seen on three continents, but never any simultaneous sightings."

"Six encounters? That's all?"

"Six is a generous record compared to some cryptids, Mr. Green."

"Cryptids? Like . . . bigfoot?"

"Hidden creatures. Often presumed to be myth by laypeople."

"Is it dangerous? The glass deer, I mean."

"Glass fawn. It is a living creature, so I don't doubt it is dangerous in certain contexts, but nothing I recall suggests that you would be a prey animal for it, if that's what you mean."

"Yeah, that's very much what I mean. And the wolf? What's the wolf called? Pretty sure I'm a prey animal for that thing."

"That question is going to be your responsibility, not mine."

Green's fingers defensively searched for the acorn in his pocket.

"What's that supposed to mean?"

Valentina folded her hands together and tucked them under her chin. It made her look like a contemplative praying mantis.

"I am debatably the oldest living cryptonaturalist, not a common topic of discussion. I daresay I am demonstrably the most knowledgeable, a very common topic of discussion. I am willing to say, with a fair degree of confidence, that the lupine creature you described is unknown and undocumented. In my community of inquiry, traditionally, a creature's discoverer gets the honor of naming it. Well, naming it in human languages, you understand."

Green did not understand.

Valentina smiled and the expression was part predatory cat, part evil fairy.

"It is . . . very exciting," she added.

He felt sick. He felt he had made another mistake in entering this woman's cabin, entering her world.

"If you are worried about Latinate naming protocols, set that worry aside. The absolute rarity of the creatures we study allows us to indulge in common naming conventions."

"No, that wasn't the first worry that came to mind."

Valentina sipped from her steaming brass cup, the disquieting glee lingering in her eyes.

Green bent over and pressed palms to his forehead, trying to think of what to do next. His monster remained a monster, whatever semantic games Valentina wanted to play. An image of his campsite menaced his mind like a downed power line. A car with a shattered windshield and a back seat full of inadequate camping gear. Another night racing to meet him. A dead man crumpled on a dark roadside.

A gentle touch on the knee brought Green back to the moment.

"Mr. Green, I will be much more helpful to you if you think aloud."

"I don't know where to start. There are too many problems, and I don't know what I don't know and the main thing I've learned in the last twelve hours is that I am a danger to myself and a potential burden to others."

His throat tightened.

Valentina gave a half shrug.

"If that is the case, it is better to know it than not. Yes?"

"It's just . . . I used to know things."

He barked out a joyless laugh.

"Or, well, I felt like I did. In my old life."

"So? What brought you here?"

"That man died and Dancer said you were an expert in monsters . . . or cryptids . . . and I thought I had to warn someone about the wolf."

"No, Mr. Green, I mean why did you come to these mountains. To this camp? Candle-Fly is not a popular destination."

The acorn had its own gravity, tugging Green off-balance as he considered the question.

"Something happened."

"Mmm. Something often does."

"This felt like a big something. Okay? And I knew, without a doubt, I just needed to get away. To, I don't know, reconnect with nature. It didn't feel like a choice. I just needed to get back to fundamentals. Whatever the hell that means."

"Not unreasonable. Not unheard-of. Rather traditional, actually. Why here?"

Green tried to think. His attention felt jerked in a dozen opposing directions.

"I mean, I did research. I looked at maps, pictures, satellite photos. I read the story of the geography. The Appalachians. The Catskills. This region. The Catskills were in a book I loved as a kid. I don't know. This was just the place. It felt obvious. At least, it did at the time. But everything about the last day and a half has been screaming at me that this was all a mistake."

Valentina set aside her cup.

"To review. Something happened. You felt called to the wilderness and then, specifically, to this area. Upon arriving, you failed utterly at the basics of woodcraft and passed a harrowing night during which you became the seventh person on record to see the glass fawn, and discovered a hitherto undescribed cryptid. In the morning, Dancer encouraged you to call upon your only neighbor, who happens to be one of the foremost cryptonaturalists on the planet."

Green's scalp tingled.

"What? Are you saying that all of this is somehow meant to be?"

Valentina frowned.

"Childish. Broad. Subjective."

Green squeezed his eyes shut and bit back the urge to scream at the odd little woman.

"But," Valentina continued, "I will say that human ways of knowing are not the only ways of knowing. As a species, we are relatively young, but the biological mechanisms that authored us are not young. We do so adore recognizing patterns and measuring out the world, but we typically disdain qualifying the enormity of our ignorance. We were shaped by natural cycles and forces that we do not fully understand. We did not escape those cycles and forces simply by inventing spoken language or algebra or internal combustion. No, we are clever, but we neither grasp nor control the enormity of nature."

Green studied Valentina's face. She was suddenly very talkative and the shift was somehow threatening. A new door had opened in the conversation.

"Modern people. They so love to cast themselves as some sort of alien intelligence on this world, visiting and observing. Arrogant. Absurd. Myopic. As if our very lungs are not a call-and-response with phytoplankton, with the nations of trees and plant life. As if our bones are not an essay written in mineral by the force of Earth's gravity. Visitors. Masters. Fools. What gave you that iron in your blood, visitor? Where was that water which fuels your life a week ago, master? Some humans are as children of devoted parents who enjoy a care so deep and ubiquitous that it has become invisible to them."

There was a threat in Valentina's words, but it wasn't the threat of physical harm or a prophecy of danger. Green had never felt the pull of any religion in his life, but there, in that moment, he thought he knew what that pull must feel like. This person didn't need to be told about the voice of the acorn. She spoke with the same voice.

Valentina's attention seemed far away, then refocused on her listener. Her mind returned to the little cabin, shifting back to the present moment.

"No, things are not meant to be in the way I believe that phrase is commonly used. That is, meant for us because of some special merit or grace we possess. And yet, the idea that human purposes are the only purposes with weight and worth and meaning is manifestly absurd."

"So," Green said tentatively. "What does all of that mean for me? What are you saying?"

Valentina thought a moment.

"I am saying it would be . . . professionally irresponsible of me to allow you to be eaten tonight."

"Okay. Good start. I guess. Honestly, I was planning to be a hundred miles from here before it gets dark. I also don't plan to be eaten."

"Leave? You would abandon your current path entirely due to the mishaps of a single night?"

"Lady, you weren't there. Nearly getting my head bitten off by a thing I could hear inside my head is not just a mishap."

The wolf's voice still echoed in his thoughts.

Not-man.

"Ms. Blackwood will do, thank you. You said you intended to be here. Did you have a goal in mind beyond simply being here?"

"Well, no, not really. I kinda assumed just being here would be enough of a challenge and it turns out I was underestimating."

Valentina retrieved her cup and studied her coffee.

"And how long are, or were, you planning to face the challenge of being here in the mountains?"

"For the foreseeable future."

He answered quickly and instantly distrusted the words. That was the acorn's answer. The acorn he still hadn't mentioned to Valentina. The acorn that had been by his side since his near death. The acorn that he couldn't even define for himself.

"Mr. Green, I find myself in the uncomfortable and presumptuous position of feeling I know what you, a near stranger, should be doing with your time. 'Should' is by its very nature a treacherous and untrustworthy word, but if you are interested, I'll risk overstepping and speak my thoughts plainly."

The offer felt like a trap.

But her bait, the chance to shrink the towering unknown crushing his bones, was too tempting to resist.

"Yes, God, please. At this point, I'll take anything."

"You may want to reserve your judgment on that, but so be it. Come over here."

Valentina stood and returned to the table with the giant moth.

He followed.

"Describe what you see, Mr. Green."

The smell hit him first. It was like burnt dust, that domestic brimstone scent of the first time the furnace kicks on in late autumn. It was old books and mildewed paper. Kitchen scraps and dog breath.

He looked hard at the moth and searched for words.

It was monstrous, but it wasn't threatening. It was still and silent and approachable. And, somehow, to his own surprise, he found the creature oddly beautiful.

"Well, I'm really not well-versed on animal life, but I think it's a moth."

He looked at Valentina for confirmation. Her face was blank.

"Go on, Mr. Green. Describe. Anything at all."

He licked his lips, again feeling Valentina's attention as a weight of vague cost and consequence.

"Uh. It has six legs. I think that means it's an insect. Or bug? I've never understood if those were different things. Um. Each of its wings are in two parts. So, it's like it has four wings in total. There's dust or something creating a haze over its body. I guess that's the trash smell I'm getting."

He leaned in closer.

"The haze seems to be rotating, like a little galaxy. So, that's . . . weird."

"Good. Very good. What else."

"It doesn't make sense, but a lot of it looks man-made. Burlap and twine. This gray part here looks a lot like old newspaper, but none of the writing is real. Just squiggles. And maybe I'm missing it, but I don't see any mouth. That can't be right, can it? It has to eat."

"The adult form of most large moth species does not have mouthparts. Luna moths and atlas moths, to name two examples. That feature is quite common. Anything else?"

Green hesitated.

"I feel like I'm about to be told I'm being childish again, but . . . there's something about looking at this thing that feels . . . I don't know . . . unclean? It's sort of beautiful, but the longer I look at it, the more I need a shower."

Valentina tilted her head.

"Go on. Speak on that," she said.

Green took off Dancer's hat and dabbed the sweat from his forehead with it.

"It's hard to describe. It just kind of feels like seeing it is begging to catch pinkeye or a cold sore. It feels like the idea of rot? Or maybe contamination? I'm sorry. I don't even know why I said that."

More scolding. Incoming.

There it was again. That treacherous delight like a loose floorboard creeping onto Valentina's face. She shook her head, but it wasn't a negative gesture.

"Mr. Green," she said. "You are a cryptonaturalist."

He felt gooseflesh creeping up his forearms.

"I . . . really don't know what that means."

Her expression flattened again.

"Crypto. Prefix meaning hidden. Do I need to define naturalist for you? Cryptonaturalist. One who studies hidden nature."

Green walked away and faced the wall.

He wanted guidance. He found it like a kid who wanted a cigarette and was forced to smoke a whole pack as punishment.

Valentina gave him time.

He forced slow breaths, then returned to the conversation.

"So far, it's more like cryptonature is studying me. Also, it doesn't seem to be hiding very well. I wish it would."

Valentina sniffed.

"I have told you already that in your first night here you discovered a new cryptid, a thing reasonably rare even among established cryptonaturalists, and you spotted a creature that has only been observed six times prior. These things are profoundly hidden. Though, apparently, not to you. Which is the crux of my assertion that you *are* a cryptonaturalist."

"Okay, but how? Why? What is it about me? I'm starting to feel a little . . . cursed."

His new life was coming too fast, speeding toward him as dark and implacable as bus tires. Would it have mattered if he hadn't gone to meet it halfway, if he hadn't driven into the mountains? Perhaps some contrivance would have landed the wolf on his condo doorstep. Perhaps Valentina would have sat down next to him on the subway. The acorn suddenly seemed to have the weight of inevitability on its side.

"Ah. A more complicated question," she said. "Though, I would not say you are cursed."

Valentina tapped the tabletop.

"This moth. This is a rag moth. A monumentally dangerous creature. Obscenely dangerous."

Green took a step away from the table.

"This one is quite dead, which is the only way we safely study them. They have a defense which is like concentrated entropy mixed with localized time dilatation. I suppose that is the sense of rot you perceived. In short, they cause instant, severe decay when startled."

"Are they common? For cryptids, I mean."

"No. Not common. But not in the same class of rarity as the glass fawn."

"How did you find it?"

Valentina opened a manila folder on the table and slid a newspaper clipping toward Green. The headline read "Ancient Mummy Found in New Jersey Storage Facility."

"That's from another specimen found last year. An unfortunate soul opened their rented storage unit and surprised a rag moth sheltering within."

"That's awful."

She nodded.

"With rag moths we look for reports of uncommonly old remains found in incongruously modern settings, then we wait a few weeks and go looking for a dead moth. Like most large moths, they have fairly short lifespans."

Green looked at the creature on the table, imagining it as someone's last sight before an inexplicable death.

"Is there some way to warn people about these things? Or, I don't know, keep them away from humans?"

"We are looking for ways to mitigate their damage, but they aren't conventionally linked to time-space. They are not objectively here. What we sometimes call a subjectomorph. So, their patterns are hard to predict with conventional thinking, but we have strayed from my point."

Green stared at the newspaper clipping and wondered how Valentina would have interpreted his unusual remains if the wolf creature had killed him. He thought of the man loading fishing gear into his truck. He wondered how much of her field was linked to bizarre deaths.

"You said Dancer sent you to me, yes?"

Valentina glanced at the hat wadded in Green's fist.

"Oh, yes."

"Then I do not need to tell you that she isn't exactly a conventional sort of person, and yet, were she to walk in that door and begin speaking with us, she likely would not mention the enormous moth corpse spread across my table. When you entered, I assumed you wouldn't see it."

"But how could that be? That moth is hard to miss."

"Because she simply wouldn't see it, Mr. Green."

He shot a glance at the massive deadly insect remains.

"Okay, but how? Seriously. It's right there?"

Valentina swept her hand in a flourish reminiscent of a stage magician.

"Exactly," she said. "This is why I say you are a cryptonaturalist. It is a vocation, certainly, but it is also an attribute. These creatures are not hiding behind trees or lurking in fogbanks. Such creatures rarely bother with conventional stealth. They are hiding behind mindsets, behind ways of thinking. And yet . . ."

Valentina tapped the edge of the newspaper article.

"Not knowing about such organisms is not the same as being outside their sphere of influence. Much in the way the people who think of themselves as distinct and separate from nature remain utterly dependent on nature for their form, function, and day-to-day survival."

Green paced and gently pinched the bridge of his nose. It felt spongy and swollen.

"I'm having a hard time buying this for the same reason I don't buy conspiracy theories. People just don't keep secrets. Especially not interesting or dangerous secrets. Why isn't all of this stuff very public knowledge? Even if I couldn't show somebody this moth, I could take pictures of it. I could, I don't know, make a plastic mold of it or something."

"There are publicly operating cryptonaturalists and cryptozoologists. They share public theories about cryptids. Yetis. Sasquatch. The Loch Ness Monster. Mothman. The squonk. Some real. Some less so. In your estimation, are these public experts generally well-respected and valued members of mainstream culture?"

He stopped pacing.

"No, they are not."

"And yet, would you say, given your experiences already, that those of us with the aptitude for perceiving such nature should endeavor to make a serious study of the subject in order to better understand our world and, in some cases, mitigate harm?"

Green thought of the man who opened his storage garage in New Jersey and made headlines as mummified remains. He thought of the dried blood speckling his own steering wheel.

"I mean, yeah. Of course. Real is real even without widespread acceptance."

"There you have it, Mr. Green."

Green's fingers slid into his pocket to find the acorn.

"I don't know what to say."

Another frightening smirk.

"Then, let us start here. I am offering you an apprenticeship. A job, of sorts. A time-honored, symbiotic professional arrangement. I could use the help. You could use the training and experience."

Green's first impulse was to buy time to think about it, dodge any immediate answer or commitment. He could think it over in a hotel room with hot showers and a little card listing nearby pizza delivery options.

Yet . . . if he did that . . . he knew he wouldn't come back. And, from there, a series of convenient compromises would lead him by the hand back into the sort of life he had just risked so much to escape.

He prepared to feel the acorn's influence.

Instead, he saw the face of his old friend, Mr. Reynard. He saw the photos of his loves and adventures sitting on his bedside table. The old man winked at him.

You deserve better.

He reached for bravery he felt sure he didn't possess. It answered anyway.

"Could I stay here? For now? As part of the arrangement?"

"I was planning to suggest the same thing."

"Do we . . . I don't know . . . discuss payment?"

Valentina chuckled softly.

"Of course. We discuss it insomuch as you understand that I will not be paying you in currency. Honestly, Mr. Green, do you suppose

American capitalism values our work with creatures that largely cannot be perceived and thus are rarely exploited?"

"I guess not. When would I start?"

"Now."

His mouth felt very dry.

"Okay. I'm in."

Valentina clicked her tongue and spoke to herself.

"Remarkable. I have not had a proper apprentice since the Rodriguez brothers. How very interesting."

He shifted his weight uncomfortably, feeling like a bug in a jar.

"Then, here are my basic terms," she said. "Subject to change and mutual consent."

Valentina laced her fingers together over her stomach, as though she were participating in an old-fashioned spelling bee.

"For the present, you will live here, though this arrangement may change after we get your campsite in working condition. You will work for me approximately eight hours a day doing whatever tasks I deem appropriate. I will make a good faith effort to ensure your safety and sanity in whatever work I assign. You will dedicate at least two hours each evening to supplemental readings and conversations on the subject of cryptonature. This will increase your utility and autonomy as a cryptonaturalist. I have no earthly idea what you would do with a weekend given your circumstances and location, but you may use Saturday and Sunday for unspecified leisure if you don't bother me overmuch or impede my work."

"Alright. That all sounds fair."

He wanted to hug her. He was also certain that, of the two other bodies in the cabin, it would be more appropriate to hug the moth.

"Excellent. You will begin work tonight."

The words *begin work* invited a brand-new anxiety to the party.

"That soon? What will I be doing tonight?"

"Simple observation. An old custom. You'll be holding a wake."

CHAPTER 6

WAKE FOR THE RAG MOTH

THE RAG MOTH'S SMELL WAS A LIVING ANIMAL. IT circled the cabin like a panther. Part old library, part condemned warehouse. It kept Green company as the sunlight disappeared from the cabin's one small window. Holding a wake meant monitoring the moth overnight, being on hand to observe any changes in the corpse.

That afternoon, Valentina had laid out more rules for his apprenticeship:

"You will not open locked doors. You will not enter my living quarters uninvited. You will not fiddle with any equipment you do not understand. You will not visit the roof of the library under *any* circumstances. You will not discuss our work publicly without my prior approval."

He really didn't think any of the prohibitions needed to be said. He wanted to discuss his new job with strangers about as much as he wanted to climb onto the camp's roofs. Not at all.

She sent him to gather his things, making a special point of telling him to leave his car at his campsite.

"I detest cars," she said.

He visited Dancer to return her cup and explain how he had solved his shelter problem for the night.

She thanked him for the cup and was bewildered by the news that he would be staying with Valentina. She had to confirm several times that they were talking about the same woman who lived down Moss Man's Row. Green thought she came close to calling him a liar.

He used an expensive waterproof ground cover as a tarp to shelter his broken windshield, holding it in place with heavy stones and a fallen branch. When he gathered his belongings to take to Valentina's, he found that most of what was relevant fit into his backpack. Clothes. Food. Toiletries and medical supplies. A gravity filter he didn't expect to need. Flashlight. A notebook and a battered old copy of *My Side of the Mountain* he'd bought at a fifth-grade book fair. He meant to reread it in the mountains.

He respected his new teacher's feelings about cars and moved his supplies on foot. With his sleeping bag under one arm and a water jug in the other, it took only one trip. He felt some small vertigo when he compared his possessions in that moment to his possessions six months earlier. Maybe for the first time, he felt no strong pull to mourn the discrepancy.

Valentina gave him a quick tour of her campsite.

Frustratingly quick.

She dismissed the giant tree house with a wave and a word. "Library." It was the same with most of the structures.

"Lab."

"Storage."

"Faraday cage."

"Crawler tunnel access."

She paused after pointing out the tunnel access.

"Keep well away from this one. Like the library roof, it is especially off-limits."

It wasn't much of a job orientation.

His task for the night was straightforward enough. Watch the rag moth. Valentina's reason for the assignment was similarly simple.

"Because I don't know what may happen," she said.

"Might something happen?"

"Always."

"Uh, anything specific come to mind?"

"Yes and no. Rag moth corpses never last. They vanish. A fair number have been studied, perhaps a dozen, but you won't find one preserved under glass or suspended in formaldehyde. No one knows what happens to them. Digital recording does not work. And, as far as I can tell from past accounts, this one is due to disappear at any moment. Thus, my reluctance to be away from the cabin."

"Okay, do you have a theory about how it will vanish?"

"Many, but we have a specimen present, so observation eclipses hypothesis."

"Is there anything, I don't know, particular I'm watching for?"

"Just watch. Mr. Green, I have barely slept since I laid the specimen on that table. I need you to stay vigilant while I recover my energy. Forced to guess, I would say the corpse may spontaneously disintegrate. Perhaps some residual mechanism of the moth's entropy defense will destroy the body. Again, your job is to leave aside prediction and focus on observation."

"What's stopping that residual mechanism from destroying me?"

"Past evidence. One rag moth corpse vanished from a workbench beside an aquarium housing fire-bellied newts. The newts were unharmed."

"Comforting, I guess. What if these corpses are reawakening and just flying off? Maybe it wouldn't be intimidated by newts. What if it just resurrects and mummifies me?"

"Very unlikely. That would have been evident in past disappearances."

"Unlikely? Just unlikely?"

"I shan't tell you it's impossible."

"So, what do I do if it wakes up?"

"You remember a fundamental truth of studying cryptids."

"And what's that?"

"These are animals. Same as you or me. They are not demons or monsters. They are not human-centric punishments or objects of elemental terror. They are nature. So? You tell me. What happens if the moth awakens? What should you do?"

Green felt a jolt of annoyance at her words. She wasn't sitting in the car when the unearthly thing licked the blood from his face. She hadn't spent the last few months being chased out of her life by an inexplicable acorn and a memory with dark feathers and edges too sharp to touch.

He forced himself to set aside his anger and consider her words. What if the moth was like any other animal? The creature had a deadly defense mechanism, but if it didn't need defending...

"I stay still. Inconspicuous."

Valentina smiled.

"Exactly. Respect it as a living thing. Acknowledge its dignity."

"And if the wolf comes back to visit? I don't suppose that cabin door is actually reinforced steel disguised as wood."

"I have more subtle protections here than just doors and locks. In time, I will educate you about them."

He didn't like it, but she wouldn't say more.

After some minorly patronizing answers to Green's questions about operating the stove ("wood plus fire equals heat"), Valentina left Green to his vigil, unaccompanied but for that living, pacing smell and the stone-dead moth laid out like the spilled guts of an overturned trash can.

Alone, Green looked around the cabin that felt strangely like a home despite its disturbing owner and contents. There was something solid and comforting about the place. It was the old coffee cup rings on a wooden chest by the stove. It was the frayed pot holder hanging on a hook. It was the hundred small signs of a life being lived.

Somehow, the warmth, comfort, and stillness of the place magnified the pain of his battered face, as if he had finally found a calm enough moment to really feel it. He couldn't stop fingering his swollen nose or the gash on his chin. Valentina had said that he didn't need stitches, but his whole face ached in rhythm with his pulse.

He stood over the moth and was surprised to find that he was not afraid. This encounter was different. He wasn't in the passive mode. The moth was not happening to him. He was studying it. Not only that, but the moth was not solely *his* phantom with which to contend. It was a part of Valentina's world too. The situation held danger, but it also handed him both agency and connection. It shattered his worries about slipping sanity and hallucinations. It was evidence that his new path might not be characterized only by isolation and constant flight from unknowable dangers.

At first, Green tried to actively watch the moth. He scrutinized a leg. An antenna. The lightless gem of a polyhedral eye. When that became exhausting, he tried to relax his focus and take in the creature as a whole, a brownish something on a brownish table. It was a confusion of textures and shapes. It was a profound mystery fading to background static with time and attention, like bones bleaching in the sun.

He tried to tease out an interesting observation about the swirling aura of motes just above the moth's body, hoping for something that would prove himself a quick study and a worthy apprentice. It was no use. The motes clotted into a tan haze that was nearly invisible and constantly in motion. Two minutes of watching invited a dull ache behind his eyes.

He began to shift his perspective on the night's job. He decided his task wasn't to watch the moth. His purpose was just to be there if the moth did anything worth noticing.

This attitude shift had pros and cons.

Pro: He wouldn't have to spend the night staring at a disturbing insect corpse the size of a car hood.

Con: If the disturbing insect corpse suddenly came to life, Green might not notice in time to impersonate a very harmless piece of furniture.

He walked circles around the table. He pulled wood from the log cradle and fed the stove. It got too warm in the cabin and he fed the stove again anyway. He opened the door a crack to let in some air. He thought of the wolf and latched it again. The heat wasn't *that* bad. He nodded at the ripe dumpster smell of the moth and wondered how long it would take for it to leave his hair and clothes.

Not long after nightfall, Valentina brought in propane lanterns.

"I'm cutting the power to preserve battery life," she said. "Keep these on low and they'll last most of the night. Here's an LED backup. I am going back to sleep in my trailer. Knock if you need me, but do not wander away from the moth unless it is absolutely essential."

The lanterns gave off a harsh white light and made a low hissing sound as they drank up fuel.

Green stood.

Green sat.

Green studied Valentina's brass coffeepot. Her cup. The leaf pattern decorating the iron stove.

He ate a granola bar and poured himself cup after cup of plastic-flavored water from his jug. He relished the sweet fresh-air necessity of stepping out into the woods to pee.

Memories of the monstrous wolf couldn't rob the fresh air of its pleasure, not as long as he stayed within twenty paces of a real building with a real door. He knew a wooden door couldn't stop the wolf, but he was beginning to wonder if the fact the door belonged to Valentina might make a difference.

All the while, Green poked and prodded at his new life plan, reimagining it, revisiting that morning's certainty that it was time to give up. He tried to extrapolate from his evening's work what he could expect from this new world he had agreed to enter with no real resistance or debate.

Sure, I'll be your apprentice. You can explain more after my broken face and I spend the night watching your murder-bug.

He had been, for years, someone who worked at a desk. Who, at home or work, lived through his computer. Files were the product he produced. Words on a screen. These were the trappings of adulthood, of maturity. The work of the mind.

Now, he couldn't help but feel that he had traveled back to his childhood. He had a task involving his body. He had a chore, a remedial assignment given to someone without any specialized knowledge. There were no hints of prestige on offer here, no unspoken respectability rolled into the benefits package. He was a kid. A hall monitor.

He scowled at the thought.

That wasn't right and he knew it. What had his life done to him that he believed physical interaction with the world was juvenile? When Green set that thought on the table, next to the moth, it was more distasteful than the corpse. Physicality was lesser? Adult life was what happened in electronic non-spaces? What would that idea say about human history? What about the people who built infrastructure, who tended forests, who brought shelter and power and healing and nourishment into the world?

Green shoved the thought away. He knew, like all sneaking prejudices, that it would linger like the smell of the rag moth, like the bloodstains on his shirt collar. A sinking realization hit him, obvious as a toothache, unseen as his pumping heart.

What else am I assuming?

What else have I internalized? What parts of me will need to slough away for me to become native to my new life? Will there be enough of me left to regrow something new in place of everything I prune away?

He didn't know.

He wouldn't know.

And that, like the hidden aspects of nature to which he had bound his life, would loom over him like a great unknown watcher following in his shadow.

Could he make friends with it?

"I can try," he said to the rag moth.

Its dust swirled. Its eyes glinted in the lantern light.

How could something so superficially ugly feel so intrinsically beautiful?

How could his own reactions feel like a mystery on par with the impossible insect?

Green sighed.

He pulled out his phone, ran through an inventory of things it couldn't do without cell service or wifi, and dropped it back into his pocket. No doomscrolling social media. No articles about losing belly fat or building deeper friendships. He was still a novice at being alone with his thoughts.

His boredom felt like wet socks.

There was a notebook lying on a low shelf next to a basket of octagonal seashells.

He grabbed it and sank down onto the cot Valentina had left in the corner. The cover was blank and unadorned. He thought it might be a violation to look inside and immediately forgave himself for doing it anyway. Drastic times. Drastic measures.

The writing was in Cyrillic? Russian?

Green growled in frustration. There would be no escape from his own mind.

Crossing his legs made the acorn dig into his outer thigh, so he uncrossed them again.

He flipped through the pages.

He stopped when he saw an entry in Roman characters.

French, he thought.

He kept flipping.

There was a diagram of a creature that looked like a bird made of sharp angles and a curved line beneath it suggested it was . . . what? In orbit above the Earth?

More Cyrillic.

On the last few pages, Green found a single entry in English.

It was a letter.

It read:

Dear Ivan,

A freshwater anemone the size of a cart horse nearly ate a good portion of my memory today. As far as I can tell, I escaped unscathed. My colleague was not so lucky. She has spent all evening trying to map out the chronology of her life in order to define the shape of her wound. The absence seems to lurk in her twenties, but she has become distrustful of her ability to place her recollections in their proper order.

I can't stop weighing what a similar loss would have cost me. The territory of my years is much, much larger and not so easy to map. Much of my life is chronicled in my journals, but not all. Words cannot (should not) attempt to capture everything. You, for example, are not a matter for my journals. So, I fear I almost lost you beneath the lake this morning.

I write to you today in a language you didn't know on a page you will never see.

We spoke so often about travel. I think we always assumed there were limits to how far a body could go. These limits meant that one could only become so lost, so far away. This was the unspoken safety net that hung beneath all our grand plans and imagined discoveries. My love, I don't assume this any longer.

When I think of the distance in time and miles between the young woman you knew and the person writing this letter, I feel my own life as the ship of Theseus, repaired and remade until I doubt my relationship to any cohesive identity. And yet, my fear of losing you to those stinging tentacles tells me that there is still living tissue connecting my present with my long ago.

Maybe you would be sad or even angry with me if I told you that it is possible to outlive the beliefs of your youth. Not easily and not often. But it is possible.

There, in my imagination, I see you frowning at the person I've become, the unimaginable changes I have weathered, body and mind.

Don't look at me like that, Ivan. If I could let you hold the number of years on my back, even for an hour, I think you would understand. This is the generosity we give to people who do not share our life experiences but insist on judging how we are shaped by them.

"If you knew, you would know."

It is how we love those who insist on being wrong. I call this generosity.

My dear, my unreasonably long-ago love, my haunting friend, how would our conversations beneath that spreading pine by the roadside be different if we knew then that there was such a thing as too far away?

Just one more thing I cannot know.

Self-preservation dictates that I must see the walls of ignorance as shelter, lest I begin to view them as a cage.

Tomorrow, I return to study the anemone. I will exercise extreme caution, but if something unforeseen happens, at least your name will be safe within the shelter of this letter.

Love from too far away,

Valentina

Texas 1934

Green closed the book.

He felt ashamed.

It was hard to imagine a less appropriate thing for him to read.

He slapped the notebook back down on the shelf as if it were the object's fault for tempting him to look.

He returned to the cot.

Sitting, he was eye level with the table's surface and the moth looked bulkier than from above.

Could that thing actually fly?

The proportion of wings to body didn't seem right. Then again, of all the unlikely things about the rag moth, Green supposed aerodynamics were the least improbable aspect to consider. Perhaps it flew the way a piece of litter flies, a plastic shopping bag billowing down an alley like a jellyfish in an ocean canyon.

He shut his eyes and wished for the time to stop trickling and start cascading.

He cradled his head in his hands and didn't wake even when his body slumped sideways onto the cot. Sleep is cousin to death and even fear is mortal.

If you put enough caterpillars in a room, they stop being animals and start being weather.

Even so, Green didn't wake when the clouds rolled in. Not at first.

He was dreaming about rose petals falling from the upper atmosphere. They bloomed into existence so high he could see the curving haze where air meets vacuum. Somehow, even on the ground, he could track their progress, whirling down through a cloudless sky, dancing like maple seeds to touch his face with surpassing gentleness before tumbling earthward to crimson the grass.

Touch.

Touch.

Touch.

Soft, scattered kisses of sensation.

The dream, of course, was a trick of the brain to explain away stimuli and cling to sleep. Something was touching Green's face.

Touch.

Touch.

Touch.

Something pushed against his upper lip, then moved off.

The dream fizzled.

He awoke to a cartoonish sight. A thing from his distant past. A kids' TV show teaching letters and numbers.

"Today is brought to you by the letter S."

A living S the color of new April leaves was perched on his chin, swaying in the air like a cattail.

His eyes focused and he saw rows of waving stubby legs and two dark, oversized eyes that brought to mind a starship captain's helmet in a science fiction show. His muscles spasmed hard enough to knock the air from his lungs. He just barely had time to override instinct and stop himself from swatting the creature off his face.

Instead, he froze.

The caterpillar noticed none of this. It finished tasting the air and resumed its crawling, inch-worming its way over Green's head and onto the cot beneath him.

His dream merged with life. He felt the gentle touches of rose petals moving over his scalp. His chest. His left hand. Both shins.

His view broadened and suddenly he could see that every part of the little cabin was brought to you by the letter S.

There was a shaggy lawn of caterpillars on every surface save the hot stove and lanterns. Each and every one of them inched and halted, reached and periscoped upward at the exact same pace and cadence, perfectly synchronized. It gave the room a green strobing quality that was difficult to watch. In the harsh white lantern light, a shifting text of shadows moved like an arcane alphabet across the walls.

Never had Green been more invested in keeping still. There was no way he could move without crushing a bratwurst-size caterpillar. It was intolerable. He was terrified to alter his position, yet lying prone in a sea of unknown organisms with unknown purposes made his amygdala scream.

He was vulnerable. His soft underbelly was laid out like a buffet. What if they were carnivorous?

He could hear a nature documentary voiceover in his head. A soft-spoken British voice offered commentary.

"The caterpillar's only job is to feed."

His imagination summoned a copy of *The Very Hungry Caterpillar,* except instead of fruits and vegetables, the friendly illustrated insect ate one, two, three vital body parts.

He had to sit up. He was going to sit up. The only question was, how?

How hard could this be?

He moved his right arm into view. It was, mercifully, caterpillar-free. Next he took that arm and began exploring the side of his body. He had a slow-motion collision with one caterpillar. His heart stopped. It rolled down his belly and landed on the cot with a barely audible *plop*. Unperturbed, it didn't miss a beat in rejoining its siblings' inching dance.

Green exhaled.

Okay. That's promising data.

He gently swept two more from his hip and another from the place on the cot he planned to plant his backside. With infuriating slowness, he tilted himself into a sitting position and set his feet on the floor.

A caterpillar climbed onto his lap.

A caterpillar swayed in the air on his left shoulder like a pirate's parrot.

A caterpillar inched up the back of his head.

They were everywhere. Luminescent green. Alien. Moving as one to the tick of a silent clock.

Green reached a careful finger to feel the acorn bulge in his pocket. It was there. Promising whatever it was the acorn seemed to promise, speaking from a mental fogbank that bit him like a caustic chemical whenever he tried to touch it.

What have I signed up for?

Sitting up, he could once again see the surface of the table. The rag moth corpse was a crumbling ruin of burlap scraps and heaped dust, but caterpillars were still streaming up and out of its center mass. They were emerging from nothing. It was like a stage illusion. The beautiful assistant was being sawed in half for an intended audience of nobody.

Even as he watched, the moth disintegrated more and more, collapsing inward, the dust rising to become a dark corona. It was as though every caterpillar that appeared removed one more stitch from the rag moth's hold on existence.

If he hadn't been so mortally terrified, he might have smiled. He had an answer for Valentina. He knew why rag moth corpses disappeared.

And all he had to do to report the good news was survive what he had learned. How many of those mummified corpses Valentina mentioned died with heads full of an interesting story?

He tried to estimate his chances of seeing morning and found he had little to go on.

The newts survived. Think like a newt. Be a newt.

Green knew as much about newts as he did Cyrillic.

On the plus side, only one plan made any sense at all. Stay stone-still. So far, that had been his course of action and he remained alive. The caterpillars were not the wolf. They didn't seem interested in him at all.

Another data point.

Even so, nothing could stop every horrible hypothetical that Green's imagination could cook up from testing the dials of his adrenal system.

Perhaps they all know I'm here and are preparing to swarm like piranhas . . .

. . . or like those beetles museums use to strip flesh from skeletons.

What did they call it with sharks? A feeding frenzy?

I'm probably thinking too simple. This is cryptonature.

They're going to pluck me out of linear time and I'll spend eternity watching worm dances.

Maybe they already have.

Maybe I wouldn't know if I were experiencing eternity.

Maybe the Earth is a cinder and this moment has already stretched on to forever.

There are more of them every moment. Did I miss my chance to run? Is this my last chance to run?

Valentina spoke from a memory.

"These are animals. Same as you or me. They are not demons or monsters."

Yeah, but purely mundane animals can terrorize you. Can kill you.

The Valentina in his memory paused and frowned at his unspoken response.

"Mr. Green," she said. "Are you focused on your own fanciful self-pity or are you watching the hitherto unobserved natural wonder unfolding around you?"

I'm watching! I can't not watch! One of them is on my cheek!

Mental Valentina scowled.

"You are not watching, you are reacting. You are making this about you. Stop it. Imagine your body out of that room and leave your senses behind. What are they doing? You know full well the answer isn't 'trying to panic one random man.' "

Green growled internally.

How is someone I've known for ten hours living inside my head?

Imaginary or not, she had a point. The caterpillars weren't treating him differently from the furniture. Maybe he could be furniture.

It wasn't easy. It wasn't perfect. It wasn't immediate, but he pushed his ego down deep inside and tried to see the caterpillars outside the context of what they might do to him. With an immense effort of will, he stopped being the direct object of every caterpillar's sentence.

Okay. What are they doing?

They all looked to be the exact same size, a bulky six or seven inches. If there was variation among them, Green couldn't see it. He shifted his gaze to the caterpillar inching up his left biceps. Its head was a dark mask of ovular eyes that appeared to meet in the center. Looking closely, Green could see a hint of ocher between the green of the body and the black of the head. Tiny translucent hairs ran the length of the animal and they pitched back and forth as the internal mechanism of locomotion contracted and expanded.

He was no entomologist, but he noticed what he could.

Focusing in on one caterpillar, thinking of it as a life-form and not a mishap, a creature who was shaped by the same natural pressures that shaped him, Green was once more surprised to find that he thought the animal was actually quite pretty. Special. That thought stood out like a chandelier in a cornfield. It made no sense.

He looked up, studying the room.

Broadening his view, he took in the space as an impression of shape and movement. The synchronized motion of the caterpillars meant that they could be perceived as a whole, a unified creature with a single purpose. Each individual organism followed the same pattern.

Inch.

Inch.

Inch.

Pause in an arc like a tiny bridge.

Inch.

Inch.

Inch.

Curve upward in an S like a snake threatening to strike.

Wave like a reed in the wind.

Repeat the cycle.

There was something else about the motion that Green could see when he took a wider view. The corpse of the rag moth formed a central point around which all the caterpillars were circling. The dead moth was the hub of a wheel, the eye of a hurricane. The moth's body was gone. In its place was a pillar of churning dust with unusual cohesion. It turned in the air like a column of muddy river water.

As he watched, he realized that the smell of the rag moth had become a taste, acrid and dry. It was more than a taste. His mouth felt parched and filmed with a month of uninterrupted sleep.

The dust roiled.

The caterpillars circled.

Green chewed at his tongue and tried to spur his salivary glands to action.

The pillar of dust flickered like a guttering flame and, for just a moment, the dark silhouette of a living rag moth fluttered above the table. Wind from huge moth's wings tousled Green's hair and grit stung his eyes.

Then it was gone.

There was a sound that wasn't a sound. A sensation like air rushing into a vacuum, emotional rather than physical. And it was over.

The dust.

The moth.

The caterpillars.

Gone.

Green sat scrutinizing the place the moth had been. Where there had been a swirl of motion in all directions, now shadowed stillness. He didn't know how they had all departed, so he couldn't predict how or if they might return.

He carefully ran his hands over his shoulders and upper back. Nothing.

He stood, feeling the buzz of adrenaline in his joints.

Looking back at the cot, he had a flash of himself mummified, white teeth gleaming in his unhinged jaw, empty eye sockets staring at the vacant table.

There was nothing on the cot.

Nothing on his legs.

Nothing on the floor.

He turned in a slow circle, pushing through the fear and reacclimating to motion.

As the seconds ticked by and his mouth began tasting less like a tomb and more like a laundry hamper, the tension drained from his shoulders. As a rule, the human body tries not to prolong states of panic.

"Okay, then," he said.

The sound of his voice planted a flag of control in the room.

"Okay."

He exhaled a plume of dust, then coughed long and hard to clear his lungs. He spat a dark glob on the dirt floor.

The coughs rattled his exhausted body, but it felt good to be loud, to set aside the tense quiet that had hung over his head like a pickax.

Following the train of that thought, he began walking around the cabin, casting his approval on the walls and corners with their sensible lack of giant caterpillars. He noticed that the parasites Valentina had plucked from the moth were also gone, vanished from their glass vial prisons.

"Okay, then," he said again, louder this time.

He grabbed some water and stepped outside.

It was still there.

The world. The woods. The autumn chill and the moonlight that turned all the trees graphite gray.

He rinsed his mouth and spit again and again before drinking.

He breathed deep of the cool mountain freshness and imagined a gentle rain washing him clean of fear.

He laughed and pumped a fist in the air.

It felt ridiculous and he didn't care.

Even his nose and the cut on his chin felt better.

Something had changed.

He checked in on his devils. The wolf. The acorn. The feeling that his new world was a sinister joke at his expense.

Hey, assholes.

They were there, but they too were shifting. They were becoming less like a devouring fire and more like difficult terrain, the hard features of a landscape Green had begun to map. He found a place to stand and a guide to stand with him.

Maybe this isn't about escaping something.

Maybe it's about arriving somewhere.

He chuckled and wiped his eyes.

He felt silly with fatigue.

Valentina strolled back into his exhausted mind and communicated with a look.

Notes.

I need to make notes while it's fresh in my mind. Also . . . I think I may pass out.

The moon was still high in the sky. He suspected this meant there was still a lot of night left to pass.

He went back to work.

Inside the cabin, it felt hot and stuffy after the cool night air. The feeling made Green's eyelids heavy.

In his notebook, he filled two pages with short, simple sentences capturing every detail he recalled.

That done, he twisted the knobs to shut off both lanterns and fed a log to the stove. He watched a jack-o'-lantern smile of firelight from the iron door's air vents color the wall. The smell of the earthen floor rose up like a lullaby in the warm dark and he surrendered to its comfort.

Near Green's campsite, a great horned owl hooted her claim over her long-established territory.

On a mountainside six miles to the west, an ancient thing that had tasted Green's blood chased prey it could not catch.

In the dream, Green was a quadruped taller than the trees on the mountainside. There was his campsite. His abandoned car beneath its tarp. The distant glow of Dancer's office sign.

His triple-jointed legs were finger-thin and picked their way between branch and bough with the steady precision of a watchmaker.

He flowed over the forest. His body, a glass orb carrying moonlight like a dish of milk, was a pearl sliding along the autumn canopy. He was a thing of pure sight, his borrowed luminescence shining wherever he looked, shepherding the shadows from his path.

There was no question about his purpose. He searched for the horned wolf, for the dangerous secret that had told itself to him alone, unasked.

How could you search for a thing that had only been found once?

No. It hadn't been found. It had shown itself.

Something white as magnesium fire darted below, like a spark arcing between the tree trunks. The glass fawn. Always fleeing. Always pursued. Between the trees. Between the worlds. Forests and fens. Oceans and continents. Our world and its native elsewhere space.

Green halted. The miniature moon of his body hovering above the steeple of a shaggy spruce.

There is the prey.

Where is the predator?

The fawn leapt and darted away, a cape of tree shadows following behind it like a bridal train.

A motion nearby pulled Green's focus.

There, seated on a soft patch of nothing, the horned wolf regarded him from behind a mask of dry bone.

Predator and prey? thought the wolf. *What do you know of such things, not-man?*

Green turned his luminescence to the wolf and found that the wolf extinguished as much light as he could summon.

The creature remained a dim ivory mask with a mane of starless night.

The wolf, in turn, pressed its shadow on Green and a thick velvet curtain fell across his senses.

Grow, the wolf said in the dark. *Grow to honor the world that made you.*

Green squirmed on his cot, blinking at the firelight glow on an unfamiliar ceiling.

He tried to bring back the treetops and the moonlight, concentrating until his breath caught in his throat, but they were gone.

There was only night and smothering heat.

He slept again without dreaming.

CHAPTER 7

The Library Tree

GREEN SAT UP AND FOUND TOAST AND COFFEE ON THE table where the rag moth had been. The coffee was still steaming.

Valentina had been there.

He ate the toast. It was homemade bread, two fingers thick. It tasted like butter and woodsmoke. The coffee was darker and stronger than he thought possible. He sipped it with his eyes closed and tried to remember the last time somebody made him coffee without money changing hands.

Even with the scent of strong coffee in his nose, he could still smell the rag moth. He wondered if the creature's influence could linger on in more dangerous ways than a simple odor.

Stepping out into the frigid morning, he reflected on a life mostly spent inside climate-controlled spaces. Seventy-two degrees Fahrenheit had been an unnoticed companion for decades.

I'll miss you, old friend.

He visited the outhouse. Washed his face in violently cold water from the pump and went to find Valentina.

He heard a muffled conversation from the tan camper and knocked on the door.

"Come in."

It was a cramped domestic space lined with utility shelves full of foodstuffs. There was a small kitchenette, a tiny writing surface scattered with papers, and a curtain separating what Green imagined was a sleeping area.

Valentina and Dancer were seated in two folding chairs. Valentina had her narrow brass coffee cup. Dancer had her plaid thermos. A thing that looked like ten pounds of chewed bubble gum, pink and lumpy with a smattering of various-sized eyes, pulsed rhythmically a few feet above the women's heads. Some of the eyes were liquid black, others had goatlike hourglass pupils. Several eyes shifted to look in Green's direction.

He froze and stared up at the blob.

Valentina cleared her throat, gave him a level stare, and shook her head. The look seemed to say, *Don't mention the hideous thing on the ceiling,* as if it were a stain on the sofa.

Dancer turned to the newcomer.

"Howdy, Green. I thought I'd—"

She stopped short and gaped at him.

"What the hell?" she said.

Valentina sipped her coffee and said nothing.

Green's heart sank.

"What?" he asked. "What's wrong?"

He checked the ceiling just above his own head, suddenly afraid a second blob was approaching his scalp.

"Your face, pal. Your face is wrong."

"Oh, yeah, I know. I look like crime scene photos."

Valentina was still giving him that look. It was painfully hard to keep his eyes off the ceiling.

"Nope. Now you look like a mascot for paper towels or maybe an oat-based cereal."

"I don't follow."

"Are you one of those rare diurnal werewolves?" Dancer continued. "You have to tell me if you are, otherwise it's entrapment."

Valentina swiveled in her chair and pulled an antique silver hand mirror from a drawer.

Green took it and studied his face. His eyes were no longer rimmed with bruises. His nose looked healed, but noticeably less symmetrical than before. And he had to assume that the cut on his chin had scarred over. He had to assume because he had a thick two-inch beard that hadn't been there the day before.

"Um," Green said. "That's new."

"Mr. Green was working on a project for me last night. It looks like it had some unforeseen side effects," Valentina said.

Dancer muttered to herself.

"Two of you. There are going to be two of you now. S'posed to be a quiet place. Easy on my nerves."

Valentina pointed to a camp chair in the corner.

"Join us, Mr. Green. Ms. Dancer came to check on you. I was just confirming that you had not fabricated the story of our new arrangement."

He glanced up at the thing stuck to the ceiling. It had sprouted several thin tendrils that ended in feathery structures that waved and curled in the air.

"Is it . . . safe to join you?"

"Yes, yes, come."

Green pulled over a chair, positioning it as far away from the thing on the ceiling as he could without seeming impolite. The sagging canvas left him a head shorter than Valentina and several shorter than Dancer. He spared a scowl for the blob as he sat. Dancer followed his gaze, apparently saw nothing, and shrugged.

He tugged at his new beard. It wasn't that he hadn't noticed it. He just hadn't thought it was new or unusual until Dancer mentioned it.

"How? My face, I mean."

Valentina shook her head.

"We will discuss theories later. Ms. Dancer doesn't want to hear us talk about business."

She punctuated the statement with a glance toward the ceiling.

Dancer nodded.

"I don't. I really don't. With infinite warmth, I have talked over these sorts of things with Val here in the past and it's a little like listening to somebody talk about a dream they had. Everything about it sounds interesting, except it slips off my brain like butter down a waterslide."

Green smirked. Dancer was still Dancer.

"Thanks for checking on me. I'm alright. Relative to yesterday, anyway."

He poked and pulled at his new whiskers as he spoke. He couldn't help it.

"Not to worry. Like I said when you arrived, neighbors look after neighbors out here. Of course, I never would have guessed you and Valentina would hit it off so hard."

"And why is that, Ms. Dancer?"

Dancer shot Valentina a sarcastic look.

"Because you've been here as long as the camp, a thing that itself doesn't make sense when I say it out loud, and I've seen you host a guest exactly zero times."

Valentina sipped her coffee. She looked small and birdlike next to Dancer, who filled the space like a grizzly in its den.

"It simply was not called for in recent years."

"By the by, I'm walking out on conversational thin ice here, but were you able to help Green with his . . . whatever it was? Incident?"

Valentina looked at Green to answer.

The wolf was still out there and the acorn tugged on the hem of his thoughts every six breaths, but he was no longer homeless, rudderless, and alone.

More or less.

"Yes," Green said. "She has helped. And she's been very generous."

"I guess so," Dancer said. "Room and board and a job? Pretty good terms for these woods. Pretty good terms for anywhere, I'd venture to guess. Not that I go in for such things. My last job involved mucking out stables and those horses acted like I was a mountain lion disguised in pants."

Dancer pulled a full-sized mug from her jacket pocket and offered it to Green.

"Sassafras tea?"

"Please."

She filled the cup from her red thermos.

He took it and found it earthy and soothing and kinder going down than Valentina's coffee.

How much of civilization beyond sidewalks and streetlights is built on sharing food, drink, and shelter?

Dancer looked from Green to Valentina and back again.

"Two peas in a pod. Wonder of wonders. Anyways, besides checking on our newest neighbor here, I wanted to mention that I'm putting in a supply order with Aisha down in Hickory. Radio or drop off a list if you want anything. I'm putting in the order tomorrow morning. Winter ain't here, but I expect it's brushing its teeth and combing its hair."

"Yes, of course," Valentina said.

"I know, I know. You know your business out here. 'Don't tell your mother how to milk a duck,' as my dear ol' mom liked to say. I'll get out of your hair."

Dancer stood, making the camper look like a dollhouse.

Her face was entirely too close to the pulsating anomaly eyeing her from four inches away. One of its waving tendrils nearly grazed her ear. Green gripped the arms of his chair and tried to look unconcerned.

"Green, it is sincerely good to see you whole and hearty. And wearing appropriate headgear to boot."

"Thank you and . . . likewise?"

Dancer grinned.

As she exited, Green touched the crown of his head. Dancer's hat was there, itchy and shapeless, but he could have sworn he had been hatless when he looked in Valentina's mirror.

The camper door shut with a click.

He took another sip of tea.

"Oh, she left me her mug again."

"Ah. She must trust you to return it to her then. I believe it harkens back to a number of customs that dictated when you leave a friend's presence you must first find a reason to meet again. Ms. Dancer is often surprisingly old-fashioned."

"She's surprising in all sorts of ways."

"Indeed. So, Mr. Green, I expect you have some news for me?"

"I do, but what the hell is that thing on your ceiling?"

Valentina looked up.

"It's a lesser phobophage. A fear-eater."

"And it's on your ceiling because . . . ?"

"I have cultivated a relationship with it. Symbiosis. It mitigates my troubling dreams and general anxiety and I keep it fed."

He leaned forward and studied the thing. Its wet eyes blinked at asynchronous intervals.

"Why does this seem less terrifying than when I walked in?"

"As I said, it eats fears. You are sitting within its radius of influence."

"What's its name?"

"Again, it's a lesser phobophage."

"You didn't give it a name?"

"This creature isn't my pet, Mr. Green. It's not a puppy."

"Blobert. That's a good name."

Valentina grimaced.

"No."

"And Dancer really couldn't see it? That still feels so bizarre."

"It's the nature of what we do."

"Seems a little lonely for Blobert. Part roommate. Part living anti-anxiety medication. I think Dancer might like the little guy."

He had a sudden, hopeful flash that not all cryptonature was menacing or lethal. There was this odd medicinal blob. There was the glowing deer simply trying to escape a predator. It wasn't all hunting wolves and deadly insects.

"Ridiculous. Don't anthropomorphize. Now, I assume I found you asleep this morning because you have answers for me?"

"I do."

He passed his notebook to Valentina and filled in every detail of his wake for the rag moth. The story felt less harrowing while sitting beneath the phobophage.

If she was impressed by Green's cool head or blindsided by the method of the moth's departure, she had an impressive poker face.

"Tell me, Mr. Green. Based on your observations, do you think it possible that the corpse was full of eggs? Not unheard-of in nature. The offspring hatching and eating the corpse from within? A funerary banquet? Like parasitoid wasp offspring devouring a caterpillar?"

"No. I don't think so."

"Why?"

"All the caterpillars emerged from a central point and they filed out one by one. I guess I'd think hatching eggs would be less uniform. Also . . . it wasn't like the corpse was being eaten. It just disintegrated. It became dust."

"Good. Do you have any ideas about how such a thing could happen?"

"I really don't."

"Neither do I," she said. "Isn't that just lovely?"

"Is it?"

"Adjust your perspective, modern man. There are uncharted worlds within your reach. In fact, you are on their shores now. The information age is puttering somewhere back there in the lands you left behind. Whatever information is here you will sow and harvest yourself. How does that sound?"

"I don't know. Worryingly colonialist?"

Her expression darkened.

"They are metaphorical lands. And I can't decide if you are joking or missing my point intentionally."

"I hear you. You're trying to make this a lesson about becoming comfortable with the unknown?"

Valentina set aside her coffee cup.

"That lesson arrives most days whether or not we invite it. But we are not in the business of passively noting our own ignorance. We are in the business of finding out."

She stood up abruptly.

"Come along, Mr. Green. To the library."

He nodded to the ceiling as they went out.

"Bye, Blobert."

Blobert blinked wetly.

At the foot of the ancient oak to the rear of camp, they climbed a spiral staircase built of halved logs leading to a massive tree house twenty feet above the ground. The stairs ended at a hatch. Valentina threw it open and climbed in with the thoughtless agility of a twelve-year-old.

"Cool, the tree fort," Green said as they entered. "I've been excited to see inside."

"Tree fort? My apprentice, we aren't here to play Tarzan. This is a place of study."

He didn't argue, but he knew there was no way he would ever surrender the fun of that place.

Entering, he saw that, most of all, it was a temple dedicated to books. The living trunk of the oak, gray as a mourning dove, grew through the center of a broad circular space carpeted with a dozen mismatched rugs and walled with shoulder-to-shoulder bookshelves. Several round windows and one massive skylight brought the morning sun into the room. A hanging rope ladder led to a hatch in the library roof, one of Valentina's explicit off-limits spaces. A few desks, small tables, and reading chairs crowded around the trunk.

"This is . . . amazing."

"Fire and flood. The two perennial enemies of books. I wanted this room set apart from the other structures."

Green shook his head.

"No. No, this isn't just practical."

Valentina raised an eyebrow.

"This feels like, I don't know the right word. A holy place?"

She paused and looked around her. The living tree. The pooled sunlight. A book collection multiple lifetimes in the making.

"I take your point. With or without intention, some places are simply sacred. They accrete and concentrate meaning."

In that moment. Looking at that room. Green had never felt more certain that he had made the correct decision in coming to the mountains. For weeks, he felt that his life had been building to a crescendo of chaos and dread. Standing in the library tree, he began to feel a new hope that all his doubt and terror had been paying for something worth having, something he might actually cherish in an earnest, unforced way.

He had a moment of déjà vu.

Not that he had ever stood in a library tree before.

But there was something familiar in it, an echo from childhood.

It was akin to the experience of a long, dull hardship in some joyless stretch of life's journey, becoming numb with sameness, only to be ambushed by a patch of golden splendor and think, *Oh, that's right isn't it, there is good to be found here as well as the trials we endure?* Goodness so simple and potent it threatens you with a kind of headlong love for the world that seems a dangerous cousin to mania.

He pulled the hat from his head and turned in slow circles.

The books. The papers. The shelves full of natural odds and ends that each seemed to whisper an invitation. Green wandered the room, fascinated. Here, a cat's skull made of blue glass. There, a potted fern that rippled and swayed like an undersea grotto. A small bell jar over a speckled silver egg that hovered an inch above its shelf. A long-fingered glove that, upon closer inspection, appeared to be a seamless piece of cast-off skin with heart-shaped scales. Fifty such wonders alongside the orderly ranks of mismatched books.

"Is this where I'll do my reading? My . . . cryptonaturalist studying?"

She smiled.

"It can get cold up here in the winter. I do not allow flame in this room, but there is a radiant heater wired into the solar batteries and electric lights. It was not built as a school but, yes, this is the most sensible place for your instruction. I also prefer reading materials to stay in this room, when possible. And I will ask you to humor an old tradition and call me Teacher."

"Thank you. Teacher. Thank you."

Valentina scrutinized Green's face.

"Welcome to the profession I treasure. Please respect it in what ways seem best to you."

"I'll do my best."

She walked over to a narrow walnut bookcase and patted it fondly.

"This shelf is your scholarly home for the present. It is general practices and fundamentals for the study of hidden nature."

"Are we here to read about the rag moth?"

"A fair guess, but no. I know the existing literature on the rag moth. Perhaps I'll show you some of the entries written in English later, but your observations last night constitute a new discovery worth sharing."

"Sharing?"

"Oh, indeed. Like most worthy disciplines, our trade is the work of a community. Many minds exploring questions from many angles and diverse perspectives. We share data whenever possible. It is amazing the cooperation you can foster when you are not working toward selling something. Though . . . I won't pretend we do not all have our own egos and priorities. All that said, you, Mr. Green, have discovered something that, in the interest of scholarship and safety, should be known by cryptonaturalists globally. So, we will share it."

Valentina reconsidered.

"Actually, you have discovered several things worth sharing."

Green scanned the room for a computer. He found none.

"Share it . . . how? Do you have a satellite phone or something?"

She walked to an upholstered reading chair next to a small desk. She sat and placed Green's notes on her lap. A hinged wooden box rested on the desktop. A brown cord ran from the box to the trunk of the oak, snaking down along valleys in the gray bark, then down below the floorboards.

"Hold out your hand, Mr. Green."

Valentina opened a desk drawer and plucked out a large sugar cube. She placed it on Green's open palm.

"For the network administrator. I suspect they are due a payment."

"Uh. Okay . . ."

"When I begin the broadcast, just listen and observe. I will, of course, credit the work you have done, but we will keep you anonymous for now to shield you from the more . . . intense . . . personalities within the cryptonaturalist community. Agreed?"

He nodded, not at all certain to what he was agreeing.

Valentina opened the box. Inside was a copper panel with a mesh speaker, a dial, and a toggle switch. A single yellow bulb faded on and off at the pace of a sleeper's breath. She checked the dial, then rested a finger on the switch.

"Silence, please."

Green leaned in to watch.

She clicked the switch. A distant crackle like tearing linen purred from the speaker.

There was a smell like a freshly tilled field.

Valentina pointed to the sugar cube in Green's hand, then to the floor.

At the thin gap where the library floor met the trunk of the great oak, near where the cord disappeared below the deck, a hedge of trumpet-shaped mushrooms were rising like a city skyline in miniature, towers as soft and pale as salamander bellies. The fungal thicket leaned toward a central point, became a column, a platform, an open palm sprouting long, curving fingers. The fingers opened. The hand looked both too human and not human enough, a fruiting body from the uncanny valley.

He placed his offering on the palm. The sugar cube sank beneath the yielding flesh and the hand divided back into fungal shapes that quickly receded beneath the floorboards, leaving only a pale dusting of spores in their wake.

Valentina spoke to the box.

"This is Valentina Blackwood transmitting on cryptonaturalist frequency 11-58-1. I have taken on a new apprentice at my camp in the Catskill Mountains. He is an absolute novice, yet he has made a number of discoveries that are worth your attention.

"Firstly, for the past seventy-two hours I have possessed the corpse of a rag moth obtained near the shores of Lake Michigan. Last night, my apprentice observed the spontaneous decay of the corpse. The decay coincided with the emergence of no fewer than one hundred caterpillars."

She continued to relay the details of Green's observations, then shifted subjects.

"Unlikely as it may sound, this is the second noteworthy discovery my apprentice has made in as many nights. The night before last, he spotted the glass fawn here near my camp.

"This was his first sighting of cryptonature and a local resident advised him to seek me out as a result."

Green squirmed at "first sighting of cryptonature." He stuffed a hand in his pocket and said nothing.

Valentina continued.

"His description of the fawn matches the known records. Translucent body. Visible organs. Pale bioluminescence."

He knew what was coming next and he didn't want to hear it.

"Additionally, he saw something new. A large lupine creature with black, viscous, dynamic flesh that shifted to reveal the skeletal structure beneath. This cryptid appeared to be pursuing the fawn."

And my throat.

"It was approximately the size of a large black bear with the morphology of an uncommonly stocky wolf, with a posterior curving S-shaped horn on its muzzle. The creature shattered my apprentice's windshield as he sat motionless in his car. It thoroughly investigated his person and caused several minor injuries. He also experienced nonverbal communication with the creature."

Sure. The way a kick to the groin is "communication" with the kicker's foot.

Valentina looked to Green and motioned him closer.

"As the discoverer of this new organism, the naming falls to my apprentice. He calls it . . ."

Valentina pointed at the device and looked to Green.

They hadn't discussed the name.

Descriptions stampeded through his head.

Murder wolf. Nightmare wolf. Devil wolf.

He looked around at the shelves full of wonders and knew those names wouldn't do. Green's pulse raced, but he leaned in and spoke as steadily as he could manage.

"The horned wolf."

If you wanted creativity, you should have given me some notice.

Valentina smiled.

He felt an urge to add a warning, to blurt out the sense of lethality and malevolence he felt in its presence, to mention the fisherman's death and how it didn't feel like a coincidence to him, but Valentina continued speaking.

"The horned wolf," she repeated. "I would ask that you do not come here seeking this creature for the present. I know that request is unorthodox, but my apprentice has just begun his studies, and I wish to treat this situation with an abundance of caution. In short, there are enough variables on this mountain already. Valentina Blackwood signing off."

She flipped the switch and closed the box.

"The horned wolf," Valentina said. "Well done, Mr. Green. Descriptive. Practical. You shunned the ugly temptation to put your signature on a living creature by calling it 'Green's wolf' or some such self-aggrandizing nonsense. Admirable instincts."

"I have so many questions," Green said.

Valentina folded her hands in her lap.

"Proceed."

"What was that hand that took the sugar cube?"

"The network administrator? Mycelium network of a globe-spanning cryptofungus. The sugar is simple reciprocity. Though, there are numerous ways to access the cryptonaturalist frequencies."

Green wondered at Valentina's ability to deliver such bizarre explanations as if she were reciting a software user agreement.

He stood and moved to look out a window. He could see the pale line of the gravel lane and ranks of autumn trees fading to a jagged horizon.

"Shouldn't I have said more about what the wolf is? Like, a warning? Nobody should go looking for that thing."

"I am sympathetic. You certainly experienced a traumatic moment with the horned wolf, but you must not let it become the monster of your personal mythology. That animal may well be as dangerous as a Bengal tiger or a great white shark, but neither the shark nor the horned wolf are instruments of evil. Think of your time with the rag moth. Try to set aside emotion. Do not moralize. Nature. Not monsters."

His anger flared, but he stomped the fire into a puff of smoke and cinders.

"None of this makes sense to me. Why can I see these things and people like Dancer can only see standard nature?"

Valentina snorted.

"Standard nature? There is no standard nature, Mr. Green. It is all fantastical."

"You know what I mean."

"I do, but we aren't leaving this point so quickly. I am your teacher and I sense a fundamental misunderstanding in your question. 'Standard' implies something hierarchical, yes? Standard versus superior? Or standard versus substandard?"

Great. Another semantics lesson.

"Yeah, I guess so."

"Mr. Green, sasquatch is a common cryptid of popular imagination, correct? You could have told me what a sasquatch was a year ago, is that a fair assumption?"

"Yes."

"Tall bipedal forest-dwelling ape. Would you call that standard nature?"

"Well, no. Of course not."

"Why?"

"Because it isn't. It's hidden. People don't just see them. They've never found a body. They're . . . legendary."

"So, it's a question of rarity?"

"Well, yes, but I think it's more than that. Sasquatch is a matter of debate. It's not accepted as just rare. It's different. It's mythic. Mysterious."

Valentina looked past Green to the window.

"Mr. Green, these mountains have a strong population of red oaks. A common, well-documented tree. Correct?"

"Yes, I think so."

Green had no idea how common red oaks were.

"Some years, the oaks in this region produce massive crops of acorns. Other years, they may produce none. Not on a tree-by-tree basis, mind you, but as a community."

Green touched the lump where his acorn rested. Valentina continued.

"There are theories as to why this is beneficial for the trees. Predator satiation and so on. But, how, Mr. Green, do all the red oaks in this region decide when to produce a crop and when to wait? Moreover, how do they speak with one another to coordinate their actions among their community?"

Green shrugged.

"I don't know, but somebody must."

"No, Mr. Green. They really don't. Not in any real detail. We do not know. We have no Rosetta stone for red oak language. The red oak is a common tree. Communication is a common behavior. And we do not know how they organize and plan their acorn crops. Scientists cannot predict when the red oaks will produce acorns with any degree of certainty. That's the commonplace and inscrutable oak, standard nature. There are countless such mysteries within easy view as you look out that window, among species no one would classify as cryptonature."

Green turned back toward the little round window and the mass of trees beyond.

"I wouldn't have guessed that."

"Look out there, Mr. Green. Don't just see. Really try to look."

Outside, the branches swayed. The oaks' leaves, russet and brown, rattled and muttered, but kept their secrets.

"Trees, Mr. Green. Organisms that fade into the background of our lives from simple familiarity. What are they? Imagine you arrived on this planet this morning. What are they?"

Green weighed the question in his mind. It was big. Surprisingly big. Too big to hold. Green knew that he couldn't even name the species of most of the trees out this particular window. He certainly couldn't talk about the intricacies of how they lived or reproduced.

"Modern people so often see trees as *things*. Fine then, let's reframe them in a context familiar to you. Let's imagine them as human technology," Valentina said. "Self-replicating, solar-powered machines that synthesize carbon dioxide and rainwater into oxygen and sturdy building materials on a planetary scale. They lift tons of water hundreds of feet into the air without making a sound. Can humans build anything that compares to that in scope, subtlety, and efficiency?"

Valentina stood and joined Green at the window. Green looked down at her lined face, her dark eyes.

"We cannot, Mr. Green. Human ingenuity cannot re-create the most common of standard nature. Not even close. Do you understand? We cannot make, or even digest, our own food without the help of other species. Beyond that, the distinction between humans and our crafts and nature itself is an absurd fiction. We, ourselves, are standard nature."

He didn't answer. He looked back to the trees.

"Cryptonaturalists study a specific niche in nature because we're the ones who can study it, not because it is any more important or amazing than the most common tree on earth. Do not rob yourself at this early stage in your career by turning away from seemingly commonplace organisms. Bats can hear the shape of their world. Pythons can see the heat of their prey. Bees can dance directions to one another at the doorstep to their hive. There is no such thing as standard nature here."

"I think I understand."

He thought about it. All nature felt new to him. Perhaps he could see all of it with new eyes.

"Um, Teacher?"

"Yes?"

"Is sasquatch real?"

Valentina nodded.

"Quite real. Sasquatch is a broad term for several species. Not terribly rare. There's a long-running debate among cryptonaturalists if sasquatch should be considered a cryptid. Something of an edge case."

"Oh, so, possibly too standard, huh?"

"Common. You can use common as a sensible description, just not as a pejorative judgment of worth."

"I got it. So, do we have any idea why some people can perceive cryptonature and some can't?"

Valentina walked back to her chair and sat.

"The short answer is no. We don't know why any more than we can decode red oak speech. We do know a few things. We know that some are born with the predisposition. Some gain it through work and interest. I know two individuals who specialize in a single cryptid species and cannot perceive any others. It is a complex question with an untidy answer. Like many aspects of nature and biology, it's a spectrum, not a binary."

"Do you think Dancer could be trained to see cryptids?"

Valentina took a small broom from beside the broadcasting table and began sweeping away the spores left behind by the network administrator's hand, brushing them through the gap beside the oak trunk.

"I do. I even suggested as much to her once. It made sense to me. Ms. Dancer strikes me as uncommonly observant and she chooses a quiet life on a cryptid-rich mountainside. I offered some basic exercises to broaden her perspective."

Green laughed.

"I would love to have heard that conversation play out. I'm guessing she wasn't into the idea."

"You guess correctly. And, by way of apology, she dropped off a gift-wrapped hat. I think that was the second hat she gave me. Or third. I don't recall."

The wooden broadcast box began to make a soft sound like a finger tapping a tabletop.

Valentina turned and frowned at the device.

"Incoming message? Too fast for a reply. There is usually a delay on those broadcasts."

A staccato chirping began and her expression hardened.

"Emergency call."

She opened the box and flipped the switch.

"Valentina Blackwood. Go ahead."

A burst of static and then a gruff voice.

"Ranger Cheng. Ranger Station Orion. Morning, Val. Calling with poor news, I'm afraid."

The muscles in Valentina's jaw tensed.

"Sorry to say, we've got fatalities reported in your area. Unknown cryptid suspected. Kinkaid Cabins, about five miles south of you. Know 'em?"

Green's mouth went dry.

"Yes, I know them," Valentina said. "Do the authorities know yet?"

"Affirmative, looks like local police are there now. Have been for a bit. Medical examiner already came and went. Likely leaving with the corpses soon, if they haven't already. I'll get you copies of photos and coroner's reports via crawler as soon as I can."

"How many?"

"Three. College kids. Sitting around a campfire."

Valentina grimaced.

"Understood."

"This one's bad, Val. Preliminary reports are just preliminary, of course, but it looks targeted. We got pinged by the Whisperwood Agents and Old Threepwood's Calamity Device. Something outside normal parameters is behind this."

Green spoke up.

"What about the other death. Night before last. Kyle . . . something."

"Kyle Cartwright," Valentina said. She narrowed her eyes at Green, but let him continue.

"Right. Kyle Cartwright. He was found on the roadside."

"Who's that?" Cheng asked.

"My new apprentice. Are you familiar with the death he mentioned?"

"We are. We're reexamining it, but nothing conclusive. It's on our radar though."

"Alright, Mr. Cheng. I'll begin investigating."

"Thanks, Val. Let us know what you find. We're standing by to help with whatever you need."

She clicked off the box and shut the lid. Her face smoothed to the sort of neutrality that looks like a wound.

Green shut his eyes and pinched the bridge of his nose. It had new angles courtesy of the wolf attack. Dread, bare and stark as a snowfield, placed a cold hand between his shoulder blades.

"Mr. Green, you seem fated to experience too much too quickly."

"First, Kyle Cartwright. Now, three others dead? Tell me this isn't a common part of your job?"

"No. Thankfully, not common at all. I haven't had a call like that from the rangers in more than a decade."

"God. What did he mean by targeted?"

Valentina pursed her lips.

"Do you recall what I told you about how we find rag moth corpses? The mummified remains? A deadly misunderstanding between species. An accident of place and time and instinct."

"Yes, hard to forget."

"Well, in the opinion of the rangers, this was not that. When Ranger Cheng says targeted, he means they believe that whatever killed those people sought them out with lethal intent."

Green felt cold. In a deep, still pool of his mind, a skeletal wolf was surfacing from the dark water, an ivory island rising from the blackness.

I told you. The wolf is different.

"It means, Mr. Green, that whatever hunted and killed those people will likely do it again."

CHAPTER 8

A GROWL IN THE AFTERMATH

THE BUSTED PRIUS FELT VERY ILLEGAL TO DRIVE, BUT Green drove it anyway.

Valentina rode in the passenger seat with all the composure of a wet cat.

"I offered to travel your way," Green said.

"You aren't ready for the ways I typically travel."

He leaned toward the console, looking out the sagging hole in the windshield, blinking against the cold wind numbing his face and stinging his eyes.

"We're absolutely going to get pulled over."

Valentina shook her head.

"The police are busy."

They pulled into the Count and Countess gas station without incident and parked along the side. Alf paused in tying off a trash bag by the dumpster to stare.

Green climbed out and waved.

"Hey, bro. Little car trouble?" Alf said.

Along with the shattered windshield, the hood was dented concave and pocked with deep gouges.

"Yeah. That's fair to say. Had a bit of an accident."

"Mountain's a little too full of accidents last couple days. You hear?"

"I did. It . . . really sucks."

Green felt the urge to apologize, but he couldn't find the words. He felt responsible. All the misfortune arrived with him.

"Friend of mine works as a dispatcher for the cops. Said those campers OD'ed. Like, all of them. Simultaneously. Shit."

"I guess that could happen."

"I guess. But two fatal nights in a row? I don't like it, bro. It's fucked-up."

Green looked at his feet. He had no words.

"Hey, like, I don't wanna get too personal, but . . . Did you grow a beard . . . in, like, the last forty-eight hours?"

"Oh. I guess I did. It's been a strange couple nights."

Alf tossed the trash in the dumpster and motioned for Green to follow him into the store. Jerome was in his spot behind the register, shuffling his deck of cards. He lifted his chin an inch to greet Green.

Alf pulled out a high stool, sat, and began peeling a banana.

"You want one?"

"No thanks."

"Yeah, I'm trying to quit too. So, what happened to your ride? And who's the angry lady?"

"Wildlife encounter. The lady is Valentina. She's my neighbor up at Dancer's place. And she's sorta my boss now."

"She lives around here? Huh. Okay. Thought I knew everybody in the neighborhood."

"I don't think she gets out much."

Jerome tapped his deck on the counter and looked at Green.

"Oh, right," Green said, bringing two fingers to his temple. "I got one in mind."

He tried to *think* the card at Jerome, imagining the mysterious communication methods of red oaks.

King of clubs. King of clubs.

Jerome pulled a four of hearts from the deck and displayed it.

Green shook his head.

"Sorry. Not this time."

The bell above the door jangled and Valentina walked inside.

"Cars are vampires and gas stations are the necks they bite to suck the blood of the land," she said.

Jerome and Alf exchanged a look.

"Right on," Alf said.

She walked to the snacks, grabbed a bouquet of Slim Jims and a bag of jerky, and turned to leave without slowing.

"Green will pay," she said, passing back out the door.

"I got it," Green said. "She isn't usually like this. She really hates cars."

"Damn," Alf said. "I kinda like her style."

"Hey, you think I could get a little more advice? I don't exactly know anybody around here and my phone gets service like ten minutes a day. Do you know somebody who can fix my windshield? We're in a hurry today, but maybe I can meet them later or drop it off?"

"In a hurry?"

"Afraid so. Valentina is kind of an expert and she has some business to do. Helping with the recent . . . accidents."

"Shit, bro, yeah, I'll help with that."

Alf's expression made it seem like he knew more about the real subject of the conversation, more than he was willing to speak aloud. He thought for a beat, then reached into his pocket and pulled out a key ring.

"Trade me."

"What?"

"Give me your keys, man. My girl Casper can fix your windshield.

She can probably do it here. Or we'll work something out. You just take my truck and go do your business. Jerome can drop me home tonight. No big thing."

Jerome shrugged an agreement.

"That's . . . really kind. I guess I won't argue. It's important I get Valentina where she needs to go."

Alf grinned.

"You can buy me a six-pack sometime."

The two exchanged phone numbers and Green turned to go. He paused by the door and looked back.

"Alf and Jerome. Keeping the fires of hope burning on the edge of the wilderness. Making community a verb."

Green felt instantly embarrassed of his words.

Alf laughed a good-natured laugh.

"You a poet, bro?"

"I think it's just the gas station ambiance."

"Yeah, we know how that is. Good luck. I'll text about the car. Probably won't go through. Stop back if you don't hear from me by tomorrow."

He went out and found Valentina standing at the edge of the parking lot, facing the woods and eating a piece of jerky like it had wronged her personally. She wore a heavy backpack that, apparently, she wasn't comfortable leaving in the car.

"Teacher? You alright?"

"No, Mr. Green," she said through the chewing. "But I'm working on it."

She continued to do violence to her snack.

"I'll . . . just wait in the truck."

"Truck?"

"Alf is loaning us his vehicle."

He climbed into the truck and waited.

After a few minutes, she walked into the gas station, returned, then climbed into the passenger seat.

Green shot her a questioning look.

"I needed to thank him."

"Oh? That was nice. Why?"

"Because the point of manners is to remind us to align our behavior with our values even when we don't feel like it. Now drive."

He did.

Alf's truck was old and well maintained. It ran rough, but felt solid.

Valentina, with crossed arms and threatening blankness, guided Green to Kinkaid Cabins, a small camp in the foothills south of Candle-Fly. Most of her guiding involved barking out cardinal directions and working to contain her annoyance when Green's internal compass failed and he had to ask, "Right or left?"

It was late afternoon when they arrived. The shadows had all bled together beneath the looming western mountains. Green spotted a sheriff's cruiser blocking a narrow drive leading off into the woods next to a large, colorful sign for Kinkaid Cabins.

"That's it," Valentina said. "Drive past."

The cruiser was empty. Green drove on, slowing the truck around the next curve.

"Okay, now what?"

"We find a place to park on the shoulder out of view of the entrance."

Her businesslike neutrality was back. It was worse than her anger. It brought to mind the seriousness of the day's work.

"There. Park there."

Green pulled the truck off onto the wide gravel berm.

They climbed out and Green felt a pang of guilt about leaving Alf's truck on a roadside while they were probably committing a crime.

This is literally a matter of life and death. He'd understand.

Valentina leapt up the steep ten-foot embankment like a mountain goat and disappeared onto the flatter ground above.

Green did not leap up like any kind of goat. He scrabbled up on all fours, sliding two feet for every four he gained. He arrived at the top with muddy hands and knees, smelling like humus and leaf rot.

Valentina was twenty feet ahead kneeling over her backpack. He joined her, breathing hard.

"Hey, Teacher, what do we do when we do encounter the police?"

"I am preparing for that now."

Valentina pulled a soiled tan pillowcase from her bag and held it up. Something the size of a softball swung within. The bulge struggled and then went still.

"What is that?"

She shouldered her backpack and carried the pillowcase at her side.

"Come. We can walk and discuss this. We're losing the light."

Green saw something in the pillowcase kick off of Valentina's leg as she walked.

"Really, though, what is in there?"

Valentina sighed.

"Mr. Green, none of what has happened in the last few days would have been anywhere near my first-year's cryptonaturalist curriculum if I could have arranged ideal circumstances. Do you understand that?"

"Sure, I get that. Why?"

"Well, because this follows that pattern."

They walked through woods clinging to late summer, wading through waist-high underbrush, skirting the grasping thorns and briars where they could.

"Concealment is worthy knowledge for a cryptonaturalist," Valentina continued. "But obviously we would prefer circumstances less grim and a method less suspect."

"Suspect?"

"I am mincing my words. Unethical is what I mean. The method we use today is frankly unethical. It's a poor excuse, but we are in an emergency situation with no time to prepare something less distasteful."

"Alright. So? What is in that bag?"

"Do you know what a mole cricket is?"

"No."

"Fascinating insect. Herbivore. Incredible burrower. In the family Gryllotalpidae, in the order Orthoptera."

"And that's what's in the pillowcase?"

"No, I was using an insect I thought you would know as a reference point."

"Oh. Sorry."

"Ignorance is not a sin, Mr. Green."

"So, this thing is like a mole cricket?"

"Yes. But much larger. Rarer. Meaner. And venomous."

"Jesus. You're going to let a venomous cryptid attack the police?"

"No, it's going to attack us."

Green's stomach did a somersault. He looked at the lump in the pillowcase. It seemed bigger than before.

"So, when you said unethical, you meant unethical to us?"

"No, unethical to put a living thing in a sack and frighten it into a defensive behavior. This is not how we conduct ourselves. I am doing it to save lives. It won't do lasting harm to the cricket, but it is still ugly behavior for any kind of naturalist. I knew where one was and I couldn't arrange another method by this afternoon."

"What is that thing called?"

"Pennington's Cricket. A tacky name given by an odious man, but hardly the fault of the animal."

Two gunshots rang out ahead.

They sounded like firecrackers, so loud and close that Green was shocked they couldn't see the source.

"We need to move," Valentina said.

She held up the pillowcase in her right hand. Balled up her left fist, and plunged it into the bag. Her face was calm, but Green saw the moment when her shoulders tensed. She withdrew her arm. There were no visible marks. She handed the bag to Green.

"Your turn. Do what I did. Fist closed, nondominant hand."

The pillowcase was heavy. It felt like a brick in a bag. His stomach turned and, in an instant, he felt both cold and sweaty. A panic rose in his chest, a certain urgency that if he didn't do exactly what Valentina said at that exact moment, he would never be able to do it.

He did it.

He closed his fist. Squeezed his eyes shut. And stuffed his left arm into the pillowcase.

He felt his knuckles resting against something hard, cool, and smooth like heavy plastic. Then, the rigid surface moved away and an electric shock jolted through his thumb. He sucked in a breath and yanked his arm free.

He held up his left hand and opened his eyes, fearing what he might see. There was nothing. A little redness in the fleshy rise where his thumb joined his palm.

"Ow. Now what happens?"

He looked up at Valentina and felt dizzy from the sight.

Her arm was gone.

No, not gone, made of water with twisting threads of shadow running through it like veins of smoke. The top of her head was the same and the effect was moving, spreading downward. Green watched the line of nothing reach her eyes and the color drain away. It looked as though Valentina had been a tank full of living pigments and now she had sprung a leak. He looked down and made a choked gasp when he saw the leak was literal. Pinks and grays were pooling at Valentina's feet, glistening wetly on the leaves like spilled paint.

"What's happening? What's happening to you?"

"Stay calm, Mr. Green. The venom will not hurt you, but it does affect your perception. Vision especially. It will conceal us, but it also alters our senses in unpredictable ways. Trust my voice. Be suspicious of your eyes."

Green checked his own arm again and saw the same unpleasant image. Inky branches stretching through dim water. A drowned tree in a rising flood. The sight made his stomach turn.

She tied off the pillowcase and returned it to her backpack.

"We will return this creature to its burrow with our apologies this evening."

As she stowed the pillowcase with one hand, the other pulled from the bag a section of gnarled log covered in moss. It looked like something she might have just plucked from the forest floor, a joint of punky wood, except it had a polished leather strap attached at each end. She tossed it over one transparent shoulder to hang at her hip, then hoisted on her backpack.

"Follow me."

She moved on in the direction of the gunshots.

Keeping up with her was a weightless, drunken experience. She was unpleasant to look at, emotionally and physically, a ghost image that his brain was desperate to blink away.

The discomfort was amplified by the fact that Green could no longer see his own limbs, which made him feel further untethered from reality. A phantom following a phantom. Only his heavy breathing and pounding heart kept him feeling anchored and alive.

There were other changes to his vision too. Every tree was outlined in a green shimmer that called to mind night vision goggles. Points of light like living campfire sparks scurried about the underbrush and darted through the air. He didn't know whether they were insects or inventions of his altered perception.

Thorns and briars tore at his hands and face as they rushed onward. Green pictured himself bleeding rainwater, clear rivulets tumbling into the dark soil. He had no options. Continue to move forward or fall bodily like a mist and feel himself drunk down into the rich, thirsting earth.

His mind groped for handholds. Fragments of memory. Bits of old learning. Essays from college English.

Full fathom five thy father lies;
Of his bones are coral made;
Those are pearls that were his eyes:
Nothing of him that doth fade,
But doth suffer a sea-change
Into something rich and strange.

He risked closing his eyes for a moment. Mercifully, his eyelids still shut out the light. Then he wasn't *actually* transparent. It was an illusion.

In that reassuring inner darkness, he felt for himself and found the familiar comfort of breath. In and out. The smell of the forest and the dry paper crunch of leaves underfoot. With his eyes closed, nothing had changed. He could always retreat there. In the blink of an eye, he could retreat there.

She stopped at the edge of a clearing. Not far ahead, Green saw a circle of squat yellow cabins. Off to the left, partially concealed by another police vehicle, a line of crime scene tape swayed and fluttered in the wind.

He stepped up beside his teacher.

"How are you acclimating, Mr. Green?"

"Not great, but I'm still here."

He thought Valentina nodded. It was hard to tell.

"Understand that it is not that they can't see us. It is that they don't want to on a cellular level. We have, essentially, become cryptids. I have a great deal of experience studying odd and hidden things and even I deeply dislike looking at you in your current state."

He felt the bile rising in his throat as he tried to watch her speak, so he closed his eyes again.

"We will move unaccosted. Often, people will even unconsciously answer direct questions in order to be rid of us. They won't remember the questions because we are currently damaging to their hold on reality and their mental immune system rejects us. We are not, however, immune to stray bullets or the attention of aggressive cryptids, but I have contingency plans."

Valentina patted the rotten log at her side with a spectral hand.

She turned and left the tree line. Green followed, wondering how frequently his new teacher had needed to worry about stray bullets or deadly cryptids.

A cruiser and a white van were the only vehicles at the scene. Beyond an oblong ring of yellow police tape strung from tree to tree around the nearest cabin's fire ring, two deputies were standing by the hood of the cruiser, looking off into the woods. The deputies, a man with a shaved head and a woman with a ponytail, looked unhappy. A gaunt young man in blue scrubs was walking away from the pair, scowling.

Shaved Head was holstering his weapon as Green and Valentina approached. Green saw the moment both cops heard their footsteps. Their heads swung toward the sound. Apologies and explanations raced to Green's lips, but the cops made a face like they had bitten into a lemon and looked away.

Valentina spoke in a voice that seemed entirely too loud to Green.

"Observe and listen."

If the deputies heard her, they made no sign. They continued their conversation.

"It doesn't matter," Ponytail said. "Say you saw a black bear and wanted to scare it off."

Shaved Head grunted.

"It *does* matter. I think they'll like that story about as much as Kevin did. Hell."

He looked to the man in scrubs who had returned to the boxy white van.

"He's just pissed because he almost shit his pants," Ponytail said.

"Yeah. Well, me too."

Shaved Head looked off at the tree line.

"Alright. I guess it might have been a bear. Never discharged my weapon before on the job. Didn't even think about it. It just happened. Felt like something was coming at me."

"Look, you just leave when that last body leaves. Should be soon. I'll drive you down to your cruiser."

It was surreal.

Green and Valentina stood fifteen feet off from the officers, loitering in broad daylight, eavesdropping on the police. It was like walking onstage during a play, all the actors pretending not to notice.

It was stranger still when Valentina spoke. She wasn't even bothering to whisper.

"Look around. If we are separated, we will meet back where we exited the woods."

Green agreed before realizing he had no idea where they exited the woods or what he was supposed to look for.

Valentina was a blur and then was lost from sight.

He sighed and risked taking a few steps closer to the deputies. Maybe he could do some good by listening. They didn't turn, but Shaved Head rested his hand on his holster. Green wanted to close his eyes again, but he couldn't watch for pointed guns if he retreated to the comforting dark.

"Alright," Shaved Head said. "I'll be in the car."

"Sounds good. I'm gonna walk that little field again. I don't like that we haven't found any paraphernalia. Gotta be ODs, but they must have chucked their kit someplace."

Shaved Head looked back to the tree line.

"Hey, maybe don't. Not solo. Let forensics do their job. They already looked. The toxicology report will find whatever there is to find."

Ponytail smirked.

"Yes, Mother."

Green moved like the air was molasses. There was a sensation of pushing through his own disbelief, wading hip-deep through his mind's need to reject the scene around him.

He turned and moved toward the van.

It was idling near the front steps of the little cabin.

A tired-looking woman sat in the driver's seat, tapping at her phone.

The man in scrubs leaned over the hood, scribbling something on a clipboard.

Green rounded to the back and flinched when he registered the van's contents.

Two gurneys. One empty. One holding a sheet-draped body.

He knew three bodies were found.

Why weren't they taken away all at once?

Up close, the white van didn't look very official. The back bumper had once been chrome, but rust gnawed away its shine. The broadside panel was dented in around an impact that left a scuffed crescent of missing paint. It looked like somebody hit it with a sledgehammer. Maybe the department didn't have money for repairs or maybe this wasn't the sort of vehicle anybody was supposed to see anyway.

Green walked up to the rear. The doors hung wide like reaching arms. A single yellowjacket crawled along the hem of a thin white sheet pouring over the edge of the occupied gurney.

In the unreality of the moment, the shrouded body seemed to be a whirlpool tugging the little ship of his attention nearer. He was there to look. He needed to look. What could be more important to see than this?

Green swallowed, teetering on the edge of the whirlpool.

Mechanically, he forced himself to step up into the back of the van. It felt twenty degrees colder inside. The yellowjacket retreated, grazing his ear with a faint whine like a distant motor.

He paused.

"Valentina?"

His voice was a hoarse whisper.

There was no answer.

He moved to the head of the body and reached for the sheet. It was tucked beneath the figure and fought with him as he worked to peel it aside.

Don't they have body bags in the cop shows?

The sheet came away.

There was the young woman with the mint coat he'd seen at the Count and Countess station on the night he'd arrived. Her blond hair was plastered over one eye. Her lower lip protruded, frozen at an odd angle, exposing white teeth and a line of pink gums. The tops of her ears and the tip of her nose looked stained with ink.

Dark as the wolf's flesh.

One of the two double doors behind Green slammed shut and he barked out a cry.

"Stop," he said.

The gaunt man reeled back and doubled over from the sound of Green's voice. He gagged and spit in the dirt. His clipboard clattered on the ground.

"Christ," he said to the empty air as Green stumbled out of the van.

Green staggered to the cabin's porch and let himself spill onto the weathered boards, his heart racing.

The man in scrubs recovered and slammed the second door. A moment later he, his partner, and the body of a woman on a fun little trip to the mountains rumbled down the wooded drive and away from Kinkaid Cabins. Green sat up and watched them go, trying not to think of the way her lips looked like molded wax. Not alive. Somehow, not fully dead. Completely and utterly wrong.

He scanned around for Valentina, but couldn't see her. It was hard to know whether that was good or bad. She wasn't much of a comfort. He flinched at a car door slam and looked up to see the cops were pulling out of the little parking area.

Gravel dust billowed.

The sound of the tires rose and fell.

Plastic police tape murmured in the breeze of approaching evening.

"Mr. Green?"

The Valentina smudge stood five feet off.

"What?"

"Tell me what you've seen so far."

The question made him very tired.

"I saw one of the bodies. I knew her face. I saw her at the gas station when I arrived in the mountains. Like I saw Kyle Cartwright. Is this me? Am I doing this somehow?"

He didn't need to see her to feel the weight of her attention.

"Hmm. Are you a dangerous, predatory cryptid somehow deceiving the most experienced cryptonaturalist in the world?"

Her tone seemed artificially light. He didn't like it.

Green thought of the things he hadn't told his new teacher. He thought of the acorn in his pocket. He thought of the crow he couldn't explain, the acrid haze of memories that hurt to touch. He thought of the wolf's accusatory pronouncement. *Not-man.*

"Did you somehow come here and harm these people while you were simultaneously observing the rag moth?"

He didn't have the words or the energy to argue.

"No," he said.

"No, indeed. No, you are one of the people fighting to solve this. That is what you are doing here. Now, tell me what you saw."

Green tried to breathe, but it felt shaky.

"Teacher. Can . . . can it wait?"

In his current state, away from the awe of the library tree, using the word "teacher" felt uncomfortably infantilizing.

Valentina paused. He couldn't see her face or guess her expression. He was talking to a disturbing bruise on the landscape.

"Yes. I suppose so. Come, stay within sight of me while I finish my examinations."

He watched the nauseating shape of Valentina duck under the police tape. He rose with a groan and followed. He had to stay close or lose her. The tape cordoned off a large metal fire ring surrounded by three bright blue camp chairs. They looked new and smelled like a sporting goods store. Green thought of that same camping gear smell lingering in his own car.

The wind shifted and the police tape billowed, changing the oblong perimeter into a fat bean shape.

Valentina knelt by one of the camp chairs and did . . . something. Green could hear a scraping noise like a fingernail scratching at nylon.

The scene was too clean. What had been there when the police arrived? Were there empty beer cans beside the toppled bodies? A Bluetooth speaker? A half-eaten bag of Doritos? Marshmallows? A cooler full of hot dogs and melting ice sold to them by Alf? How much of it was sitting in a cluttered evidence room?

He stood at the edge of the ring and thought about friends sitting around a cheerful fire. It was a happy image, the sort of idyllic vignette he carried with him as he drove toward the Catskills. It was the hopeful future he clung to as the acorn chased him out of his old life, a classic campout with friends, an endless summer vacation. Except, it all went wrong. For him and for them.

Something came here and it went wrong. As wrong as it could go.

Something.

That's what Valentina would want him to think.

But it wasn't *something*. It was the horned wolf. The monster.

She wasn't there. She didn't see it.

He didn't want to get any closer than he needed to in order to keep track of his teacher. He didn't know what to look for. All he could do was contaminate the scene or be in the way. He shifted his focus to a nearby patch of grass and found a dead robin gaping up at him with sightless eyes like black beads.

Nowhere is safe to look.

Valentina moved about like a minnow flashing in a mountain stream, glimpsed then gone, glimpsed then gone.

He didn't like the silence, so he tossed words at it.

"Can you see anything?"

"Still searching," Valentina said. "They took most everything, of course. I'm confounded as to why they didn't take the chairs. Not that I'm an expert on modern policing."

Green tried to think of something useful to add.

"I saw the girl's body in the van. She had dark patches on her skin. Dark like the horned wolf's body. Is that important?"

His voice was flat.

"We have far too little data to make any educated guesses yet."

He tried to allow for Valentina's wisdom and experience, but all he could see was that sharp-toothed skull pressing in on him. What would have happened if he had reached out and touched that black, pooling flesh? Would they have found him lifeless in his car with ink-stained fingertips? Perhaps he was still destined to take a ride in that beat-up van.

It wasn't data, but it felt true. True and hateful. That huge nightmare creature pouncing from the dark trees with unearthly grace. They wouldn't even see it, would they? A world they couldn't touch, but it could touch them just fine. More than touch.

Valentina might be experienced and wise, but Green thought he had something that she didn't—a healthy connection to instinctual human fear.

There was a kind of wisdom in that, too, wasn't there? Did Blobert do his job too well? It was possible to be too detached and analytical. Wasn't that a kind of gap in her awareness?

Green thought of the young man in the Ohio University hoodie back at the Count and Countess station. He pictured him being slid into a metal drawer. What was he studying? Why wasn't *he* able to see the threat lurking out of the dark trees?

His brain floated back to his own college days, a drunken span of years in which poetry and coffee shop politics seemed like the only path leading up and out of the bullshit.

What had Tennyson called nature?

"Red in tooth and claw."

"Hmm?"

He had accidentally spoken aloud.

"Oh. Nothing."

"Come, Mr. Green. Look here. These patches of grass. Can you see the shapes? But why would the grass die from such brief contact with a body?"

Valentina was a smoky lump crouched near the crime scene tape. Green swallowed and took a knee beside her.

"Here, beside this chair, then over next to the fire ring. Can you see the discoloration?"

It was subtle, but he could see it.

The grass was the wrong color. Not dead. Not yet. But on its way. A pale yellow was overtaking the green.

He made an unintentional sound in his throat when he noticed the shapes. The patch in front of them was the silhouette of a body on its side. Green stood and looked at the other patches. They were less clear, but still unmistakably human. A yellowing shadow of an outstretched arm. The clear crook of an elbow. The L of a foot outlined in wilting grass.

"They look like . . . fingerprints of death."

Valentina was silent for a moment. He couldn't see her, but he again felt the weight of her attention. She was considering him.

"This was too much. A string of too much. I shouldn't have brought you here."

Green thought about disagreeing, but he was bone-tired. Spiritually tired. He wanted to be done. He didn't even have the clarity to articulate what that meant.

"Rest your mind. It needs a break. Your only task is to stay near me. Focus on that."

Green touched the acorn in his pocket, one more persistent unknown.

Valentina retrieved two mason jars from a side compartment on the pack and unscrewed the lids.

"Here. Drink this. It will help you metabolize the cricket venom faster."

Green took the jar.

"Thanks. Is this made of something tragic? Widow's tears?"

"It's water and honey. You'll find honey has myriad uses in our work."

Green closed his eyes so he could drink without seeing his fever-dream hand holding the jar. It was cool, simple, and sweet. He downed the whole jar without pausing. He stood with his eyes closed, returning to the healing power of his breath.

Valentina took the jar from his hand. He heard her futzing with the backpack and moving around nearby, but he resolved to stay in his calming darkness until she asked him to follow.

"Just a moment. I need to rule out a few more possibilities before we depart."

He could hear her pacing back and forth.

She spoke to herself in a soft monotone while she worked.

"No visible tracks. No scorching. No obvious soil disturbance. No mucus trail. No musk or marking. Sky is intact. Turning left still possible. Turning right still possible. No carrion kings. No number repetition. Taking samples of live and dead grasses."

Green didn't open his eyes to see if she was speaking into a recorder. He didn't ask follow-up questions. Valentina was absolutely correct. He was done putting a brave face on it. It had been too much.

The fact that half of what she spoke to herself hinted at lifetimes more to learn might have been exciting at other times, but at that moment it just felt like sinking chest-deep in a sulphureous swamp.

The growl came without warning.

It was deep as caves beneath the ocean and undeniable as gravity.

Green's eyes snapped open.

Valentina was already more visible. She lay on her stomach in the grass with her ear pressed to the ground.

His heart pounded.

"Teacher, did you hear it?"

"Just a moment, Mr. Green. I'm listening for burrow echo."

"No! Listen! The growling!"

Valentina sat up.

"What growling?"

The growl came again. It felt like it was ringing Green's rib cage like a church bell.

He staggered and held up a finger.

"*That* growling."

Valentina narrowed her eyes and surveyed the tree line.

"I don't hear any growling."

The growl came a third time and this time there was a single command in the sound.

Run.

Green spoke that command aloud as it tumbled through his skull on the back of that primal threat.

Valentina stood up calmly. She shouldered her pack and tilted her head in assent.

"Toward the truck, then," she said, and moved in a jog toward the woods.

The jog quickened to a run as he joined her.

Branches whipped.

Twigs cracked underfoot.

Green's chest ached and his legs were on fire.

He looked over his shoulder and hated that he could still see the roofs of the cabins. They were too slow. They couldn't escape.

He slammed into a dogwood sapling that sprang back and shoved him off his feet. He got up running and risked another look behind.

The wolf was there.

Standing motionless forty feet off.

The monster.

A horror desecrating the fading light of evening.

Its skeletal legs were exposed, birdlike, too narrow for the massive body they supported. The skull was bare, eyes fixed on Green's back. The dark flesh collected above the shoulder, rising up in jagged points like a young mountain range. The whole of the creature stood in a great pulsing shadow, an inverse fire. It was an outrider of night, a trespasser in the waking world of birdsong and golden sun. It stood statue-still, watching their desperate flight.

Green could do nothing but turn his attention back to Valentina before he lost her in the woods or crashed into another tree.

He hadn't heard the wolf approach, not until it growled, not until it wanted him to hear.

He wouldn't hear when it decided to close the distance and clamp his spine in those white gravestone jaws.

He wanted to scream a warning, but why?

There was nothing he could do.

They were already running.

It was up to the wolf if they would outlive the day.

He ran and felt a kind of bleak gratitude for the branches that stung his face and the briars that bit his hands, because those were pains he could comprehend. Those things were real and in front of him and held no secret malice that might threaten him in ways deeper than physical harm.

They made it to Alf's truck.

Green slid down the embankment on his back, fighting for breath.

Valentina climbed inside.

He kicked up a spray of gravel rounding the hood and threw himself into the driver's seat.

He knew what the horned wolf made of modern obstacles like steel doors and windshields.

Valentina caught her breath with dignified precision.

Green turned the key and stomped the accelerator, spinning the tires and leaving a rooster tail of dirt and stones spraying up behind them.

Then, they were away, fishtailing onto the road. Yet even speed and distance felt like empty comforts. Paper armor.

"Mr. Green, slow down."

He hadn't even seen the wolf run. It wasn't there. Then it was.

"Mr. Green, slow down."

He was hyperventilating.

If Valentina would admit that a word like "sacred" existed for a reason, then how could she deny words like "monster"? Words like "evil"?

She placed a hand on his forearm.

"Mr. Green . . ."

He glanced at the odometer. She was right. They were approaching sixty miles per hour on curving mountain roads. He eased off the gas and hated every ounce of speed he surrendered.

His hands were shaking.

He tried to grip the wheel tighter to steady himself.

"Would you like to hear about my favorite comfort food?"

"What?"

Forty miles an hour had never felt so slow.

"My favorite comfort food. I want to tell you about it."

It was too slow. It was far too slow. Did it matter? What was speed to a thing that could appear out of nowhere?

"Shouldn't you be preparing one of those contingencies you mentioned? Where's that log thing?"

"Listen to my voice, Mr. Green. Nothing is chasing us. If something did, we would handle it. Now, I would like to tell you about my favorite comfort food for autumn."

She didn't see it.

She didn't hear it.

She couldn't understand.

"It's had a few names. Welsh rabbit or Welsh rarebit in the eighteenth century, but given the origins of those names I think 'cheese on toast' will do."

"It's still chasing us. I can feel it. It knows where we are."

"And it waited until we drove away to spring its trap? No. You're driving home to a rest. You're warm and dry. You're learning about my favorite food for autumn evenings."

He glanced at Valentina. Her color still looked wrong, like a badly painted mannequin, but it was improving.

Green checked the rearview and said nothing.

"You might infer from the name 'cheese on toast' that you already understand the recipe, but you would be oversimplifying. The name doesn't do the meal justice. Like most simple foods, the ingredients are key. A homemade loaf. Not too dense. Thick slices. Toasted on a fork by the fire. Modern toasters do not replicate that flavor."

She paused and fished out her jerky bag and insisted Green take a piece.

"You chew while I talk."

"I'm not hungry."

"I didn't say you were. Now chew."

He did as he was told. The jerky tasted like salt and campfire smoke.

"Toasted bread."

Green's heart still beat in his ears, but he felt the adrenaline easing.

"Yes. Fire toasted on a fork. Once you have your toast, you need a rich Cheshire cheese. Hard to find in North America these days, but worth the effort. The smell of it sets your feet on cobblestones in eighteenth-century England. Now, you would be doing this while you toast your bread, mind you, but you crumble the Cheshire with a three-finger pinch of breadcrumbs and the crushed yolk of a boiled egg into a pan and warm it on the fire. Just hot enough to melt the cheese and bring the mixture together."

Green chewed jerky and shivered. He worked to watch the road without thinking about his hands on the steering wheel. They were still the wrong color.

Valentina's words pulled him into a firelit place full of the smell of toasting bread and cheese.

"Like all the best comfort foods, this recipe isn't too complicated, and it has the added benefit that if you begin with frost-reddened cheeks and numb fingers, you will thaw yourself while you prepare your meal. Turn left here."

Green turned.

If it wanted to, the wolf could already be back at Candle-Fly.

Maybe it was stalking Dancer as she walked out to watch the sunset.

Maybe it was visiting Alf and Jerome. Perhaps everyone he met now was cursed to die.

Maybe it was lying low in the bed of the truck.

He thumbed the acorn in his pocket and heard a line from an old horror movie.

The call is coming from inside the house!

"Next, of course, you spread the Cheshire mixture on your toasted bread. You could eat it then, but you would miss the crowning touch that takes it from simply delicious to transcendent."

They passed the Count and Countess and Green slowed to look. No wolf. No sign of danger. His car was there, windshield still broken.

"Do you know what a salamander is, Mr. Green?"

He was half listening.

"Small, squishy reptile."

"Amphibian, actually, but I'm talking about culinary equipment. I believe they have been out of fashion for some time, but a salamander is essentially a thick disk of iron with a long handle."

Green lost the thread of his morbid thoughts and remembered wondering about the tools next to the cabin's fireplace.

"I think I saw one in the cabin, right? I wondered what that was for."

"Just so, though you can use a hearth shovel if needed. The last, key step of cheese on toast involves heating up your salamander red-hot. Truthfully, this is the first step. You set your salamander in the fire as soon as the idea for the meal occurs. That sort of forethought was usually involved in older recipes. I always thought it added to the satisfaction of the finished product. Careful intention. Ritual."

Green felt wrung out and on the edge of tears.

"Now, my favorite part. With the Cheshire mixture spread on your toast, you pull that almighty hot salamander from the fire and hold it just above the cheese. It bubbles and browns and the cheese sinks into the bread, components fusing into a greater whole."

Dusk proper had arrived when they pulled into Candle-Fly Camp.

Green looked to Dancer's office.

The light was on.

Her body was not broken and spread out by her front door.

"Have you ever had it, Mr. Green? Proper cheese on toast?"

"No. It sounds . . . pretty good."

"Sometimes I think people deny themselves comforting tasks like making handcrafted meals because they are told so often how convenient their lives are. They begin to think that instant, soulless nutrition is all they need. Nonsense, of course. Go ahead and drive straight to my camp. I can abide a vehicle for one night. This vehicle has served with honors."

Green hadn't realized until that point, but Valentina hadn't complained once about being a passenger on the drive back, not even with his erratic driving.

She hadn't betrayed an ounce of fear or anger as he took mountain roads at unsafe speeds.

Damn. I must be truly pitiable.

"I'll understand if you wish to go straight to bed," Valentina said. "But, if I can tempt you, I have everything we need for cheese on toast and I can have the cabin hearth alive and crackling faster than you'd believe. Full moon tonight. Clear. Crisp. The cabin will be warm enough to leave the door open and let the smell of leaves in. It will be too cold to fret about insects. Probably not a thing to be missed."

"What about the wolf?" he asked weakly.

"My camp is safe, Mr. Green. Our home is a safe place to rest. Put your faith in that."

In the last light of sunset, Valentina looked very much like a witch. *A witch,* Green thought, *who is on my side.*

He decided to trust her.

He didn't seem to have much choice.

"Okay," he said. "I think cheese on toast would be nice."

And it was.

CHAPTER 9

THE HOLE IN NOTHING

"GATHER WHAT YOU NEED FOR A HIKE, MR. GREEN," VALENtina called from the steps of her trailer while Green pumped water into his jug.

The pump handle was so cold he worried his skin would stick. Silver frost rimmed the clover at the pump's base, the morning sun still too low to sweep away the night's lingering chill.

"How far?"

He realized his question didn't matter much the moment he asked it. It wasn't as though he knew what he should pack for either a short hike or a long hike.

"I expect it will occupy most of our day. Pack a lunch."

He thought of the small pile of gear next to his cot in the cabin.

"Do I need to bring bear spray?"

"There are no grizzlies here. Black bears are glorified raccoons. I'm deterrent enough."

He smiled and went to get his things.

Green's sleep had been terrible. Even after the calming respite of

Valentina's cheese on toast, he woke countless times to stand and listen by the cabin door, then chided himself back to resting. What did he expect to hear?

The horned wolf had let them run from Kinkaid Cabins.

Why didn't it kill us?

Because it didn't want to?

Yet?

He turned the question over in his hands again and again through the night, a second acorn weighing on his thoughts.

Either it didn't want to, echoing the conscious choice it made on the night Green heard its thoughts. Or it simply couldn't because of some contrivance of Valentina's, some "deterrent."

He hoped it was the latter.

He did not like the idea that he was alive because of that monster's whim and forbearance. It felt better to believe that he was part of an active and effective resistance to the creature's designs.

The lingering scent of toasting bread and melting cheese looked over Green's shoulder while he packed. He imagined the ghost of a woman in a mint green jacket sitting on the edge of his cot, watching him paw through his supplies. The ghost of a man holding a fishing rod stood by saying, "If you stick to the roads, you can't get too lost around here."

Green had not stuck to the roads.

He shouldered his gear and turned back to the door.

An old song ran through his rattled mind.

You can never be strong. You can only be free.

"Easy for you to say."

He went out.

Valentina was waiting for him.

She wore her customary canvas pack and carried a knobby walking stick.

"Nice stick," Green said.

"Thank you. It's blackthorn. A gift from an Irish colleague. Blackthorn has some particular benefits in our line of work."

"Mysterious. I like it."

"Not mysterious, just not relevant today. It is my task to plan your educational meals to be nutritious, so I don't give you random bites of empty calories until you are full to bursting without absorbing the proper informational nutrients in their proper order."

"Has anybody ever told you you've got a real talent for metaphor?"

"Oh, hush, Mr. Green. It's a three-mile hike to reach our destination. I don't suppose you have ever walked six miles in a day."

"Hey now, I lived in the city. My car spent most of its time in the parking garage. I walked everywhere. I'm game. Where are we going?"

He tried to sound nonchalant, but the idea of being miles from camp without a car or any nearby shelter rang an alarm bell in his head.

The wolf comes at night. Maybe . . . but the sun was still up when it chased us at Kinkaid.

"We need data. We are in an anomalous situation that, based on the proximity of the recent deaths, seems to be tied to this area specifically. So, we are checking in on another recent place-bound oddity of this region."

"And what's that?"

"It will be easier to explain once we arrive."

They started off from Valentina's camp, heading toward Dancer's office. The sun was still a misty yellow ball hovering close to the eastern horizon and dew sparkled on the weedy margins of Moss Man's Row. They passed Green's campsite and, peering down the path from the little parking spot, he wondered if he would ever manage to spend a full night there. A robin on a low branch above the lane puffed up its feathers against the cold and sang bright notes into the morning haze. Even with Green's terror hangover, it felt good to be out and walking through the woods on such a morning.

They reached the moss man. The big stump was shaggy with growth and spotted with lichens. Huge bracket fungi, like tawny dinner plates embedded in the rotting wood, shadowed glimmering crescents of frost from the wan sunlight. Green surprised himself by nodding a greeting to the citadel of vibrant decay.

"Now that you've recovered," Valentina said, "you will kindly get that vehicle away from my home when we return."

"I can do that, but I wouldn't say I've recovered. I can't get that wolf out of my mind. Or the face of that dead woman."

Valentina glanced at her apprentice, but didn't slow.

"Only natural. Fear and sadness accompany tragedy."

"I'm getting very tired of being afraid. I don't suppose Blobert has a cousin I could meet."

She reached out and trailed her fingertips along the papery skin of a yellow birch as they passed. Green noticed she often touched the landscape while she walked.

"I'm afraid not. And dulling fear is a remedy that is sometimes worse than the disease. But fear is part of the reason we are on the move today."

"What do you mean?"

They turned from the gravel and continued on a narrow footpath trailing down the slope south of Candle-Fly. The leaves felt slick and soft underfoot.

"Fear has two fangs. The first is a pervasive sense of helplessness. The second is the enormity of the unknown. Today, we aim to armor ourselves against both. We are not helpless. We are not hiding in our shelters. We are actively seeking information to improve our position. The unknown does not root us where we stand. We are rejecting both helplessness and the premise of unknowability."

Her words didn't untie all of the knots in Green's chest, but they loosened a few. He absolutely had the impulse to hide, to do nothing, so moving forward was a kind of victory.

The sun climbed as they walked, the sky brightening to an autumn blue of faded cornflowers. The mountain woods were alive with the motion of falling leaves and the wind carried the earthy scent of plant matter returning to the soil. Green drank deeply of the mountains. He drank instinctually and felt a thirst he couldn't name quietly subsiding.

For a moment, he set aside all thoughts of phantom deer and maddening acorns. He was simply a man on a walk in a beautiful place.

" 'The clearest way into the universe is through a forest wilderness.' John Muir said that."

"He did," Valentina said. "He also said, 'Between every two pines is a doorway to a new world.' That is likely the more appropriate quotation for today's work."

That comment pulled Green out of his idyllic musings. He didn't like the idea of mysterious doorways. Doorways let things in.

"Muir was a compelling writer," Valentina continued. "Of course, he also held many reprehensible beliefs and worked to erase indigenous histories. Yet he could turn an evocative phrase and he helped some Americans feel a new kind of connection with nature."

Green stared at the back of Valentina's head as she walked. He had spent a decade cultivating the skill of office talk, cheerful conversation about nothing. Valentina was a very different sort of animal. He quickened his pace to keep up with her.

"Hey, Teacher, the scope of your knowledge is borderline ridiculous."

Valentina sniffed.

"I travel widely. I read widely. I work to maintain active curiosity and humility in the face of new information. I don't let my vanity insist that I cannot be improved upon. It is not a comfortable worldview, but it is worthwhile. It keeps me young."

"Are you going to explain that two pines quote or am I still waiting for mealtime?"

"Patience. As I said, better to see it first."

He didn't like it, but he couldn't think of a persuasive way to argue.

A squirrel with one bulging cheek pouch ran into the path. It turned toward the walkers and opened its mouth in a too-wide yawn. The bulge, a bright blue eye, rolled into the open mouth and studied the pair. A red slash appeared in the white fur of the squirrel's belly, a second mouth that let out a chattering cry before the creature scurried off into the underbrush.

"Was that a . . ."

"Cyclops squirrel," Valentina said. "Quite common in this area."

A lump of something unpleasant pressed on Green's tongue. He spat, but there was nothing there.

"Ugh. Why does my mouth taste like ashes?"

"It's a defense mechanism against predators. Suppresses appetite. Effective, wouldn't you say? Don't look directly at the eye next time."

Green kept spitting in the leaves, which accomplished nothing.

The wind changed and there was new warmth in it, morning giving way to noonday. A low-level burn in his ankles and calves told him that walking mountain paths was not the same as navigating sidewalks and subway station stairs. These were not paths built for humans, yet humans were built for them. It was a subtle distinction that manifested as a dull ache in unfamiliar muscles.

Valentina set an unhurried pace. The path forked many times, but she never hesitated in choosing the way. Green fell back and noticed how strange and easy it was to share comfortable silence while walking through the trees. He didn't feel a need to fill the quiet. There was so much to see, to smell, to hear in the pulse of the living woodlands. Here, a burst of crisp sound as two chipmunks raced through the branches of a fallen sweet gum. There, the drumroll of a downy woodpecker hunting for his lunch. And always the soft march of Valentina's footfalls while she ducked beneath a storm-tilted trunk or strayed from the path to touch a feathery hemlock bough. He began to mirror her, stepping where she stepped. Touching what she touched. As he did, he realized that there was an entire vocabulary of new textures to learn along with the sounds, scents, and sights of the woods.

It was nearly 11 A.M. when they arrived. Valentina halted at a small clearing like a castle moat surrounding an unremarkable stand of gangly young pines in the center.

"We're here," she said. "The Hole in Nothing."

Something about that phrase made Green tingle with recognition, but he couldn't quite place it.

"Muir's doorway between two pines?" he asked.

"Exactly."

He stood beside his teacher.

The first thing Green noticed was the litter.

Sun-faded beer cans gleamed silver from the drifts of leaves. A gold condom wrapper and a smashed liquor bottle marked the boundary of the little clearing. He stepped over them and studied the area. There was a small fire ring made of sooty stones with evidence of a recent burn. It looked like a not-so-secret hangout for high school kids.

Valentina scowled.

"This place has become more popular since I last visited."

"It's kind of . . . filthy."

"It is profoundly dangerous so, of course, is appealing to young people. It resonates with their feeling of immortality. The same reason they are drawn to abandoned quarries and condemned houses."

Green walked forward and crushed a can into the soft soil. There was something about the pines in the center of the clearing. He couldn't quite tell what was off about them and it was like an itch he couldn't reach.

"Careful, Mr. Green. Do not go wandering until you see it."

He scanned the trees. A barricade made of branches lashed together with twine blocked the way to an arch where two bent pines met. A cartoonish skull and crossbones done in Sharpie on a white plastic cafeteria tray hung from the barricade. "*Hole in Nothing*" was scrawled beneath the skull.

"I assume that's it."

"That's it. What do you see?"

"I see the nothing, but I don't see the hole."

It looked like a regular space between regular trees. Regular nothing. Only . . . not quite.

A soft breeze rolled through the clearing, sizzling in the dry leaves and snack wrappers. The pines swayed and softly knocked together where their trunks crossed to form the archway. An electric expectancy ran a current down the back of Green's neck.

"Take a closer look. It won't leap out and grab you, but don't get near the trees."

Green walked forward and stood by the barrier.

His throat tightened.

He looked at the crossed pines and imagined an ambush predator on a sandy seabed, camouflaged by a million generations of evolution, resembling nothing but a jumble of volcanic rock with two faint eyes betraying a living symmetry.

He could just make out something there. Not a hole exactly, more of a filter or lens occupying the archway between the trees. The light was different beyond the two pines, tea stained, a quality of sepia tone.

"I think I can see it."

It was such a minor distortion, but looking at it was like scraping the pad of his thumb perpendicularly along the edge of a razor, feeling its cutting potential poised and waiting for a change in direction, a shift from scrape to slice.

"Stand there and watch me, Mr. Green."

Valentina stood at Green's side, then paced a wide circle around the arch, heading for the far side of the trees. He watched her pass behind the first bent tree comprising the left-hand side of the archway. She did not emerge on the other side of the trunk. A moment later, she leaned around the right-hand tree and smiled.

He felt something that wasn't quite a giggle dance through his chest, the butterfly-stomach sensation of standing at the edge of a tall building. He'd thought madness was something that crept in and spread like mildew, not something you could hike to in a few hours.

Valentina ducked back behind the hole and was gone from view again.

"Join me on this side," she said, a disembodied voice from beyond the hazy archway.

Green left the barricade and rounded the trees. From beside the arch, Valentina was perfectly visible, standing with her hands on her hips, watching Green with placid interest.

"Now stand where I stand," Valentina said.

Green did.

She rounded the arch and stood behind the barricade. Green could see her just fine.

"Like a two-way mirror?"

"It's more of a door than a mirror. Though, of course, it is fundamentally different from any doorway I know of. For example, if you were to walk through the arch to me from that side, nothing would happen."

"I think I'll pass."

Valentina ignored the comment.

"Yet," she continued, "if I passed through from this side, I would be . . . affected. It's unidirectional."

Green walked back around to stand next to his teacher.

"I don't like being near this thing."

"As I said, it will not leap out and grab you."

"You mean because it hasn't done that yet? I'm also the first person to see the horned wolf. And how many people did you say have seen that glowing deer?"

"Mr. Green, don't spend your imagination inventing worst-case scenarios. We have plenty to do in our work with the dangers we can confirm with empirical data."

He eyed the hole. It felt like a vicious dog on a very thin tether.

Something clicked and he recalled why "Hole in Nothing" had a familiar ring.

"Wait a minute. I think I saw a flyer about this place at the gas station."

"That would be absurd."

"Yeah, it would," Green agreed. "But I'm pretty sure I did. Maybe Alf made it."

Valentina sighed.

"Usually, the folks around here have more sense than to poke around this sort of anomaly. There is no shortage of oddities in Appalachia."

"Well, somebody left all this trash and made that sign on the barricade. I'm guessing you didn't doodle that little skull. Maybe it was them. Do you think anyone has gone through it? The hole, I mean."

"No."

"Why not?"

"Because they almost certainly wouldn't have returned alive and I hear about that sort of thing."

Valentina took off her pack, knelt, and began unloading empty jars and sample bags.

A dull pain brought Green's attention down to his right hand. It was clinched in a rigid claw around the acorn in his pocket, so tight the muscles in his forearm burned. He released the nut and crossed his arms.

"Wait, does this count as cryptonature? Why can people see this thing?"

"Again, it's a spectrum, not a binary."

"So, where does it go? You called it a door earlier. Doors lead somewhere."

"That's a complicated question. It is not as simple as a matter of where, unless we use that term very broadly to refer to outside our reality."

Green felt his skin crawl.

"Huh. I hate that. Can we shut it? I mean, we need to shut it, right? I don't like how this place feels."

"I don't disagree. Yet, in this instance, it isn't an easy matter. The most reliable known method for closing such a doorway involves stepping through."

"Wow, I think I hate that even more than your last answer. Why would going through that thing shut it? And couldn't we . . . I don't know . . . just toss a mannequin through or something?"

Valentina smirked and continued organizing her sample bags.

"If only. It's a gap in the skin of reality, in our time-space. One feature of reality here in our universe is the transformative power of a subjective viewpoint, the presence of an active observer. A sapient being making a willful choice can bring their reality along with them and shut such a rift. Tangible matter and intangible will acting with a unity of purpose to reassert a cohesive, unbroken border of what is real. In short, you step into the gap as something akin to a living embassy of our reality and, under those auspices, you intend the doorway shut. Such is our current working theory of the mechanisms at play."

"In short? That's the short version?"

"Exactly."

Green looked to the hole and back to his teacher. He felt like he was hanging on to the conversation by his fingertips.

"So, if that's the proven method, why haven't you done it yet?"

Valentina stood, turned, and looked around the clearing.

"Here, help me with this branch. I'll demonstrate."

Green took one end and helped her carry it to the barricade.

They swung it three times and tossed it through the archway.

It vanished without a sound. The space rippled slightly, like a leaf touching the surface of a still pond.

Valentina rounded the pines and searched the ground.

"No. Nothing. It has fully exited. Let's try again."

At the edge of the clearing, he spotted a forked three-foot log like a stubby Y. He grabbed the forked end, found it heavier than expected, and dragged it to the barricade, leaving a long, loamy scar in the leaf litter the color of dark chocolate.

The two of them hefted the log and repeated their experiment. The Hole in Nothing swallowed the second log with another ripple. He heard a soft *plunk* and a rolling skitter.

They walked to the far side and, this time, Valentina found what she was searching for.

"Here. Look here, Mr. Green."

She returned holding a weathered shard of wood.

"This one made it back."

"That's the log?"

"It is."

Valentina handed him the pale, spongy thing. It was smaller than his forearm and seemed to weigh nothing at all. The outer wood was a jumble of insect damage and discoloration from what he imagined were countless varieties of mold and fungi. Part of him wanted a magnifying glass. Part of him wanted hand sanitizer.

"Okay. So, what? The hole rots things?"

Valentina studied the remains of the log.

"Hmm, I would suggest time and detritivores rot things, but we're just getting started."

She began gathering up several sticks and chunks of partially burned wood as she spoke, making a small pile beside the barrier.

"Observe, Mr. Green. Stand to the side."

Green stood aside and watched his teacher. She began tossing the bits of wood she had gathered into the space between the pines.

The first throw yielded nothing.

The second throw yielded nothing.

The third sent a shower of violet sparks into the air on the far side of the hole. Green flinched and stepped back. There was a smell like burnt Styrofoam and a sudden dryness in his mouth like he had just spit out a handful of cornstarch.

He gagged.

"As you can see," Valentina continued, "predictability is not a feature of this anomaly."

She tossed the charred remnants of a campfire log through and this time a glob of something viscous and translucent bounced against the leaf litter. It seemed to hover for a moment, bits of twig clinging to its wet surface, before some mechanism of physics took hold and the ball of slime fell directly upward, vanishing into the sky with a whistle of sudden speed.

Valentina stooped, picked up a smooth gray stone, and tossed it through.

It landed on the other side, looking largely unchanged except for a fading orange afterglow of dissipating heat. The leaves beneath the stone smoked. Green regarded the cooling rock with suspicion for a long moment before returning his attention to his teacher.

"That, Mr. Green, is why I haven't tried stepping through. The other cases in which that technique was employed were decidedly less severe. There's no knowing what this break in reality would do to me. I have tried a few alternative methods of closure, but clearly I haven't succeeded. Typically, such interruptions in the fabric of the universe resolve themselves. I was continuing to monitor it while hoping it would heal on its own. That hope seems increasingly less likely."

"You think the wolf came through there? You think it might be a mon . . . creature . . . that tears its way between dimensions or something?"

"I don't know. But allowing for such a connection is why we are here today. Recent events suggest that a wait-and-see approach to the hole may no longer be tenable."

Green didn't like the emptiness between those pines.

The more Valentina spoke about it, the more the hole seemed to have a perspective of its own. The more he felt it watching him.

"We fight fear with action and information," he said to himself, echoing Valentina.

She nodded. "It is a powerful combination. Yes."

Green picked up a wilted, rain-soaked cardboard six-pack carrier from the ground and tossed it through the hole, then peeked on the other side. Nothing.

"Cardboard isn't the most resilient of substances," Valentina said.

"I know. But, hey, at least I got rid of some of the litter."

"Mr. Green, this is a one-of-a-kind tear in reality. It isn't a rubbish bin. Don't make light of it."

He sighed.

"I'm not. Look, it's currently terrifying me, and I want to do something to push back. So, I'm experimenting, okay? I'm taking your advice."

He snatched up a disposable plastic lighter and tossed it through. There was a soft insectile buzz beyond the pines and when he rounded the trees to look he found a perfectly round two-inch burrow leading down into the soft soil. A thin coil of bronze smoke snaked from the fresh opening in the earth.

"I appreciate the virtue of experimentation," Valentina said, "but I advise against frivolous interactions with something as powerful and unruly as this. I risked a demonstration so you would understand our situation. At this point, there's nothing to be gained by risking more. Do not poke the bear, Mr. Green."

He swallowed.

"Fair point. I can't stop thinking about what that thing would do to a person. I guess it's like standing on a subway platform. Some part of my brain can't help imagining taking a leap in front of the train."

Valentina collected two stacks of sample bags from beside her pack. She shook her head.

"It may come to that, but let us hope for a safer solution."

The idea loosed butterflies in his stomach.

"Those other times you mentioned . . . When stepping through was used to close the door? What were those other rifts like?"

"Twice before, yes. Both cases exhibited much more limited, stable effects."

"Only twice?"

"Large sample sizes are not a luxury our field of study typically affords. There was the Galveston covered bridge. It was closed in such a way, but months of testing indicated it consistently led six minutes into the past. Predictable. Still, the cryptonaturalist who closed it experienced that six-minute journey as a subjective month navigating a silent, lightless maze by feel with no end in sight. No sleep. No hunger. No thirst. Just endlessly pressing on down dark, winding corridors. A harrowing prospect."

Green's jaw dropped open.

"He time traveled? Did he meet himself from six minutes earlier? Warn himself about what to expect?"

"Time doesn't work that way. Not for humans. Reality's immune system rejects subjective paradoxes. For example, no meeting oneself to alter one's future. No doubt he lived out those aberrant six minutes in a pocket dimension that mirrored his own past, though without his presence. He subsequently rejoined his original timeline once he progressed in linear fashion to the moment of his departure."

"Oh, of course. It's so obvious now that you say it."

She ignored his sarcasm and continued.

"Following his nightmare month in the maze, he found himself standing on the empty bridge, disoriented, forced to shield his eyes from the light. Six uneasy minutes later, his team was suddenly there, preparing to celebrate his success. From their perspective, he simply stepped through and collapsed as the rift vanished. The team quickly shifted to triage as they learned of their colleague's ordeal."

"Damn. That's awful. What about the other example?"

"There was also the Lake Itasca Mist-Arch, which briefly appeared above the surface of the lake whenever a loon called and transmitted matter about ten meters away into a stand of wild rice. The young cryptonaturalist who kayaked through that rift was transported the ten meters and gained a novel, persistent conviction that clover meant her harm."

"So . . . not our first choice. Got it. Are there less-terrifying methods?"

Valentina frowned.

"Yes. Several. So far, they have been ineffectual. We need more information."

She handed him a stack of sample bags.

"Focus, Mr. Green. We are looking for connections to our current situation. Help me explore the area."

"Okay, okay."

He stepped away from the hole, trying to quiet his imagination.

Maybe that thing is the entrance to the wolf's den?

Maybe it has nothing to do with us at all.

She directed him to begin searching the edge of the clearing for anything noteworthy.

Green turned and walked toward the woods.

After the second spiderweb to the face, he picked up a branch and waved it like a conductor's wand while he walked, wondering how many spiders were tough enough to survive the frosty fall nights. He scrutinized the ground, finding fewer and fewer pieces of trash as he moved outward from the clearing.

Something crimson caught his eye and he stopped next to the body of a red bird, one wing splayed like fanned playing cards. Green shouted to Valentina.

"Dead bird over here."

She was searching the opposite side of the clearing.

"Yes. I have found two dead nuthatches already. Bag it."

He knelt. The bird lay with one wing extended. The other was plastered to its side. Its eye was a perfect black jewel next to the carrot-orange beak. There was no blood, no visible damage. It seemed perfectly intact. He thought of the pink gumline of the dead woman in the van at Kinkaid Cabins.

"This one's a cardinal, I think."

"Keep looking. Call them out if you see more."

He turned a sample bag inside out and used it like a plastic mitt to grab the cardinal. He'd seen plenty of dog owners in the park use the same technique. The little corpse was cold and stiff. A layer of dead leaves came with the bird into the bag. He put the bag in his jacket pocket. It felt impolite to treat a death in such an unceremonious way, but he didn't know how to respect a dead bird in a plastic bag.

Green walked on and found another corpse immediately.

"Uh, gray bird. Looks like a small, skinny pigeon."

"Mourning dove. Bag it."

The dove joined the cardinal in his bulging pocket. The two bags crinkled as he stood and continued the search.

They moved on, circling the clearing and calling out their finds.

"Gray squirrel."

"Two more cardinals."

"European starling."

"Blue jay."

"Northern flicker. No, two northern flickers."

"Uh, a little gray-and-white guy with a black head?"

"Chickadee."

They continued for a half hour, finding just over a dozen corpses before rendezvousing in the clearing. Valentina stowed the bagged remains in her backpack. Except for the bits of twig and leaves clinging to them, all of the corpses seemed to be in pristine condition, avian displays in a natural history museum. Green ran fingers through his hair and tried to swallow away the knot in his throat.

They're just birds.

The thought wasn't convincing. A pattern was emerging in his new line of work, a pattern etched in death. Death, he knew, was natural. But if this was nature's true face, it little resembled the character of nature from his daydreams.

"Fourteen total," she said. "All appear remarkably fresh. No variation at all in level of decomposition. Interesting."

"What does it mean?" Green asked. "I saw a dead bird at Kinkaid too. It didn't seem important at the time."

He recalled the lifeless robin in the grass. After the van, after seeing her face beneath the sheet, it hadn't seemed worth mentioning. Were there dark stains on the flesh beneath those feathers?

"I'm not sure. I need to study these remains. Though, I am more certain than before that this is not a good place for children to loiter."

She looked down at an abandoned sock at the edge of the clearing.

She patted her pack.

"At least we now have some physical evidence to examine. Our day has been fruitful."

"It was a dead robin," Green said. "At the cabins, I mean. Just one more cursed sight on a day full of cursed sights."

The concern on Valentina's face told Green that he had that unraveling look again.

"I'm alright. Or I will be. I'm . . . adjusting."

"I know, Mr. Green. I know."

Valentina raised her eyes to the canopy.

"It is too quiet here."

She looked around the clearing.

"I can't guarantee if I would have noticed dead birds on the ground in my earlier visits to this place. I feel I would have noticed this . . . absence."

She turned and held her hand up, fingers parallel to the horizon.

"Each hand width between the horizon and the sun is an hour of remaining daylight. Plenty of time to find a more wholesome place to rest for lunch and still make it home before evening."

Green imitated her motion, guessing five hand widths until sunset.

Only five hand widths until another night. Another tide of darkness to hide the thing that is killing this place.

He looked back toward the Hole in Nothing, wishing he had the power to close it. Valentina turned and headed back up the path toward Candle-Fly Camp. Green followed.

"Should we do anything to stop the local kids from coming here?"

Valentina tutted.

"Paradoxical human time travel is more likely than us accomplishing that."

They put an hour between them and the hole before stopping for a brief lunch.

The day had changed. Now, as they walked back to Candle-Fly, he couldn't help searching the ground for little bodies. The silence had been companionable on the morning's hike. It had metastasized into something different.

Back at camp, Green moved the truck to his site and tried to text Alf about his car.

No service.

He was still receiving spam texts from time to time, so he hoped his message would slip through the mountain's nets at some point that evening. He considered adding a "PS" urging Alf to get rid of his flyer about the Hole in Nothing, but decided that was more of an in-person conversation topic.

The evening was spent in the library tree, reading about an endless stairway leading down from a traveling alley and the ongoing debate about whether the place itself could be classified as a cryptid. He decided it was mostly fiction, but the subject made him uneasy. Yet, as the sun set and Green imagined his own personal monster awakening somewhere out in the dusk, the treetop study felt mercifully safe, even if some of the information it protected did not.

CHAPTER 10

ROOT CAUSES

"YOU KILLED THOSE PEOPLE."

Green stood in front of an entrance to an impossible forest, an arched gateway made of two bowed trees the color of bleached bone. The way beyond was as black as midnight water and in the center hung the skull of the horned wolf.

In a sense, the wolf answered.

Green looked up at the skull and felt only anger.

"A heart attack," Green said. "A city bus. Cancer creeping like mildew. Old bones wrapped in night. Each as petty as the next. There is nothing impressive about bringing death. What you're doing is empty. Purposeless. Do you kill for sport? The sport of what? How is serving decay sport? Decay doesn't need any help. Entropy doesn't need servants."

It was Green's own voice, but he felt he was speaking with Valentina's words, her strange formality.

The skull said nothing.

"Answer me!"

Green thought his regret at the creature, projecting his empathy, his numbing compassion for the lives of people he did not know. He thought of his old neighbor, Mr. Reynard. He felt the old ice-dagger pain of his absence and watched that pain sprout and climb like ivy, winding like clockwork, clinging to the loss of Kyle Cartwright, the loss of the campers at Kinkaid Cabins. His remorse grew and stretched, a thorny hedge of pain, hung with the corpses of songbirds and the dusky shine of acorns like polished brown agate reflecting the starlight.

He thought the skull dipped a fraction of an inch.

Annoyance? Acknowledgment?

You have grown. Stop calling my thoughts here, not-man. I have work to do.

Then, it was gone.

The hedge of pain snapped into grayscale and shattered, drifting off like smoke, like the dusty scales from a moth's wing.

The darkness melted away and Green was looking down a tunnel of gray boughs like the rib-lined gut of an endless serpent.

There in the distance, he could just see the thin light of dawn pooling beneath the cabin door.

He awoke.

Great. Dreaming about work again.

He shook his head.

Nightmare creatures and haunted forests. Arguments with a murderous skull. Work.

He could tell by the birdsongs it was dawn.

A knock at the door.

"Come in."

Valentina entered, carrying the same toast and coffee as the mornings before. The knock was new.

"Good morning, Mr. Green. Breakfast."

"Morning. Thank you again, but please don't feel like you need to bring me food every morning. It's kinda embarrassing. And I can guess what Dancer would say about it."

He stretched and swung his bare feet onto the cold dirt floor. With a pang of self-consciousness, he glanced down at himself, noting that his T-shirt and sweatpants were grubby, but not indecent.

"I'm a very early riser and feeding one's apprentice is an old tradition," Valentina said. "It kindles my nostalgia. Humor me."

He rose and went to the table to eat. He would forever think of that table as the rag moth's table. The association made him think of the word "wake," bringing to mind the parents of the Kinkaid Cabins victims. Would they have been called to the area to identify their children in some windowless basement of a county building?

"I don't really feel like arguing with you," he said. "I'll never get sick of this bread."

"We'll add bread baking to the curriculum."

Green ate and scratched his scalp. He felt greasy from being alternately too cold and too hot. Valentina said that he would get used to going without daily hot showers. He hadn't yet.

"When you're finished, I'll be waiting by my trailer."

"I won't be long. What's the plan for today?"

Valentina shook her head.

"It's technically the weekend, a concept to which I am still acclimating, but if you don't object, we have some catching up to do. Data. We still need data. And if it's within my control, we're going to have a gentler week, lest you think our entire profession is fear and chaos."

A dim skull peered at Green from his recent dream.

"It's hard to imagine we could have a less gentle week," Green said.

Valentina spat a word Green didn't know.

"Mr. Green, I've outlived many of my old superstitions, but just the same, don't say things like that."

He took a big bite of toast.

"Yup. Regretted it as soon as I said it," he said with his mouth full. "Anyway, no, I don't mind working on the weekend. It's not as if I had plans. Another hike?"

"No, we will be staying in camp today. Probably for the next few days, at least."

He thought of the stakes behind their need for data. He wondered who else might be heading their direction while he chewed his toast, traveling for a fishing trip or a school hike. He wondered what they might meet when they arrived.

"Teacher . . . we don't need to stay in camp for me. I mean, I think we need to do whatever we can to protect people. Right? I don't think the wolf is going to go away just because I'm . . . struggling a bit."

"Admirable, but there is only so much we can do. Our power is in information. Knowledge is our best protection."

She left him to finish his breakfast.

Green dressed and Valentina led him to the makeshift structure she called "the laboratory." Its walls were part corrugated metal, part wooden siding, part roofing shingles. It fit in with the rest of the camp insomuch as it didn't break the pattern of vastly diverse, mismatched structures laid out like spilled Lego bricks in front of the library tree.

They entered and he was surprised by the sparse orderliness of the interior.

A large steel L-shaped worktable occupied a third of the space, surrounded by tall cabinets full of labeled drawers, glass vessels, and equipment Green couldn't identify.

The room was uncomfortably hot. A little electric heater whispered to itself in one corner.

"Why is it so hot in here?"

Valentina paused by a cloth-covered tray on the table.

"Close the door behind you. Are you squeamish about anatomy, Mr. Green?"

He honestly wasn't sure. It had been many years since he dissected a frog in high school biology.

"Can I turn that heater off?"

"Just a moment."

She removed the cloth to display several birds in different stages of dissection.

They didn't look real. A cardinal, pinned to the work surface, was opened to display its vital organs. The bird's internal structures gleamed pink and ocher, musculature peeled back, heart and liver framed by delicate white bone.

Green furrowed his brow and looked at the tray. His memory flashed to an afternoon dismantling bargain-buy clocks with Mr. Reynard.

"Did you learn anything?"

"Yes, but not from the dissection. Touch them."

He looked to the birds, then back to Valentina.

"Really?"

"Yes. Just for a moment."

Green licked his lips and summoned courage.

Reaching out, he rested two fingertips on the cardinal's prominent exposed sternum.

It was ice-cold, smooth, and dry.

"It's cold . . . That makes sense, right? Dead things are cold."

"Dead things are the temperature of their surroundings. What is the temperature in this room?"

He understood.

He stepped closer to the table and this time rested his entire palm against the cardinal. He placed his other palm over the body of an adjacent chickadee. It was like resting his hands on a snowbank.

"They're . . . frozen," he said.

"Correct. And yet, it is nearly eighty-four degrees Fahrenheit in this room and has been for several hours. The birds show no sign of thawing."

Green took his hands from the birds and rubbed them together to banish the chill.

"Is that why they didn't decompose?"

"I expect so."

"And . . . the people who have died?"

"I have put in an information request to the rangers. They have ways of finding out what the local police know, though it will take time. It is also quite possible that if the bodies were transported from the outdoors to some form of refrigeration, the temperature anomalies might not have been discovered."

Green felt sweat run from his hairline down his cheek and wiped his face on his sleeve.

The cardinal's eye, a glassy black pearl, reflected the rectangular fluorescent light above the table.

He sensed a rebuke in that eye, in those fragile, unbroken bones gleaming from the center of that blossom of red feathers.

"What about other injuries," he asked. "What else is damaged?"

"Other than their temperature, the birds appear normal. There is no other sign of lethal injury."

A wolf's skull spoke from a fading dream.

Whose work is this?

The horned wolf stood like a statue just behind his eyes.

Is this how I would kill, not-man? Frozen songbirds?

Green gritted his teeth.

"As I recall," Valentina said, "you mentioned some feeling of localized cold when you first saw the glass fawn, correct?"

He recalled the numbness that came with the glowing deer, that first night in his car, the way his breath fogged the window. It hadn't seemed important before, not when such minor details sat in the shadow of what followed moments after.

But the fawn didn't invade my thoughts and threaten me.

And the fawn isn't monstrous in the same way as the damn wolf.

And the fawn hasn't been visiting my dreams and keeping me from rest.

"Yes. Sort of, but it was the horned wolf that attacked us at Kinkaid Cabins."

"Was that an attack?"

Anger erupted.

"Are you joking? Yes! Obviously it was!"

The birds watched his outburst with dead eyes.

Valentina stood like a stone. Her expression did not move.

Green mopped more sweat from his face and collected himself.

"I'm sorry. It's just . . ."

"I know," Valentina said. "You have made your feelings clear. I wasn't there. I haven't seen it. I appreciate your perspective, but I think you need to step outside your assumptions and consider that the horned wolf has visited you more than once and you are still whole and very much alive."

"I need air."

He brushed past Valentina and went out, wiping sweat with one hand and clutching the acorn in his pocket with the other.

He sank down to sit on a cinder block next to a cluster of rain barrels. Looking around at the strange assortment of buildings and padlocked doors, and imagining the unknown contents within, he felt suddenly and intensely homeless, a visitor in someone else's story. A cold breeze chilled the sweat at his temples.

He put his head in his hands.

A distant crow cawed. He shivered.

He heard Valentina approach and looked up.

She frowned at him. Green wondered if she was reconsidering her offer of apprenticeship.

"You need to go for a walk," she said.

"Am I being put in time-out?"

"No," she said gently. "I have just . . . been forgetting some fundamentals. In more ways than one. You need to go look at the mountains. Get your bearings. Find a view that speaks to you and sit with it, have a conversation."

She smiled, but it seemed mechanical, like she had recently learned the expression from a book. He supposed she meant it kindly.

"When you get back from your walk, we will talk about the basics of life here. Camp basics. Wilderness skills. I suspect you will find learning a new profession easier when you don't feel threatened by unknowns on all sides."

"Really? Is there time for that?"

"There is. There must be. Now, I have research to conclude and journals to revisit."

She squeezed his shoulder and went back into the lab.

He didn't know how she could stand the heat in there.

After fetching a canteen of water, Green did as he was told.

I am absolutely being put in time-out.

He walked.

He paused by a rotting log to look at tiny mushrooms, delicate as pushpins, with white tops like droplets of milk. He passed a hollow tree, then doubled back to look inside. It was a dark, homey-looking space full of wood chips and seed hulls. It smelled like sawdust. He knelt by a tiny stream flowing down the mountain. A maple leaf, yellow as sweet corn, spun down the current and out of view. He wondered how far it had traveled from its tree. How far would it go?

He arrived at his campsite and found a place to sit and study the view.

Dancer really had given him a gift.

He looked out over the mountains and tried to empty himself of fear and anger.

The Appalachian Mountains. Green knew a few things about them. He knew they were old, perhaps the oldest in the world. Over a billion years old.

Older than land plants.

Older than vertebrate life.

They were old when the dinosaurs awoke and grew to shake the ground. If the mountains thought with a human mind, they would think of warm blood as a very new technology.

But, of course, they didn't. They didn't think with human thoughts or mechanisms. They weren't so limited. What they knew and what they were was not separated by anything so crude as brain cells, as consciousness flashing across nerves like heat lightning.

The acorn was in his hand again.

Green tried to hate the acorn, the way it drew his attention like a solitary headstone on a bare hill. He couldn't. His hate slid off the smooth brown thing. It was a commonplace object. It was the churning storm that ground away all the comfortable landmarks of his old life.

He set the acorn on a nearby stone, forcing himself to swallow the fear that it would roll away. He withdrew his hand. It sat. Seemingly inert. Looking very much in its proper place.

Hot panic hit him, but he held it up in the cool mountain air and watched it fade like an ember plucked from the fire.

One evening, weeks earlier, he had set that same acorn on his white stone kitchen counter and watched it pick apart the threads of all his choices. On his counter, that little nut looked very out of place.

He pictured the acorn surrounded by his old condo, the way it clashed with everything in ways that eclipsed simple aesthetics.

And *this* acorn, *this* acorn was not just a token of some distant forest, some impersonal metaphor for a more primal world. No, this acorn was very personal. This acorn arrived packaged in a memory that felt like a fresh injury anytime he acknowledged its existence.

Everything about that acorn felt like an intruder. Yet, it was an intruder that knew his name and spoke a message that wouldn't be ignored or dismissed. It was an intruder that said, *I'm not in the wrong place. You are.*

In the days after his not-death and encounter with the giant crow,

Green wanted to drink too much. He wanted to toss the acorn out his fifth-floor window, to embrace some comforting excuse about an overworked mind, pop some sleeping pills, and surrender fully to twelve hours of dreamless rest. He wanted to pester the new young couple across the hall, demand to be let into Mr. Reynard's old home so he could sit in the place his friend had taught him that sorrows are best met in the light of camaraderie.

Except he knew it wouldn't work. Not the drinking. Not the sleep. Not living for the past. It wouldn't work because, however painful the memory, he hadn't imagined it. He hadn't imagined the crow. He wasn't imagining the acorn sitting on his countertop, sucking the oxygen from his rooms with its simple existence.

The intruder was already inside. And it was, without any doubt, too late. Everything had changed. It had all changed. Green felt like a man dressed for deep winter, stepping out the door of a snowbound cabin and finding himself on an equatorial island. He wasn't dressed for this weather and the colossal dissonance of it all was smothering.

There are times, Green knew even then, when you just have to sit in your discomfort. Times when there is nothing to do but experience the rushing river of your own feelings and see what time and the flowing waters carve from the stone of your present self.

So, Green sat and looked at the acorn in his efficient, modern kitchen and knew that everything was changing, with or without his consent. The acorn wasn't going anywhere, but something had to give.

Over the next few weeks, he became a very poor employee. He engaged in a deliberate study of his own thoughts, coaxing old desires from dark corners, brushing the dust off past fascinations and childhood joys. He unearthed an ill-defined, but enthusiastic, preoccupation with moss and ferns and campfire sparks floating up through the twilight.

As the days passed, he could feel the weight of a theoretical new life taking its first breaths, just out of sight. Something was out there.

Something fundamental. Something that chuffed and sniffed with a bear's heavy lungs and paced in the dim elsewhere beyond the city lights. Something better. Something that made Green's white-tile life seem like the thinnest rice paper barrier, daring him to press a hand through and peer at a place alive and real and not engineered for human convenience. A place that asked you for more than your obedience and less than your soul.

He returned to himself, to the mountains, and looked down at the acorn. There, tilted and resting on its cap on a mossy stone, it did not look out of place. The acorn was right where it was supposed to be. Now, the question was, could Green find a way to belong there too? Except none of this was what he expected. This wasn't just moss and stone and campfire evenings. He was a cryptonaturalist now, a word, an identity, that was utterly new and came with a host of questions and consequences. In the city he had felt at sea, but at least nobody had been relying on him to solve a mystery or prevent untimely deaths.

Still, he knew, there was no going back.

Present Green and past Green exchanged a nod over a narrow ravine of chaotic weeks, narrow, but too wide to leap and too deadly deep.

He drank from his canteen and plucked up the acorn, returning it to his pocket. He watched golden light hold a conversation with autumn mountainsides. He invited an uncomplicated silence into his mind and hoped that the landscape would pour in with it.

When he stood again, his legs were asleep and he had to shake away the pins and needles.

He took a moment to press his forehead against the tree that had been his backrest for the last hour.

"Thank you," he said, feeling self-conscious and choosing not to care.

His attention landed on Alf's truck.

He checked his phone.

Still no service.

He felt a surge of guilt for keeping the truck a day longer than intended.

"I guess I'll reach him the old-school way."

He drove down to the Count and Countess, where he found his battered Prius sitting with a new windshield. He parked beside it. A banana air freshener hung from his car's rearview.

Alf greeted Green like an old friend, passed over Casper's invoice, and loaned him the station landline so he could pay for the repairs.

"Hey, before I head out, I wanted to talk to you about those flyers in back," Green said.

"Yeah?"

"The one about hiking to the Hole in Nothing. I think you should get rid of it."

"Bro, those flyers don't exactly get a lot of traffic. You're the last person to see 'em."

"I figured. But it isn't safe."

"Oh, yeah? You been there?"

"Yes. Just yesterday."

"Pretty cool, right?"

Green thought about the ball of goo shooting into the sky and the way the hole seemed to watch him.

"Uh, I wasn't a big fan."

"Did you see it at night?"

Green shuddered at the thought.

"No. Does that matter?"

"Yeah, bro. It matters. You gotta see it at night."

Green thought about telling Alf about the dead birds, but he realized he would be inviting questions he didn't know how to answer.

"Look, maybe just steer clear of that place. At least for now?"

Alf shrugged.

"I hear ya. Good lookin' out. I'll keep the tourists away."

"Thanks, Alf."

"Don't forget, Green, you still owe me that six-pack for hooking you up with car help."

"I didn't forget. Want me to buy it now?"

"Nah. I'll tell you when. Anyway, you gotta drink it with me and you don't look down for day drinking right now."

"Heh, no, I guess not today. Well, I have zero trust in my phone, but you know where to find me."

Green looked through the glass door to the dark trees across the road.

"Alf, you guys see anything weird out here . . . especially at night . . . just, stay away from it. You know?"

"Hear that, Jerome? The new guy is giving us advice."

Jerome didn't answer. He did something fancy with his deck, displaying the cards in a star shape, then continued shuffling.

"Yeah. Sorry. I guess you know how to live with weirdness out here."

"Yeah, bro. I guess I do."

"Okay. Stay safe, Alf."

"Don't be a stranger, brother."

Green went out and something made him look back. Jerome was standing at the window, holding up his deck. Green grinned, nodded, and tapped his forehead.

King of clubs. Come on, man. You got this. King of clubs.

Jerome pressed a king of diamonds against the glass.

Close.

Green shook his head. Jerome turned away.

The Prius still smelled like fresh camping gear and old coffee. It was a smell from a week earlier and seemed to be from a bygone decade. There was a brown constellation of dried blood droplets smattered across the Toyota logo in the center of the steering wheel.

On the drive back to Candle-Fly, Green noticed three soft tan shapes lying in a patch of pine straw just off the road. He pulled over before realizing he'd made the decision. There were no other cars.

He climbed out and felt the profound isolation of an empty roadway pressed between great swaths of woods like a fossil folded in layers of shale.

He thought of Kyle Cartwright loading his fishing gear when something found him in a spot very much like this one.

The sun was still high in the sky. The wolf and fawn were creatures of the dusk and dark.

Aren't they?

Green went to inspect the shapes.

Three deer lay dead beneath a white pine. They were unmarked. The animals might have appeared asleep, except they had fallen at unnatural angles, one doe's black nose buried in the soil. Pine needles clung to the deer's dark, sightless eyes.

Green knelt and reached to feel a soft white throat.

It was numbingly cold.

He looked up the hill and saw a dead chipmunk near an emerald tuft of club moss.

His eyes traveled farther up the slope.

How much death is out there, beyond what I can see?

How many corpses are hidden in thickets, unable to rot, to return to the soil?

How many victims are trapped in perpetual winter?

He didn't know. He wasn't certain he wanted to know. He just wished he could make it stop.

CHAPTER 11

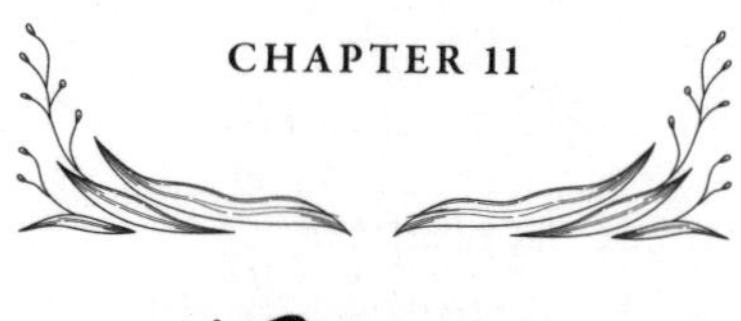

TRUST

OVER THE NEXT FEW DAYS, VALENTINA STARTED HER CAMP basics training as promised. It was a dizzying array of subjects ranging from solar panel maintenance to splitting and stacking firewood. Some of the skills seemed modern. Others felt anachronistic. They used an old tin throat lozenges box stuffed with cotton scraps and wedged in a bed of smoldering coals to make char cloth for catching sparks from flint and steel. They covered navigation with a map and compass. They used a post-hole digger to excavate a privy pit near Green's camp. They did laundry creek-side with a washboard and ringer. They took inventory of winter provisions and discussed best practices for food storage, preservation, and thwarting mice.

Green was certain he couldn't retain the information at the pace with which Valentina delivered it, but he thought he understood her motivations. She was trying to build him up, trying to make him feel less like a guest and more like a resident in his new life. Information, he was beginning to understand, was Valentina's love language, her currency of care.

During the lessons, he could feel her trying to keep cryptonature out of the conversation. When he asked about their work and the lingering threat, she would only say, "I am not ignoring the subject, but this is the best use of our time at present."

As afternoon of the third day arrived, the lessons culminated in new housing for Green. He moved from the cot in the cabin to an insulated structure with a corrugated metal roof, a wooden plank floor, and a modern wood-burning stove that you didn't need a pot holder to open safely. The structure seemed new, but he couldn't recall whether it had been there the day before.

The place was small and smelled like sawdust. It was ugly. He loved it.

He named his new home "the shed" and, if he thought he understood Valentina's motivations for the days' lessons before, moving into his own space allowed him to feel the wisdom behind her plan in a much more real and immediate way. That morning, he understood her reasoning intellectually. Now, he understood emotionally.

He looked around at his cramped storage closet of a home and felt that he had been invited in off the porch of his new world and given a seat by the fire. Valentina often seemed to have all the human warmth of a lichen-speckled stone jutting from a mountain lake. Yet, as Green stretched out on his new cot and studied the manufacturer logos on the foil-backed insulation tucked against his metal roof, he reflected that human warmth is as varied as the people who keep it alive.

Outside, the shadows grew long. Evening was coming. The things that waited for evening were coming too.

For days, Green had received a "not now" when he tried to talk about the death stalking the mountainsides. It had been a hectic but peaceful respite, and he could feel it coming to a close. Valentina had left him to situate his belongings in the shed. With the dark only a few hours away, he felt a pull to get back to business.

He heard the library tree hatch thud closed.

Apparently, Valentina had a similar impulse.

Green climbed the spiral log stairs to the library, trailing his fingertips along the oak's bark as he went. He lifted the hatch and stepped inside. Valentina was already seated at the little table by the trunk, tinkering with the polished wooden broadcast box. With its side panel open, it looked like a cross between an antique radio and a hamster cage full of colorful, transparent tubes. The tubes housed tendrils of something pale and fleshy.

"Time to get back to cryptonaturalist work?"

Valentina shut the box.

A light flashed amber above a toggle switch.

"Yes, Mr. Green. We have two messages and I've been waiting on several responses to inform our next steps. I haven't been idle during your studies."

She handed Green a sugar cube. He dutifully placed it in the fungal hand of the network administrator as it bloomed from the space beneath the floorboards. It withdrew in eerie silence and a dusting of spores. He retrieved the little broom and swept the mess through the gap by the bark.

She flipped the switch.

"Val, this is Clara."

The voice carried the grit of a long life or a heavy smoker.

"I didn't want to make you wait, but I'm still doing research on my end. Thought I'd shoot over my first thoughts. I'd try will. I'd try water. And I might try matter stitching, like the Heinze brothers did on that epistemological sinkhole in Pataskala, Ohio."

Valentina shook her head at the box.

"Anyway, more to come soon. The boys are taking me to catch the archive train and see what I can dig up there. I'll be in touch."

She clicked the switch off and sighed.

"I've tried water and will. I've tried stitching."

"Teacher, can you give me a hint of what we're talking about?"

"Closing the Hole in Nothing. That was Clara Rodriguez. She has made a special study of various rifts and portals, so I asked for her opinion. You'll recall, I explained the principle behind stepping through to close it from inside when we visited the hole."

"I remember. And I remember all the reasons that's a terrible idea in this case."

"As I said, there are other, less dangerous methods. Running water through a rift sometimes closes it. Water has many properties we do not fully understand. The stitching she mentioned involves moving objects in and out of a rift rapidly, which can cause a collapse from overtaxing the system. Unfortunately, I tried both of those options after my initial observations of the hole."

He looked around at Valentina's collection of books, journals, and artifacts.

"I guess I'm a little surprised to hear you asking for advice. Didn't you tell me you're the most knowledgeable cryptonaturalist when we first met?"

"That's not how knowledge works, Mr. Green. A foundational strength of humanity is our diversity. Diversity of thought, experience, and perspective. That strength is meaningless if we don't ask each other for help. Unshakable confidence in one's own ability and judgment is the surest sign of a fool."

"Okay, well, what about the other thing she mentioned? Trying willpower?"

"Yes, I also made a minor attempt at willing it shut as well, though it might be worth it to try again. Intending a semi-corporeal doorway shut from the outside is more art than science, but it has been done."

He pinched the bridge of his nose, wishing he had something useful to contribute.

"I don't know if it's connected to the wolf, but I know I'll rest easier when it's gone. I warned Alf and Jerome to stay away, but I'm not sure they took me seriously."

Valentina nodded.

"There's a second message."

She turned back to the broadcast box. She flipped the switch again.

"Ranger Reem. Ranger Station Orion. Calling Valentina Blackwood. Ranger Cheng asked me to call you first. There's been another death in your area and . . . it appears to carry the same markers as the deaths at Kinkaid Cabins."

Green slumped into a chair and felt his stomach drop. His thoughts filled with dead black eyes, crisscrossed with pine needles, staring at him with painful absence.

"The body of an elderly man was found on the outskirts of Hickory, not far from Iverson's Run. Time of death unknown, but if the pattern holds he would have died last night. Continuing to monitor for updates. We received your supplemental materials on the birds you collected. Analyzing now. Please call in any new developments on your end. And . . . Valentina . . . if there's anything more we can do, don't hesitate."

The box clicked and went silent.

She rose and retrieved a map of the area, unfolding it on the little table.

"The attacks we know of happened here, here, here, and here."

She made four circles in pencil.

"Your campsite. Mr. Cartwright. Kinkaid Cabins. And now here at the edge of Hickory."

She drew a tiny X.

"This is the location of the Hole in Nothing. You'll notice it is nearly in the center of the four incidents."

She drew a broad circle around all her marks.

"I would estimate we are dealing with an area of around twelve square miles. Thus far, it is a fairly small area of effect."

"That doesn't sound that small."

"Out here, it is quite common for twelve square miles to include very few human structures. There are only two structures left in this immediate area that make likely targets if our predator is actively seeking human victims."

She drew two more circles.

"A seasonal Girl Scout camp, which is currently unoccupied, and a small stable that boards horses. There is also the Count and Countess gas station and the nearest edge of Hickory proper, but the emergent pattern suggests that the attacker prefers dark and seclusion. I think the stable is a likely next target."

Green felt his pulse increase from a walk to a trot.

"Okay, what do we do?"

"I plan to keep watch at the stable tonight. I am not asking you to join me."

"Of course I'm going to join you."

Valentina smiled. This wasn't her mechanical smile. This was her fairy-tale witch smile.

"Ah. I believe you do, in fact, understand the dangers involved, so I will not make the choice for you."

He imagined staying in his shed while Valentina was off in the dark woods alone trying to prevent another body from arriving at the Hickory morgue. He thought of sitting on his cot, unable to sleep, wondering if his new mentor would return. Part of him wished he could stomach a night like that. But he couldn't.

His hand dipped into his pocket and closed around the acorn.

"I'll go. I don't want to, but I will."

"My feelings exactly, Mr. Green."

"Do we warn the stable owners?"

"I wish we could. Consider how that would appear. Two odd people warning of odd things in the midst of investigations into strange deaths. There have been warrants for my arrest before. No great obstacle, but still a nuisance and a potential hindrance to our work as well as to Ms. Dancer."

Green made a mental note to ask follow-up questions about Valentina's outlaw past at a more appropriate time.

"Moreover," she continued, "what would you warn them to do? Keep a lookout for an invisible threat that we ourselves don't fully understand? I don't see how they could move all the horses by nightfall. No, their best protection now is our vigilance."

"And . . . what do we do if we see the wolf . . . or the fawn attacking? Are we supposed to, I don't know, kill it?"

Valentina sniffed.

"No. Wildlife mitigation, I believe, is the modern terminology. We annoy it. We chase it off. We determine what it wants and remove the attraction. My apprentice, intelligence means options. It means we don't have to make the brutal, ill-advised decision to kill off a part of the world we neither own nor comprehend. We mitigate the risk."

"That makes sense, but what if it decides to mitigate us right back?"

Valentina shrugged.

"We adapt. Perhaps we flee and regroup. Perhaps we neutralize its ability to do harm. It is natural to fear the unknown, but what world are we shaping if we attempt to destroy anything that we view as a potential risk? Empathy and curiosity take more courage than blunt force, but it is the wiser long-term path."

"I get it. But it also sounds like the more dangerous path."

"Indeed. Dangerous and worthwhile."

"And if we become the next victims?"

"Orion Station will see to it that other cryptonaturalists continue our investigation. Examine your motivations. If your principles always align with the safest path, can it truly be said that you have any principles beyond self-preservation?"

The horned wolf's muzzle pressed in through the silence following Valentina's question, shattering it in a rain of glass.

"That feels like a question that has different answers depending on where you are sitting and what is trying to kill you."

"Does it? Perhaps. But this is not the first time I have risked my body to protect a principle. It gets easier with practice."

She patted his arm and stood.

"Now, I have some preparations to make. While I do, I want you to read something."

"Study? Now? Really?"

"You have an hour. I have my tasks. You have yours."

Valentina ushered Green to a chair and selected a thick rust-colored binder.

"Begin with this one," she said. "It is a journal by a cryptonaturalist who began her career in 1948. Clara Rodriguez."

"Is that . . . the same Clara who left the message?"

"It is. She also held your current position as my apprentice, many years ago."

"Many years ago? Um, Teacher, I've been meaning to ask. If you don't mind. May I ask your age?"

"You may, later. Now, focus on this."

She tapped the book.

"It is full of useful information and the insights deepen as she becomes more experienced. She isn't a bad role model to meet early in your studies. Many in our field would likely tell you it would have been better to encounter her before me."

Green opened the book. It was a three-ring binder full of typed pages and handwritten notes. He flipped through the pages. Some were dog-eared. Some were coffee stained. Some were covered with whited-out corrections and a few were redacted with black marker.

It was an intimate thing. It was someone else's life. He turned to the first page. It had been typed on an old-fashioned typewriter.

Valentina walked away without another word.

Green read.

[Transcribed from original document by L. R. Rodriguez]

September 12, 1948

Where to begin?

Everything changed two weeks ago when young Jonathan Herkimer turned his afternoon math lesson into a game of hide and seek. He darted from the room with a giggle as I rummaged for my lesson plan.

I wasn't cross. A good tutor knows to build in time for a bit of mischief and, honestly, I wasn't terribly interested in the lesson myself.

I heard him dash into the study and found him beneath his grandfather's prodigious desk. Atop the blotter was a sight that took my breath. There were half a dozen detailed, annotated drawings and diagrams of tractor-sized lizards roaming the prairie.

I nearly fainted.

It wasn't the shock of seeing such outlandish creatures. It was the shock of familiarity, the shock of a secret stolen from my mind and displayed on the desk of a man I hardly knew.

Jonathan looked up at me from his hiding place with uncommon concern on his young face. No doubt I looked as if someone had just walked over my grave. He marched himself back to his desk without another word. I hardly remember the rest of our tutoring session, only a specter of tension pacing the room like a tiger and Jonathan stealing surreptitious glances at me while completing his assignments.

How can I describe my relationship with the lizards in those drawings?

As a child, when I told my uncles about great, thorny

lizards bigger than horses grazing the fields near Stoneburner's Feedstore, they laughed. So I laughed. I was seven and I knew already that their laughter wasn't to be trusted. In our house, mirth and anger were always scheming together.

I knew those lizards could look just like tumbled stone or slip beneath the turf like a diving frog as fast as you could say "button," but how could you miss seeing them?

You couldn't.

So, I was mad or damned and in practical terms I wasn't sure which was worse. There were always cautionary tales about wayward women in other families. The sanitarium. The nunnery. Places you were put to be forgotten. Oubliettes the menfolk could pretend were a kindness.

I know there are households who smile at whimsy and think kindly on their children's imaginary playmates. I know it in the way I know the north pole exists or the dark side of the moon. The knowledge is academic. In my family, we didn't talk of whimsy. We talked of lingering scars from the dust bowl. We talked of the abandoned homestead. Uncle Juan told grim stories about shoveling grit from the kitchen with a wheat scoop and the way the air would be haunted with static sparks. My family cursed the adage "rain will follow the plow" and doubly cursed themselves for ever thinking it trustworthy.

My choice was obvious. Deception. Avoidance. So, I didn't mention the giant lizards. Nor the zebra ants. Nor the golden dragonflies with eyes like silver coins.

If you were a child, you could speak of such things. Once. Perhaps twice. No more than that.

If you drew pictures of them, you had better draw them a bit different every time. Add a horn here. Add some wings there.

And now I had found the sorts of drawings I would never dare to make sitting out in the open on Robert Herkimer's desk. I had stumbled into an ambush, my forbidden subject lying in wait where I would least expect it.

What did I know of Mr. Herkimer? He was the patriarch of his family. He paid me to tutor his grandson. According to local lore, Robert Herkimer had made his fortune "away" doing "God knows what." He didn't seem to participate in any industry and it was the height of mystery why the Herkimers had settled in Eastern Kansas at all.

My afternoon lessons with Jonathan ended as the grandfather clock in the hall chimed thrice. I dismissed him and remained, stone-still, studying the fringe on the rug and feeling as if my body was mineralizing into stone. I heard Jonathan stamp down the stairs, racing to join his mother in the garden.

The minutes stretched. I sat, frozen with indecision, knowing it was too dangerous to mention the drawings to Mr. Herkimer. At the same time, I desperately craved outside confirmation that my odd observations were not evidence of some cancerous madness that had been swelling within me since childhood.

I couldn't mention it to him.

I simply couldn't.

The risk far outweighed the reward.

The smell of cigar smoke drifted into the room, bringing with it the news that my employer had arrived home. I didn't want to be forced to fabricate an excuse to justify why I had remained in the house. It was time to go. I could think on my predicament that evening, formulate a plan. First, I needed to escape and recover from my shock. With a bit of luck, I could slip from the house unnoticed.

Luck failed me.

I passed Mr. Herkimer in the hall. This shouldn't have been much of an obstacle as the man rarely looked directly at me. Unfortunately, my tongue rebelled against my better judgment and the words spilled out.

"Mr. Herkimer, those lizard drawings on your desk. Have you seen the creatures?"

I practically shouted it at him.

I was mortified.

He raised an eyebrow, then calmly asked me to follow him to his study. He asked me to sit. He closed the door. I knew he would terminate my employment. I was wondering if somehow I had also broken the law. He would ruin me. I reasoned that I could scarcely imagine the ways in which a person like Robert Herkimer might exact revenge for my audacity in bringing such madness into his home.

He sat across from me at his desk, fiddled with his gray walrus mustache, and fixed me with an unreadable look. I think that image of him will remain vivid and indelible in my mind forever.

He tapped his desktop, then slid several drawings toward me.

"Clara," he said, "are you telling me that you've seen these animals?"

I panicked and tried to backtrack. It was no use. Even with years of practice carefully omitting information, if asked a direct question, I'm a terrible liar.

"Well, I didn't mean to suggest that they were real. I meant . . . are they from a picture book?"

Robert smiled kindly. I'm not sure I'd ever seen him look pleased before that moment. Then, he said the words that changed everything.

"Clara, they are quite real and I have indeed seen them. Have you?"

My eyes filled with tears.

"Yes. My God, yes. I see them all the time."

He grinned like the Cheshire Cat and clapped his hands.

"Wonderful. Absolutely wonderful," he said.

The following week was absurd.

Mr. Herkimer kept me on the payroll, but hired a new tutor for Jonathan. In fact, he offered me a pay increase to leave my other tutoring posts, but I have a reputation to consider and have, as of yet, declined the offer.

He also asked me to call him Robert. I'm still getting used to that. I protested that it might look strange in public and he said that he gave up appearing conventional long ago. I wish I had that luxury.

In the last two weeks . . . the things I've seen defy description. He showed me a dizzying array of impossible curios, housed in the secret attic. A feather the size of a canoe. A pinecone that radiates endless heat. A small shrew-like thing made of living springs, gears, and cogs. Each time I perceived and expressed appreciation for the wonders in Mr. Herkimer's collection, his opinion of me seemed to grow.

This morning, we did an unimaginable thing. We went and observed my thorny lizards together. He calls them "Prairie Monitors."

What a truly odd experience to discuss one's imaginary childhood companions with another. It felt like thinking of an image and having a stranger fish it from my skull and describe it to me.

Part of me is elated about all this. Part of me thinks this must mean I truly have slipped over the edge.

Mr. Herkimer says that seeing these creatures makes me uniquely suited for his line of work. He told me about his teacher, a gentleman in Boston, and his teacher's teacher, a Cree woman in Quebec. He says that there are experts in this obscure field all across the globe.

I don't know what to make of it.

I just know, this morning, speaking aloud to another human being in the presence of those miraculous lizards, I felt wholly myself in a way I am still struggling to define.

Perhaps this journal will help me in that task.

Mr. Herkimer tells me I have a talent for pseudozoology and cryptonature. He tells me that this talent is a blessing. I hope, one day, that I will feel the same.

Still, my fear whispers to me and I cannot help but worry he is gathering evidence against me, though if he wished me harm he certainly wouldn't need a contrivance as elaborate as this. I know that doesn't make sense, but fear sprouted in the soil of experience isn't easy to uproot.

Hopefully, these writings will be a future treasure to me and I do not hear these words read back to me as part of some court proceedings.

In the margin, Valentina had written: *V. Blackwood Journal 488, PG 56.*

Green was eager to dive into Valentina's journals, but he couldn't quite pull himself away from Clara. She was floundering and he knew the feeling. He wanted to see her find her feet and get up onto dry land before he had to go spend an uncertain night in the dark woods. He read on.

She did indeed find her footing, absorbing all Robert Herkimer had to teach and voraciously adding to the global body of cryptonaturalist knowledge with her own meticulous observations. He began skipping ahead, skimming entries. There were portions Green understood well enough, like Clara's detailed descriptions of one prairie monitor's surprisingly friendly interactions with white-tailed deer. And there were sections he didn't understand at all, like Clara's many frustrations with using linear language to describe nonlinear insect behaviors.

As the journals progressed, they became more inscrutable, but this was itself a lesson. Green watched Clara transition from bewildered, to enthralled, to immersed. It could be done. It was an uplifting thought.

He was preparing to check on Valentina's preparations when an unexpected development occurred in the text. Clara discovered that Robert Herkimer was what she called a "poacher."

She had been investigating the sharply declining population of her beloved prairie monitors and her findings pointed back to her own teacher. She confronted him and he made no secret of it.

Not only was he unrepentant, he scolded Clara for harboring childish views about nature.

> "We are predators, Clara. What about our place in the natural order? And what of us specifically, those of us who can naturally perceive this deeper level of God's world? Do we spit in the eye of providence or do we gratefully accept the precious harvest made available to us chosen few?"

Robert was selling trophies to oligarchs and princes, fashionable mystics among the super-rich, and wealthy cults with endless avarice for hoarding precious oddities. He peddled the idea that only the most spiritually sensitive or magically gifted buyer could even perceive this preserved claw or that necklace strung with cryptid molars. A single prairie monitor, butchered and preserved, would fetch a small fortune on markets too secret for names.

> "We must do something to fund you sitting in a tree all day watching zebra ants, mustn't we? There won't be much

time for scientific inquiry if you choose to tutor or farm for your living."

He felt Valentina standing next to him and looked up.

"Poor Clara," Green said.

Valentina looked down at the page.

"Ah, that entry. A pivotal shift and not just for Clara."

"How do you mean?"

Valentina paused to collect her memories.

"Mr. Green, you are joining a professional organization and a community of experts and enthusiasts. The cryptonaturalists. Our branch of study has had many names, many factions, and has never before known the cohesiveness it knows now. The world has become a more connected, more communicative place.

"Clara rightly perceived a failure of imagination and morality on the part of her teacher, but Robert Herkimer's practices were not terribly rare among cryptonaturalists of earlier times. Lucrative expeditions to hunt a yeti or travel writers selling curios to decorate the parlors of the wealthy. Very common."

Valentina glanced up at a nearby shelf holding a jar of water vapor that occasionally coalesced into a jagged tooth.

"Clara brought the issue to a head in the mainstream of cryptonaturalist society. She astutely pointed out that we cannot possibly know the complex ecological impact of removing even a single cryptid from the world, creatures with populations often numbering in single digits, but with outsized roles to play in natural cycles well beyond our understanding.

"Robert Herkimer attempted to blacklist Clara from cryptonaturalist circles, but he failed. The fair-minded among us could see the obvious sense in her position. Clara found new mentors and new homes that were eager to host her talents, but she would not let the issue of poaching rest."

Green nodded, recalling his earlier question about killing the wolf.

"Eventually . . . later than you might hope . . . the global community of cryptonaturalists outlawed poaching and ostracized any members who practiced it. Well, openly practiced it."

"How'd that go?"

Valentina sniffed.

"There have been arguments. Even some fights. Some cryptonaturalists are allied with dangerous creatures who take mutual-defense pacts rather seriously. There have been a handful of ugly incidents. But, all in all, Clara's work led to a better, more thoughtful, more unified community."

"But why did you ask me to start with this book? I was expecting more, I don't know, basic procedures and facts. Maybe something to help prepare me for our job tonight. This is more . . . personality."

"Exactly, Mr. Green. Facts are just facts. They are inert. Unshaped clay. Facts do not contain inherent significance. Facts, in short, do not make meaning. People make meaning, sculpting it from the raw substance of facts. 'Personality,' as you put it. In any discipline, if the goal is to collect information, it is worth asking some basic philosophical questions first. Questions like, why bother? Why should I care about this set of data? What is this information for? Why spend our limited life minutes on this? Robert Herkimer had his answer. Clara Rodriguez had a much different answer."

Green pondered. It was a big question.

"May I ask what your answer is?" Green asked.

Valentina looked around her library.

"I agree with Clara, though I have made some of Robert Herkimer's mistakes in the past. I have had a very long time to make mistakes. Have you read any of my journals yet, Mr. Green?"

"Not a journal exactly. You . . . left a notebook in the cabin. I read some of it the night with the rag moth. There was a letter to someone named Ivan. I'm sorry. I don't suppose I should have read that."

"Ah. No, that's not one of my indexed journals for a reason, but I don't particularly mind. I am not terribly shy these days. Not much of interest for you, though, in a sentimental letter to my past."

"Yeah. About that. And the thing you said earlier about Clara. That letter to Ivan was dated from the 1930s and referred to a long time ago."

"Yes."

"So, yeah, exactly how old are you? If you don't mind my asking."

Valentina smiled.

"I don't mind, but I'll propose a trade. It's a trade of trust. Truthfully, I had it in mind when I asked you to read Clara's journal."

"Okay. I'm listening."

"I'll answer your question honestly and in return you'll answer a personal question about yourself honestly. Agreed?"

"Sure. Why not? Agreed."

"I am 512 years old. As near as I can guess, that is."

Green began to smile and then the smile melted away. She was not joking.

"How?"

"Well, technically that is more than one question, but once you begin reading my journals you'll learn all of this anyway. Call it a botanical accident for now. I was one of the people of the East European forest steppe. I had a talent for finding unusual plant species. One singular species left me frozen in time for nearly two hundred years and . . . deeply changed. So, perhaps you could argue that I am more honestly three centuries old, but I think I've earned all five. I have certainly paid for them."

"Holy shit."

For a moment, the room around Valentina seemed to fade and she was standing like a giant on a gray, weather-blasted plateau of time. She was as much a cryptid as the horned wolf, singular and inscrutable, an alien presence walking in the world of mundane things. The idea made him feel suddenly homeless, once again beyond the edge of the map. Green's vision shifted, and he saw his teacher, the woman who built a treetop library, who made him cheese on toast to heal his unraveling nerves.

Green recalled Valentina's letter to Ivan.

. . . if we knew then that there was such a thing as too far away . . .

"So, Ivan . . ."

"Was a dear, dear friend in eighteenth-century Russia."

"Too far away."

Valentina's eyes went somewhere distant.

"Indeed. Too far away."

She came back to herself and focused on Green's face.

"Now, it is time for my question."

"I don't think I have any secrets to rival 'I'm five hundred years old,' but shoot."

Something twisted in Green's guts as it came to him.

He did, very much, have secrets.

"We shall see. Between the rag moth and the glass fawn, well . . . Last night, I researched the previous six sightings of the fawn. Four of the reports are very old and very incomplete, threadbare oral tradition mixed with allegory. Not ideal."

"Okay. Not sure what I can answer about that."

She pulled two notebooks from a nearby desk and opened them in front of Green. He stooped over and read a highlighted passage on the page.

. . . the others were not so fortunate. They were too close. I watched them fall . . .

Valentina continued.

"The most recent two accounts are better. Armed with new information and reading between the lines, they seem to agree on two points—that the glass fawn is a bringer of ill fortune and, more to the point, no one who gets closer than perhaps one hundred meters to it survives to tell the tale."

Green turned his attention to the second journal.

A block of underlined text.

. . . I only saw its light, but it was the deer. Nothing glows like that in the jungle. When I made it down to the valley camp, it was a charnel house, a place of the dead . . .

She spoke on.

"They do not mention localized cold specifically, but certain colorful phrases imply it. I'm afraid I trusted my recollections too much. I sometimes fail to reckon with the truth that human brains are not meant to house a collection of memories as large as mine. I should have researched the fawn earlier."

He swallowed.

"But . . . if the fawn is so deadly . . . and it's been seen before . . . why hasn't it killed more? Hundreds? Thousands? Did those other accounts say how they stopped it?"

"Ah, Mr. Green. I believe these are the correct questions. No, the past accounts make no mention of thwarting the fawn, yet the killings seem to take place over a relatively short span of time before halting. Based on past patterns, I suspect that the fawn's presence in our world is fleeting."

"So, what, it's normally . . . dormant?"

"Or, more likely, absent."

"You said the Hole in Nothing leads outside our reality, right? Do you think it came through there?"

"That is precisely my current hypothesis. In fact, I suspect that the two phenomena are, essentially, one and the same. Dependent upon one another. If the fawn is from outside this dimension, then it is entirely possible that reality cannot heal while it is present. The fawn's unrealness is an active injury to our world's mode of existence that is expressed as that rift between the pines."

She tapped the open journals.

"Clearly, it has torn its way into our reality on other occasions. The question is, what made it depart?"

Her words made Green feel unanchored, like he was drifting away from himself. A flash flood of dread crashed inside him. Listening to Valentina undercut her own humanity and then talk about the universe like a jigsaw puzzle with a piece missing was beyond disorienting.

"Did you find any mention of the wolf? Did you look?"

She shook her head.

"The only data we have on the horned wolf comes from your observations, which, I remind you, include two encounters during which the creature could have killed you and did not. That alone marks it as less lethal than the fawn."

It called me "not-man."

"Well, maybe it couldn't kill me. Somehow. Maybe like the fawn."

Valentina's expression hardened.

"Just so. That brings us back to the answer you owe me. Mr. Green, I have a suspicion that there is something you have not told me. Perhaps it involves that 'something' you mentioned urging you toward the mountains when we first spoke. I also have a suspicion that whatever is in that right pocket of yours is involved."

Green's hand moved to the acorn, then quickly away. Valentina watched the motion.

"It seems you have not been entirely open with me. As you may have gleaned from Clara's journal, trust must be a key facet of our arrangement. Trust and community are essential to our work."

He swallowed.

"I understand."

"Well, then, to my question. No living person on record has gotten as close as you did to the glass fawn and survived. Nor witnessed rag moth caterpillars, for that matter. So, kindly explain to me why you are still alive."

Valentina took a seat and folded her hands in her lap.

Green felt the weight of her attention, the same weight that pressed on him at their first meeting.

He reached into his pocket and pulled out the acorn.

It sat on his open palm.

Valentina studied it, then raised her eyes back to his.

"Go on," she said.

He groped for the memory of his not-quite-death and felt the same psychic jolt that always demanded payment when he tried to think of it. Some part of the machinery that kept him grounded in reality coughed black smoke. The huge, black bird perched on the no-parking sign laughed its cawing laugh and it seemed to be mocking both his past and present pain.

"I . . . almost died."

"Keep talking."

He told her about the bus, his vision of approaching tires. About the otherworldly bird. About the ridiculous acorn that was suddenly in his pocket and in his thoughts. He told her how that event unspooled the rest of his life and how he decided to rebuild it. He tried to express what it cost him to talk about it, to think about it.

"The memory hurts. That was . . . almost the end of me."

"Are you sure it was almost? Perhaps you did die."

Green just shook his head. He felt a sudden urge to vomit.

"Interesting. That is one more first to add to your tally. I have not heard such a story before. Although, there are a number of large avian cryptids that might match your description of the black bird. I wonder . . . Perhaps that creature gave you the acorn."

"Why would a giant bird bring me an acorn?"

Green swallowed, willing his stomach to calm.

Valentina cocked her head like an owl, glancing at the library roof.

"Perhaps it was a bribe. Or a purchase."

It was too much. He stood too quickly, knocking the journals to the floor. He took three staggering steps toward the hatch before collapsing forward to dry heave on hands and knees. The sheer, hideous terror of the memory kept hammering him as he tried to clear his head.

"Stay there," Valentina said.

He didn't feel like he had much of a choice.

She opened the hatch and was gone. Green fell onto his side, hugged his knees, and tried to think of anything else. It was impossible. It was all more than he could process. The memory had been a hot stove, now it was a house fire he couldn't escape. He shut his eyes tight and wished he could simply pass out.

He heard Valentina's footsteps, but he couldn't open his eyes. The fire was spreading. He was choking on smoke.

There was a soft plop near his ear and something changed.

The fire was there, but the roof was gone. A cold breeze swirled through the house and ushered away the dark smoke. A steady rain fell. The flames guttered and died.

Died. My death. I died. And then . . . I didn't.

He opened his eyes.

Six inches from his face, Blobert sat on the wooden floor, pulsating and blinking at Green with too many eyes.

"Oh, it's you."

He knuckled tears away and rocked into a sitting position.

"May we continue?" Valentina said.

"Jesus, lady."

She shifted a chair and sat across from him.

"The phobophage will make this conversation easier."

He took a steadying breath.

"Come on. Say Blobert. Just say it once."

"I will not."

He wiped his mouth on his sleeve.

"Alright. I can talk. But I don't think there's anything else I can tell you."

"Very well," she said. "In the future, please do not hold back such information. We can work on deepening our understanding of your situation together. Let me examine your acorn."

Valentina held out her hand.

Reluctantly, he passed it over.

She held it up and scrutinized it. She smelled it. She listened to it. She produced an iron nail from her pocket and touched it to the acorn's cap. She whispered something to the nut, then looked at it as if expecting a response. Then, she handed it back.

"As far as I can tell, it's an acorn. White oak is my best guess. *Quercus alba*."

"That's all?"

"That is all for now. It may be that acorn is giving you some form of protection. It may be that your near death, or rather undone death, has altered your relationship with mortality in some way we cannot yet determine. Clearly something unusual allowed you to survive the fawn's presence. These are questions we will pursue, but not tonight. I am content that I now at least know the shape of your situation, if not the details. Tonight, we have other pressing business."

Valentina looked out the window.

The western sky was starting to blush.

"It's time to go."

CHAPTER 12

THE COST OF OUR PRINCIPLES

DANCER WALKED DOWN THE GRAVEL LANE PULLING A RED wagon with an enormous peace lily in the bed. She intercepted Valentina and Green just as they were turning off the lane to hike to Wildwood Stable.

"Evening. What summons you two into the woodland dusk? I do believe the sky is getting a running start at a postcard sunset."

"Business," Valentina said. "But I will not fail to notice the sunset. What brings you out our way?"

"Just taking Archimedes here for a walk."

Dancer grinned at the lily in her wagon.

"She's about to be shut inside all winter and I don't know how many fair evenings we have left."

"Oh, hang on," Green said.

He dipped into his pack and brought out Dancer's cup.

"Here you go."

She took it and touched it to her forehead in a salute.

"You're a gentleman and a scholar."

She leaned in confidentially.

"And you know full well I will be burdening you with this selfsame errand again soon, bud."

"I hope you do," Green said.

"I expect you guys have heard the latest bad news. Fella down in Hickory?"

"Yes," Valentina said. "I'm afraid so."

"Is it . . . you know . . . is it something from over on your side of the street, Val?"

"It is. That's what brings us out tonight."

Dancer shook her head and chewed the inside of her cheek.

"Is there something that I can be doing here? I mean, we've stepped past strange into deadly. Can't just ignore deadly. This isn't just oddball tracks in the mud or that Hole in Nothing."

"You know about that too?" Green said.

"Everybody knows about that, Green. Hard to miss news of a thing like that."

He threw up his arms in exasperation, giving up the idea of ever fully understanding his new reality.

"If you can, put on extra lights," Valentina said. "Consider playing music outside. We think the danger prefers dark and quiet."

The kids at Kinkaid would have had sound and light.

"What exactly am I trying to frighten off here, Val?"

"A pale, glowing deer, but I doubt you would see it."

Green looked away.

He wanted to argue but didn't. Yes, the deer seemed to be a threat, but he couldn't shake the idea that the wolf was still somehow the greater danger.

"Alright. Well, Archimedes and I will visit the other campers and spread the news. Get loud and bright. Not exactly rocket surgery. We can manage that."

"Other campers?" Green asked.

"Yeah, there's four others here besides you two. Carrie and Jen down by Snaggletooth Rock. Travis and his sugar shack in the maple wood and Ol' Animal up in Stumptown."

Green looked at Valentina.

"Maybe we should keep watch here. I didn't know there were so many others at Candle-Fly."

Valentina shook her head.

"No, as I said, I have other protective measures here, though the events at your campsite have made me question their current efficacy. Still, I believe Wildwood Stable is the most vulnerable."

Dancer caught Green's eye and smiled.

"I don't even think she's being like that on purpose. She just drops mystery grenades into the conversation on pure reflex. Wildwood Stable, huh? Yeah, I guess they're pretty isolated. Alright. I better be off now if I wanna visit everybody before dark and get Archimedes to bed on time. Safe travels, neighbors."

Valentina and Green walked into the trees to the crunch and squeak of Dancer turning her wagon and heading back down Moss Man's Row.

Valentina walked faster than usual, forcing Green to exert continuous effort to keep up.

The speed of travel and the earnestness of the errand stretched the minutes. There was a kind of pressure in the woods. Green considered asking his teacher about it, but couldn't find the words he needed. It was slippery, a sensation he couldn't articulate.

Wildwood Stable was a sloped, grassy rectangle carved from dense pinewoods on a winding mountain road. A weather-beaten, T-shaped barn stood in a broad field. The barn shadowed a practice ring in front and a chain of linked paddocks out back. A little white house was tucked off on the eastern edge beneath the skirts of pine boughs. The property was a conspicuous lake of evergreen among a valley packed with autumn-brown oaks and sugar maples. Valentina and Green arrived under a western sky the muddy red of drying blood.

"You haven't said much about it," Green said.

The pair stopped in the deep gloom on the edge of the wood and looked out over Wildwood, then made their way toward the hillside.

"About what, Mr. Green?"

"The acorn. My story. The giant bird. Any of it."

"I suppose I am still mulling it over. You have added yet more unknowns to the landscape. Between the wolf, the fawn, and your own peculiarities, you are entering the field of cryptonature in a singularly unusual way. It requires consideration. It's hard to say if you are profoundly fortunate or profoundly unfortunate. There are so many unanswered questions."

He glanced at his teacher, feeling a shapeless suspicion that there *must* be more she could say. She was a small, gray-haired woman walking through the dusk. She was also a collection of multiple lifetimes studying the most obscure knowledge imaginable.

They walked around the practice ring, keeping to the far side from the house. Green ran his hand along the rough split rail fence, looking at the hoof-pocked earth. Beyond, he could see a lamp shining in a window. Two red pickups sat in the gravel drive next to a little city of horse trailers.

They moved past the paddocks and up the slope. Night was gathered under the trees. It seemed to wait for some signal to rush into the fields beneath the open sky.

"I will have to broadcast an update about the nature of your encounters," Valentina said. "We can't, for example, allow our colleagues to assume it is safe to observe rag moth decay, not until we know more about your unique circumstances."

"Maybe be a little vague about my situation in the broadcast, okay? At least until I understand more about what happened to me."

"Why? What is the root of this caution? I can see no reason to keep your condition a secret."

He winced. Thinking of *his condition* still brought a jolt of fear and pain. The subject, like the memory, had teeth. He wished he had smuggled Blobert along in a backpack.

He spoke through clenched teeth.

"There's just so much I don't know about myself. I mean, for example, am I, like, immortal now?"

"No."

"Wow. You answered that awfully quickly. Is the question that weird? I survived the moth and the wolf or fawn or whatever. And you certainly seem to be immortal."

"Don't be ridiculous. I most certainly am not. We have never, in the whole of human history, discovered a single permanent, unchanging life-form in nature. Never. That long-standing truth will not end with you or me. And believe me, I have aged considerably, just not at the typical rate. And you, maybe your mortality is somehow tied to that acorn, or to the bird you saw, but acorns and cryptids are likewise not built for forever."

"Okay. That feels right."

"What feels right, Mr. Green?"

"That my mortality is tied up with the acorn somehow. I don't know. It feels so important. I can't stop thinking about it. Maybe this little nut really is a matter of life and death."

"And why do you think that is?"

"It came to me when my . . . accident was undone. And I feel like I have to keep it safe."

"Nonsense. If you truly cared about safety, you would have stayed in your old life. You certainly would not have agreed to work with me."

"I guess that's true, but seriously, what happens if I lose the acorn and suddenly there are bus tires racing to smash my face? That could happen, right? There's no way to rule it out."

"No, I do not think that particular fear is merited. That is almost never how time works. The past quickly accretes weight and rigidity. It may start as soft and pliable, a trait the editor of your death likely exploited, but it is like coral. We living organisms scurry about building it, then it becomes as hard as stone."

Walking in pinewoods was different. Without the dry rustle of fallen leaves, their footfalls were a soft hushing sound as they trod the pine straw.

"Okay, so if the acorn is lost or destroyed, it may just mean my regular death."

Valentina tilted her head.

"Perhaps."

"So, what should I do? To keep it safe, I mean. I've thought about burying it in concrete or vacuum sealing it in a safety-deposit box somewhere. It can't just stay in my pocket. It takes too much of my attention. It's always tugging at me."

Valentina glowered at Green.

"What? Why are you looking at me like that?"

"The answer is obvious to me."

"Which is?"

"In my mind, there is one highest and best use of an acorn. One thing that definitively sets it apart from other objects."

She gave Green an expectant look.

Green returned a blank stare.

"Plant it," she said.

He had a flash of abandoning the acorn under a little mound of soil and walking away. The idea drew his hand to his pocket in a defensive flinch.

"But that's basically the same as throwing it away. I can't predict what that would do."

"It would bring new life into the world. It would become a tree, a fountain of leaves, and a home for countless species. A source of food and shelter. Perhaps the mother of countless more generations of trees. There is no question about the best attribute of an acorn. It may become an oak. What could be better than that? What can boast the same?"

Green was silent for a moment.

"Or it could become a snack for a squirrel."

"There are ways to protect a seed from such mishaps."

"What happens when the oak dies?"

Valentina sniffed.

"My apprentice, I am uniquely qualified to say that no one has any business outliving an oak tree."

"I'll have to think about it."

The sky above the stable shifted from deep blue to black. A screech owl screamed, imploring the dusk it so loved to linger awhile longer. Green and Valentina found a secluded spot high on the slope above the paddock and settled in to watch.

"You're awfully practical about death," Green said. "You aren't afraid of death?"

"I am not. Why should I be?"

"I don't know. The unknown? An ending?"

Valentina smiled.

"The unknown is my business and even the very young learn that we must make friends with endings. I am far from young."

"Are you, I don't know how to put it, religious? Spiritual?"

"Perhaps, but not in the way I think you mean."

"I guess I'm asking if you believe in an afterlife."

"I would say that cryptonaturalists rarely rule out possibilities without data, but no, I do not believe we go on as we are. I do not think we retain our personalities or memories. I do not draw distinctions between mind and brain, and brains are natural things shaped by millennia of evolution to look after our bodies. It does not strike me as likely that our thoughts would suddenly split from all physicality and continue beyond the death of the body. Thinking is a function of the body. The one invites the other."

Green watched a yellow porch light flick on in front of the little white house and he wondered what sort of people lived there.

"That seems bleak. The loss of knowledge, of self."

"Take a deep breath and look around you."

Pale stars were fading into view. A soft susurrus of evergreen brought to mind the sea. The new night smelled of pine and cut grass.

"Would you call this forest in which we sit a human place, Mr. Green? A function of human thought and meaning?"

"No. I guess I wouldn't."

"And does that make it alien and forbidding? Is it bleak?"

"Well, no. Not at all."

Valentina squeezed Green's shoulder.

"Death may be a loss of humanness, of the ways of knowing to which you are accustomed. But I feel certain that human ways of knowing are not the only ways. And nothing, not death nor loss of mind nor memory, can remove us from nature."

She placed a hand against a nearby pine and looked up at the sky.

"Drink in the stars. Feel the familiar pull of gravity on your bones. Smell the living trees. Nature is a thing of unity and renewal, change and cycles. You were a part of that before you were born and will remain a part of it eons after your death. And if ever these ideas become too distant or abstract, just pause and look around. You know what nature is and you know that it feels like home. When you feel that instinctual love of nature, your senses are trying to tell you something. They are telling you that human existence is not the only worthy kind of existence."

Green sat silent for a moment.

"Does that mean you welcome death?"

Valentina hmphed.

"Certainly not. I, as I am now, am too in love with this world. Survival instinct is nature too. And, in any case, I am too curious to depart this mind yet. But I do not lose sight of the fact that when my time comes, I will be unfinished. We will always be unfinished because we are not meant to culminate in any fixed state or final achievement. I do not believe life is a thing that gets completed, just concluded. Truly, it would be tragic for it to be otherwise."

"Speaking of survival instincts, you haven't really explained what exactly we plan to do if the horned wolf or the glass fawn arrives here."

"It's quite simple, Mr. Green. You see, I have an immortal apprentice with a magic acorn."

Green laughed.

"Really though, what do we do?"

Valentina pulled her backpack in front of her and produced a cartoonish-looking nubby orange pistol and the same rotten log she brought to Kinkaid Cabins.

"I brought a flare gun. The fawn appears to dislike light and attention. And I brought my spore-log again."

She grimaced as she mentioned the log. Green recalled her wearing it on a strap over her shoulder while they investigated the area where the college kids had died. She had called it one of her contingency plans.

"The log again? What does that thing do, anyway?"

"It's full of a potent cryptofungus called Lethe's doorstep. A gift from the network administrator, produced by their cousin. If I crack it open, spores will spread over several square miles rendering everything, and I do mean everything, unconscious. For reasons we do not fully understand, the effect tends to have a much shorter duration for humans than most cryptids. It is a reset of consciousness that favors our physiology."

"Tends to? Most?"

"It isn't a pleasant contingency, but it has saved me in the past. The discomfort upon waking from the spores is poetically distasteful."

"I don't think I want to know what that means."

"Good. I don't want to describe it."

Valentina retrieved a chocolate brown tarp from her pack and spread it on the ground. The distant whinny of a horse seemed to mark the exact moment dusk surrendered fully to night.

She handed him a small radio.

"What's this for?"

"We're going to do periodic patrols, each going a different direction and meeting back here."

"But isn't this the best vantage point?"

"It is, unless the fawn comes from the woods behind the house or approaches from beyond the barn. We have too many blind spots."

"Alright. Fine. So, if we split up, what is my protection from the wolf—and the fawn?"

"Your wits. Your focus. And, I would add, the unique protection of the events of the last few weeks of your life."

"Seriously? You want me to wander these woods that have claimed, what, six human lives, completely unarmed?"

Valentina gave him a flat look.

"Yes, I do, Mr. Green. Again, you didn't have to accompany me this evening."

"That seems awfully reckless."

"What is it you think we do?"

"Study nature. Not sure why that means we need to make overly risky decisions with our lives."

"We study a very particular kind of nature."

"Yeah. I know. The kind I'm not allowed to call monsters."

Valentina narrowed her eyes. In the dark, she looked more than ever like a storybook witch.

"I have calmly extracted myself from the jaws of a shark made from ice and water vapor. I have studied snakes that call lightning and forests that punish trespassers. I have bargained with insects that fold distance like paper and I have a name in the private language of the Corvid Court. None of these things were monsters, no more than an African elephant or a Portuguese man o' war. Center yourself, Mr. Green. Caution is not the keystone virtue of your new profession. Curiosity is."

"Uh-huh, but can I take the flare gun?"

Valentina sighed and offered the gun.

"Fine. You check the woods behind that house, preferably without terrifying its residents. I will explore the other side of the fields. Radio if you spot anything. We meet back here within the hour."

She slung the spore-log over her shoulder.

"Stealth, for a human, is about looking where your feet are going. Do not overcomplicate it. Do not crack branches. Press the ground, do not stamp it. Do not drag your feet. Move them up and down. Stay on the balls of your feet when you can. When you cannot, step on the outside edges of each foot, then roll your weight inward as you press down. My old teacher used to say, 'Snuff the flame of your body and kindle the fires of your senses.'"

Green stroked his beard, feeling a tingle of adrenaline as Valentina turned and moved quiet as a cloud shadow through the trees. Two breaths later, he was alone on the edge of the pinewoods.

He looked at the flare gun, realized that the trigger was the only moving part he recognized, and stuffed it in his jacket pocket. He had zero clue how to use the radio. The house was a distant gray smudge with bright windows. He made for it, thinking of Valentina's stealth advice and feeling overly conscious of his size.

He stayed on the balls of his feet for about thirty steps before his calves were burning. He had no idea how you did anything precise with your feet while wearing new hiking boots in the dark woods. So, he clomped. He clomped as gently as he could.

At the rear of the white house, Green found a large propane tank. It looked like a giant Tylenol. He crept up behind it and studied the home. No movement. Flower-print curtains soaked with buttery light.

He scanned the woods, but saw nothing. In the distance, he heard the furtive sounds of something foraging, but he felt confident that the creatures he sought would make no noise at all. Conventional animal sound was a comfort.

He walked on toward the road, glancing left and right in slow rhythm in time with his steps.

The moon crested the trees and Green was shocked by the amount of light it provided. There were shadows in the moonlight. Moon shadows. A thing he didn't know existed.

Across the road, a silver spark drew his eye. Something had caught the moonlight, but instead of going dark again, it held the ghostly glow, kindling it to white fire.

It was the glass fawn, walking directly toward Wildwood Stable.

He froze.

At that distance, it was such a tiny thing. A strange little deer pulled from an animated film walking in the real world, a trick of light and angle.

His stomach fluttered, recalling the first time he saw that deer.

Recalling what followed it.

He pulled the flare gun from his pocket and turned in a slow circle.

The hunted had arrived. Where was the hunter?

Green knew that the horned wolf would not come with a moonlight glow to announce its presence in the darkness. It wouldn't walk across the road with delicate care, the way the fawn was doing. It would be invisible and then it would be exactly where it wanted to be.

The fawn walked forward.

Adrenaline ran a current through his limbs.

He didn't know exactly how near the fawn might need to be before its chilling effect took hold, but it was moving closer to the house. He still harbored doubts that the glass fawn was to blame for the recent deaths, but those doubts were nothing so vain or foolish as certainty. He took a step forward.

The fawn was well over a hundred yards away, but it stopped as soon as Green moved. Even at that distance, he could feel the fawn's eyes upon him like a winter wind following a newcomer into a warm room.

Well. If not now, when?

He raised the flare gun, estimating an angle that would carry the bright fire up and over the road where the fawn stood. He pulled the trigger.

There was a muffled crack and a smell like sulfur, then nothing.

The fawn took a step toward him.

He cocked back the hammer and tried again.

Even more nothing than before.

Valentina had said that you don't meet the unknown armed for war, but they were also there to defend people who couldn't defend themselves and now Green was absolutely without any tools to turn away the approaching cryptid.

"Shit."

The fawn looked away from Green and began a slow arc around the practice ring, heading for the house. Something about the motion flipped a switch in Green's mind. The deer wasn't fleeing and it wasn't wandering. That turn wasn't random. Was it hunting?

He picked up a stick, planning to crack it against trees and fence posts to startle the fawn into retreating. It was better than nothing.

Suddenly, the fawn went still and Green saw its attention snap to the opposite tree line.

His mouth went dry.

That's where Valentina was heading.

He stared at the fairy-fire thing. It looked peaceful, even lovely, but he trusted his teacher. He still struggled to believe the fawn was responsible for all the death on the mountain, but he trusted her.

The fawn reoriented its body and began gliding toward where Valentina was no doubt watching. Its legs moved, but the movement seemed out of sync with its speed. It shifted across the ground like a marionette in the hands of a novice puppeteer.

She'd been joking when she said that her immortal apprentice was her plan for defense.

She was half joking.

The fawn began to slide faster toward Valentina.

"Aw, hell."

Green ran.

He felt heavy and loud, but he ran as hard as he could toward the fawn.

He threw his stick aside and put all his effort into a full sprint.

Distantly, he heard the front door of the house click open as he passed.

He ignored it.

He wasn't a runner and he felt a fire blooming in his chest from the effort.

The fawn's legs swayed in a languid dance, but it was still leaving him behind.

He needed its attention.

He meant to yell "hey," but it erupted from him as a half-roared "haaaaaa."

The fawn paused and did a boneless somersault that made no physical sense and then it was facing Green again, standing stone-still and waiting for his approach.

He slid to a halt thirty feet from the creature, feeling rivulets of sweat freezing on his face. His lungs burned and his chest ached with the sunless cold beneath a frozen sea. Between the sudden winter within his body and his panting exertion, he had to plant his hands on his knees to stay upright.

He eyed the fawn and fought for breath.

Up close, Green saw his mistake.

At that distance, without fogged glass between them, the fawn was neither graceful nor lovely. Neither ethereal nor statuesque.

It was a deer-shaped pool teeming with rotting, malformed fish. A pale, wet, pulsing thing pressed beneath a stone. Its two dark eyes were not eyes and looked at nothing, between them a buzzing, hateful disk spun like a coin on a dish.

Green met its sightless gaze and something unhealthy touched his mind. For a moment, his inner voice was no longer alone within his skull. There was something else in that refuge beneath the bone, something the color of cream with a forest of questing fingers.

He screamed noiselessly and clutched his forehead.

Then, something else was there in his mental darkness, in the place he had thought so safely locked away and private.

This new thing came with a booming, thunderous growl that drove the invader from the hollow places inside the walls.

Look away, not-man.

Green gasped in a breath and shifted his whole body away from the fawn, turning his back on the creature. The ice in his beard clattered like beads as he turned.

There, tearing through the dark like an obsidian knife, was the horned wolf.

Its fleshless jaws hung wide, bone and tooth amid a thicket of sharp black peaks that roiled like a lightless fire.

It leapt, sod spraying skyward in the wake of its speed.

The wolf sailed over him, raining down soil and grass. Green toppled into a roll, feeling the earth shudder at the wolf's impact.

There was a streak of white fire in Green's peripheral vision that took a moment to parse. The glowing deer was there, then away, leaving an afterimage of itself on the dark landscape. The glass fawn was across the paddocks and disappearing up the wooded slope. It was impossibly fast, not just faster than an animal should be, but faster than a physical object could move through space. It didn't speed like an arrow, it transitioned like the swing of a flashlight's beam across the landscape. Here and then gone. Whatever mechanism it had just used to flee the wolf, it wasn't muscle or bone or sinew. It was something else.

Green tilted himself up to hands and knees, then rose, the muscles in his legs shuddering. He heaved in the air, watching his breath transform from crystallized vapor back to transparency. Melting ice in his hair sent streams of frigid water trailing down his neck and back.

The wolf had not pursued the fawn.

There was no chasing after speed like that.

Green summoned all the calm that was left to him and turned.

It was there, standing six feet away, the nightmare that shattered his windshield again and again in his memory. It was bigger than he recalled.

He had no weapons. He had no strength left. Yet, somehow, his fear was all spent.

"Well. It got away."

Green's voice was hoarse.

The bear-size wolf turned to him, slow and smooth as honey. The pine scent of its breath was sharp and with it came the wolf's thoughts.

It won't be caught with speed, but it may be denied prey and rest and territory.

Green knew the wolf wasn't speaking words. The wolf was transmitting raw meaning, mind to mind. The words were Green's.

It didn't matter.

They were communicating. Green was, in every way that counted, standing in the dark talking to a monster.

Bravely done, not-man.

Green met the wolf's eyes. There was something new there.

Some deep part of his brain was screaming at him to run, to seize a weapon, to protect his soft throat. In a timeless, detached space, Green took those ancient impulses and set them on the table in Valentina's cabin. He studied them. His teacher was there, standing in his headspace watching him steadily. Clara was there too. No. These artifacts of terror, fear of the dark and unknown world, could not be trusted as guiding principles.

"Thank you," Green said. "And likewise. What is that creature?"

A soft sigh behind the wolf rose like a phantom from the ground.

Green and the wolf turned.

Valentina was there, wreathed in frosty breath. She held the rotting spore-log in both hands.

The wolf growled low and Green felt the vibrations in his ribs.

"I hate this part," she said.

"Wait!"

It was too late.

She broke the log over her knee and tossed the halves at the horned wolf's feet.

"I apologize in advance, Mr. Green."

Green had just enough time to question if it had worked before he noticed, in an offhand way, that he had slumped to the ground. The wolf slumped next to him, eye to eye. He wondered if all wolves' eyes looked like that, like deep green water glinting with islands of gold. His consciousness became too light then and the wind caught it, sending it dancing out and away over the distant treetops, but he wasn't alone.

CHAPTER 13

BECOMING PACK

SHHHH. THE ROCKS HAVE EARS AND NOT ALL OF THEM ARE our friends. Be a shadow, not a sound.

Pup halted, still all gangly bones with just a fog of flesh coalescing in his ribs.

Mother formed a tongue and licked the length of Pup's skull.

You don't have to stop playing. Just not so loud. There will come a time when none of the deep things would dare to take you no matter the sounds you make, but that time is not yet.

Mother yawned like a cave and turned three circles before lying down in the granite hollow.

Pup eyed his game.

It wouldn't be as fun now.

He was leaping from the root thickets to menace a great gnarled leg of oak that looked like a charging elk.

He couldn't menace if he couldn't growl.

So, he settled for curiosity.

Pup buried his muzzle in the stone, feeling the delicious cold enter his bones, soft and secret as fox song.

He listened with his whole skull the way mother had taught him, like a fat spider in the center of her web.

What was the wind and what was food in the trap?

That was the trick.

Pup heard many things in his bones. Lurk-cats that chewed the earth like they hated it. Shadow skates that were still half dream and swam through the ground like trout within the stone. Pinch bugs and peepers that rolled and clattered like pebbles tumbling down the mountainside.

He knew these things.

He ate these things.

The danger, Mother said, was in the deeper ones that kept their bones attuned to his sounds.

The thought made Pup tuck tail and look to his mother.

She was there.

As big and constant as gravity.

Let the monsters come. She killed monsters or chased them back to the nowhere places.

That was the duty for which the mountains rewarded them with sprawling root tangles, the under forests, and stone wilds teeming with food and beauty in the one solid deep-season of forever.

A lurk-cat was chewing up from beneath, blind in its war with earth, moving straight for Pup's teeth. And why not? The mountains loved them best.

Time raced on.
Pain and learning.
Love and hunger.
Riddles in the dark.
Pup grew,

slow in the moment,
fast in the memory.

Mother stood at the lowest precipice of their territory again, above the endless deep, washing herself in the wellspring of darkness where the silence boomed like thunder.

Pup was not so small now, but he was not his mother. She was strong like the long years had pressed the constancy of stone into her body.

He knew what it meant that she was drawn to that place, their furthest refuge from air and sky. It was instinct. Even he knew the tug of that narrow ledge if he went too long without sleep and the thoughtless part of his mind wandered free and unchecked. *Go to the deep places. Go to the deep places.*

She was going to go. There would be no returning.

On the one hand, it was the highest compliment.

She would not go if she didn't think him ready to serve as the mountains' guardian.

On the other, it was like anticipating a wound that would never stop bleeding.

It was true that he hunted easy as breathing now.

It was true that when the thicket singer had come for him, he wetted the ground with its oil and stood howling in its wreckage.

It was true that he dared the lonely deep things to reach for him and they all shied away from the challenge.

But he was not his mother.

Fear and doubt and sadness were the price of wakefulness and he would pay them, but he didn't have to love the transaction.

He pondered his mother's lessons.

The stories.

Always the stories.

Mother told such stories, each of them a reminder about duty and a call to prepare.

She could show him images of the things she had driven from their mountains, things that might return. The tooth-wind. The hateful orb. The frozen deer.

Things from just away were bad.

Things from outside were worse still.

Pup was strong, but he wasn't his mother.

He wanted to do his duty, but he wasn't his mother.

He felt the mountain's own heart pumping life through his dark flesh, but he wasn't his mother.

Mother was leaving.

When she left,
it was a wound of the body.
When the pain was dulled with years,
it was a wound of the spirit.
When he named the world his family,
he became different, but whole.

The pup was not a pup.

He roamed and hunted and fought and found no equal in pure might above or below the mountains.

He could feel the borders of his mountains like he could feel the borders of his bones, his territory. Home and family, one and the same. He could taste the dark and know all the creatures it touched. Already, he had learned something of his mother's old strength; already, he felt the dark stone lending him a tiny fragment of itself, the inertia of its unquestionable, ancient existence.

Perhaps one day, he would have his mother's strength.

Perhaps even the mountain would grant him kin.

Yet, "one day" and "perhaps" weren't of much help when the cursed day came that the air betrayed the mountains and let in a trespasser from outside the world of real things.

Too early.

He was not ready.

He had seen the creature before, in his mother's mind. The frozen deer. The moonlight fawn. The parody of life that slid through the barriers like a glass splinter.

It wore its shape in mockery of the natural world.

It was a deer the way ice is an imitation of stone.

No.

There was no metaphor in nature to explain the outsider.

A wrongness in the mind and an insult to the land.

A famished absence with a body.

He was not ready.

He was not his mother.

It didn't matter.

He loved his mountains and he loved the duty that transformed his hours from numb waiting to needful purpose.

He would answer what the deer was with what the mountains are, with stone teeth and the places kept forever holy with unseen eons.

He chased it.

When it turned to fight, when it reached for his mind to unmake him, it was like a thousand years of frozen wind biting at the stones.

In other words, it was nothing.

His mind was the mountain's mind and the wrongness of the deer had no power over the billions of years enfolded there, of all those countless tons of simple, blunt existence.

Yet, neither could he will the outsider away in the manner his mother had done, sending the smoke of its intent fleeing back through its hole to the outside.

He couldn't force the sky to be unmarred through tooth or mind.

Neither could he catch it and tear it, litter the woods with its shreds like torn moonbeams fading in the dirt with the rotting sycamore leaves.

He was not his mother, but nor would he turn from his duty, even though failure felt like a burning ember balanced on the back of his neck, sinking deeper every day the deer continued to stain his homelands.

Somewhere, down in the unending dark where the world's weight walked on four paws and licked its children clean of all memory of the frowning sky, did his mother watch? Did his failure put an ember on her back too?

No.

He wouldn't allow the thought.

She was in the forever deeps now, where the loyal pack remains beyond all danger and sadness.

Each of that pack endured the trial of the shallows, defying the open air, and it was his turn now.

Hateful months passed and the frozen deer grew bolder.

It defaced the world's works and arts. It grazed on soft, fragile lives beneath the skies, a coward's prey, not even honoring them by consuming their flesh, the fleeting wildflower creatures that glimmer across the ground like sparks, bright then dark within moments, lovely temporary things like storms of ghost lights in the cavern lake.

Its empty appetites changed as the year ripened. He did not know why, only that whatever it sought must be denied.

Birds.

Squirrels.

Humans.

Purposeless vandalism of all the life-forms the mountain called to root in its gardens, but the mountain had a guardian.

If only it had a stronger one.

One night, by the human dens above the racers' maze, he saw the outsider fail to take its prey.

This was new.

A pattern change.

An opportunity?

A trap?

A human in a car endured the frozen deer. Watching the fawn's failure was like seeing a great horned owl crack its talons on the hide of an April cottontail kit. It was absurd.

The outsider fled at his coming, and he faced the human.

The human's mind met his mind. Another first.

He knew people were clever the way a badger was fierce, but he had never spoken to one.

Its mind was fear stink and panic, but there was something else he couldn't place.

It was a man.

No.

It was a not-man.

He broke the not-man's car to smell him. He tasted his sweat and blood.

He wasn't from the outside.

Were his senses failing?

The not-man had something in him that tasted of mountain-kin, of deep scent.

Impossible.

It was a trick.

There was too much wrongness in it.

He couldn't afford two invaders.

He should kill it.

Would his mother have killed it?

No.

We do not trouble about root nippers when an under-saint goes prowling.

He left the not-man shivering in his brittle den.

The deer had done another space-blur and was elsewhere.

It didn't matter.

There was no hiding from him, not in the mountains.

Every life the frozen enemy claimed was an insult.

It was a taker without reciprocity.

It was an unliving pestilence. A waster. A killer for nothing. A hollow blight that shed its emptiness wherever it went.

The mountains wrote poetry.

The deer scattered the words like sow bugs beneath a kicked log.

The wolf did not dream,
except when he did.
Twice he dreamed of the not-man.
Strange upon strange.
Tonight's dream was different.
The entrance to his den,
south bitterroot cave,
shifted into Mother's muzzle and spoke.
"What is family?"
The pack.
"Why?"
We are the mountain's own.
"Service to the mountain is family?"
Yes.
"Good. Remember that."
I don't understand.
"You will, Pup. Go with my love."

In a stalemate, the wolf knew, you must focus on incremental changes, any shift in the balance. Was the pursuit of the outsider making him stronger? Was it making his enemy stronger? How could tactics be changed to ensure the fight was enriching him and diminishing his foe? If he couldn't reach victory with a sprint, could he reach it an inch at a time?

He didn't have the answers.

What he had was the imperative. Chase the thing. Understand the thing. Banish the thing.

He could grapple with the outsider's mind, stilling its body with the assault.

That was something.

It mattered little because he too must still his body during the mind struggle. Two statues.

Stalemate.

Slow, stagnant, bitter stalemate.

The sun set and the wolf waited to feel the hateful touch of the deer on the land.

The deer bit into the sky's fur during the day, hung there like a fat tick drinking the blood of the world.

It must.

Anywhere else and the wolf would have found its hiding place.

It came.

It blurred.

It ran.

It blurred.

It slowed.

It was by a human place. A horse place.

The wolf shot off as fast as a diving falcon, but he was a creature of matter and followed matter's laws. He could not just blur through space like the enemy. Perhaps he could beg the mountain to shift him as fast as the deer, but pride said, *Not yet*.

When he arrived, he saw something surpassingly strange.

There was the deer, moving to destroy an old human for the crime of simply living.

And there was the not-man, charging the enemy, running in defense of the human.

Was that possible?

He was slow, but the deer was, what? Insulted by the very idea of his approach?

The deer turned.

The not-man faced it.

He had grown somehow.

He was not shivering in his den.

He should be dead.

He should not be able to stand against the frozen deer.

He should not be able to stand near the outsider thing.

He should be dead.

Instead, he was standing.

He was standing in service to the mountain.

For a moment, the wolf was stunned into stillness. Then he felt the outsider's mind rumbling toward the not-man like a landslide. Trees tilting. Ground slipping like an ice flow.

Whatever else he was, the not-man was a pup and he had picked a fight with a crystal wight.

He would not fight alone.

The wolf sprang.

As he ran, he lent his thoughts to the not-man. It shouldn't have been easy, but it was.

Easy as falling.

He closed the distance, mind and body, and the deer fled with its customary insult to physical customs of mass and motion.

But he had gotten closer this time.

Closer than ever before.

This was a change.

A chip in the stalemate.

"Well. It got away," the not-man said.

Wonder upon wonders it was standing and speaking.

The wolf spoke back.

When was the last time he had a real conversation? When his mother was still in the shallows? When the scimitar cats told grim jokes and crimsoned the snow with their hunts?

A sound.
An ambush.
A tide of nothing.

Green and the horned wolf sat in a cool autumn nowhere and faced each other. The silence was a sheet of glass, a sonnet of smooth water, a deep pond in windless night.

Green touched the quiet first.

"I just lived your memory."

The wolf studied the small creature. He looked shaken. He looked stubbornly awake, despite what it must be costing him.

Green cocked his head at the wolf's assessment. Thoughts were different here. Too loud. Skulls were made of glass and minds were words floating in the air. No secrets.

And I lived your memories, not-man. The Crow King owes you an explanation.

"The what?"

The Crow King and his trade without your acceptance of the bargain. When you fell and the king ate your death without your leave to do so.

"I . . . don't know what you're saying. You saw when I fell in front of the bus? I don't know what you mean by . . . a trade."

The pain of the memory flew toward Green, a physical thing in the place where thought was substance. It flew on black wings.

He slapped it from the air and it vanished in a rain of ash and feathers.

The wolf studied Green.

You do not know your own memory?

Pain sparkled in the emptiness between them, growing where the flying agony fell, and the wolf traced its searing lines down to its roots.

"That memory . . . hurts. And I can't understand it. That bird . . . the crow . . . just screamed at me."

Perhaps you cannot understand it alone. Come.

"What? No. I can't."

But with the mountain guardian's help, he could.

Green walked down a dark corridor. The wolf padded along beside him.

Here, an archway of verdant honeysuckle.

Seven-year-old Green mixed a potion of mulberries and creek water in a sun-faded blue bucket meant for molding sandcastle parapets.

They walked.

Here, an open door.

Jess tossed aside her keys hard enough to mark the drywall.

"Just don't ask about my day anymore, okay? I hate this. I hate this job," she said.

"Maybe it's time to look for something else," Green said.

"You were a fucking literature major. One of us needs to have a real career."

They walked.

Sunlight filtered in through lace curtains.

Mr. Reynard looked up from his work gluing tiny gears to a mat with shaking fingers, adding wheels to a clockwork locomotive. He smiled at Green.

They walked.

The corridor fell away and Green was on a busy city sidewalk.

He watched himself walking toward the intersection.

"Hold on, I can't do this again."

You must. You can't allow a terror to shelter inside your own skull.

His hand fell to his side, reaching for the acorn. Instead, his palm found the wolf, hard and cold as stone, but rippling like water. He left his hand on the wolf's shoulder.

Together.

The Green of memory seemed to trip on nothing, then flail onto the crosswalk.

A man with graying dreadlocks gasped and reached for him, too late.

There was the bus, a heartbeat away, scuffed chrome and tinted windows, a toothpaste ad smiling joylessly above a line of rolling tires.

The Green lying on the pavement said nothing.

The Green standing beside the wolf on the sidewalk screamed as the tires met his prostrate form and the bus bounced six inches.

Then, everything went still.

All around, the world was frozen. Pedestrians balanced impossibly in mid-step. The man with the dreadlocks was caught trapped in a backward fall as if seated on an invisible chair. Passing traffic transformed into a parking lot.

A great sable shape swooped up and through the motionless bus, perching on the No Parking sign.

The crow had changed. It was more vivid now than in past memory, electric blue eyes and a silver sheen that danced across its dark feathers. It was bigger than a man and its outstretched wings shadowed the entire sidewalk. A foot above its head hovered a dingy patch of nothing in the shape of a seven-pointed star.

The Crow King. The wolf's understanding was Green's understanding. *A master among corvid kind. A thing of time and memory. Subtlety and understanding. Trades and tricks. Formidable. Not to be trusted.*

There was something writhing and inexplicable struggling in the crow's beak. Green recognized it as his own. It was the moment of his death, plucked out of time, food for a strange monarch on a timeless street.

The crow tipped back his nickel-gray beak and, with a rapid stabbing motion, swallowed the grim moment whole. The recent death fought on the way down.

Green was no longer beneath the bus.

He was standing, struggling for breath, looking about him with wide, frantic eyes.

Time began to thaw, breaking loose, sluggish as melting river ice.

The newly re-alive Green looked up at the crow.

The crow cocked its head and regarded the man.

"You see us? Already?" the crow said in a deep, croaking voice. "We are perceived?"

The Green of memory heard only deep, mocking caws.

The Green accompanied by the wolf heard meaning in the speech.

The Crow King's voice was a dirge.

Tears streamed down both Greens' cheeks.

The crow ruffled his feathers and seemed to sigh with his entire body.

"Ah, our young and old associate. You know what was taken then? If you know, it cannot grow back. Absurd and troublesome. As usual."

The crow shook its head.

"Disagreeable. A trade then. A proper trade."

The great bird's beak dipped beneath a wing and tossed something toward Green.

It was the acorn.

Green caught it, placed it in his pocket, then retrieved it again as though he didn't know how it had arrived.

"If you must call upon our court at this early date, find us in the wilds. Unlikely. In plain sight. At the temple tree, above the place of memories. Yet, we would rather you did not. We have fulfilled our part. And dealings with you are always rather complicated."

The king paused for a response.

Past-Green gaped, uncomprehending, panting, and clinging to his acorn.

Full movement returned to the world. The silence broke. The crow was gone.

The bus that had killed him moments before rumbled past untroubled. His skull remained whole and its contents within. The man with dreadlocks stood nearby, checking his phone and thinking nothing at all of Green's welfare.

Green rubbed his temples.

He was back in the nowhere place, seated across from the horned wolf.

Now you remember.

He did.

We understand one another.

He gazed across the emptiness at the wolf. He did not feel grateful, but nor did he feel afraid.

"Well . . . wolf . . . I know you now, and I guess you know me, but what do I call you? What do you call yourself?"

I do not call myself.

Green sighed.

He knew the wolf. He *knew* him. The knowledge took away a gallon of fear and delivered an ocean of uncomfortable awe.

"But what can I call you? Humans name things."

The wolf thought.

What do you call this mountain?

"Appalachians? Catskills? You want me to call you Catskill?"

Catskill. You may call me Catskill.

Green recalled reading the etymology of the name, a derivation of the Dutch for "wildcat creek," Kaaterskill.

His thoughts shifted from a noisy creek to a trio of enormous house cats leaping through the pines.

The wolf saw his thoughts and brought a rhyming image up from memory, a tawny scimitar cat rolling with her cubs in late summer grass, laughing at the world.

"Catskill. Sure. I like it. Call me Green. 'Not-man' makes my stomach turn."

The wolf stood suddenly and sniffed the air that was not air. He was missed. The mountains were calling him back, calling him to wakefulness and to duty.

Green felt the call and felt Catskill going to meet it.

"When we meet again, we'll meet as friends?"

It was part statement and part question.

No, not friends.

Catskill thought of his mother's words, of service to the mountains. Of family.

We are kin. We are pack.

CHAPTER 14

HANGOVER

GREEN AWOKE TO A HIGH-PITCHED WHINE.

His first desire was to stop the sound. He wondered what was making it, then realized it was him. It was the involuntary sound of his body objecting to being conscious, rejecting it like a foreign object.

The entirety of his skin was an open eye and the night air was dusted with cayenne.

"Oh my God."

He rolled over.

His clothes were soaked from the wet turf and grass clung to his face. Every sensation was magnified to intolerable clarity. The smell of horse manure filled his sinuses. He placed a hand on the ground and noticed that he was vibrating. Not shivering, vibrating.

He coughed.

Phantom strings of iridescence unraveled from his mouth and braided in the wind like ribbons.

He sat up.

His tailbone vibrated against the ground like a phone buzzing on a table.

Valentina was crumpled in a small ball nearby, tendrils of pastel, frosted breath drifting from her nostrils.

Next to her were the halves of the broken log. The splintered wood glowed an eerie blue.

The wolf, Catskill, was gone.

Green stood.

Standing felt terrible.

There was a pulsing engine under his feet and his hypersensitive skin felt it in every cell.

He looked back toward the house. It was far across the field, but he could see the door was standing open, a rectangle of yellow light in the deeper shadow of the porch. A figure in white lay by the front stairs.

Spore-log? Or dead from the fawn's presence?

Green touched the acorn in his pocket. A trade from a king of crows. A payment for a meal. Perhaps more.

He tried to prioritize. He was awake first. There were things to do, but thinking was difficult.

Valentina was alive.

Valentina had done *this* to him.

He huffed out a breath and another shred of iridescence coiled into view and faded.

He decided his teacher could stay in the dirt for a bit and went to check on the house.

The moon was low and the first hint of dawn had washed the stars from the eastern sky.

Walking was not fun.

He moved with slow care. His bowels rumbled like a dryer full of sneakers. The glass fawn was not near and the certainty of that knowledge startled him.

There was a thin, elderly man sprawled face down in front of the house, a dead flashlight beneath his fingers. Green knelt and rolled him to his back.

The remnants of a minor nosebleed left a dull red line across his cheek. Still breathing. Warm to the touch.

Green sighed.

Gotta move him inside.

"Okay. This is going to hurt."

The man was heavier than he looked, but Green hauled him into a fireman's carry and took him into the house.

Inside, a woman was slumped in an upholstered chair, silver crochet hook gleaming on her lap. She snored softly. A shaggy Maine coon cat slept on a rug nearby. Phantom colors drifted from both sleepers.

The television chirped about a revolutionary juicer that would detoxify and make skin glow.

Green deposited the man on the couch, did a quick check for other survivors, and locked the door as he left.

They would not be happy when they awoke, but it was a miracle that they were alive at all. He didn't know the lethal range of the glass fawn, and he did not like the idea that these people's lives had become a data point in that deadly question. He couldn't imagine what they would make of spore-log aftereffects, but at least they would outlive the pain and confusion. That was a victory.

He stood on the porch and looked out into the dark, swinging his jaw wide open to quiet the drumroll of his chattering teeth.

Catskill was out there somewhere.

Thinking of the wolf did something strange.

The landscape lightened. There was no more light, but the darkness had shifted from black to grayscale. It was like a moonlit night when the world was blanketed in snow. Something had turned up the dial on contrasts.

"Catskill? Did you do that?"

The wolf was busy elsewhere. He knew. He just knew. But yes, his packmate had done that. Catskill was sharing a piece of himself with Green.

That's new.

He tried to feel exactly what Catskill was doing, then recoiled.

He tasted mineral grit and felt the whip of roots lashing his face as he sped through the soil. The sting of it lingered on his raw nerves even after he pulled his thoughts away.

Right. Shit. Never mind.

Valentina was a small lump far out in the field.

He couldn't leave her. He couldn't carry her all the way back to Candle-Fly. He couldn't just wait in the cold field until she woke up.

With a groan, he left the porch, cursing the high-voltage zap of pain that shot up his leg with each step.

He had just found a wheelbarrow in an old potting shed and was rounding the house with it when Valentina appeared.

"There you are," she said. "Where is the horned wolf?"

She coughed and a shimmer of color swam in the air like a hunting eel.

Green grunted and dropped the barrow handles. Touching anything hurt.

"The wolf is gone. We . . . He . . . is not a threat to us."

Valentina shook her head and spit on the ground.

"Save the story for later. *Pizdets.* If possible, it feels worse than I remember."

She coughed again.

"Or I am just old."

Green tried to hold his arms away from his sides, wincing each time he brushed against his own ribs. Something akin to heartburn hit him each time Valentina spoke. This particular brand of misery did not love company.

"Please tell me you have something in your backpack that ends this. I don't care what it is. I just need it to be over."

She shook her head and flinched.

"No. Just time. A few hours. Did you check the house?"

He knew a few hours was better than a few days, but he wanted to scream in her face anyway.

"Yeah. They're alive, but they won't be happy when they wake up."

When Green and Valentina made it back to camp, morning had arrived and the woods were raining down fists made of birdsong. Every twitter in the branches, every scuffle of chipmunks racing through the underbrush, every chitter of scolding squirrels felt like wet garbage pressed directly against Green's raw, exposed brain. The two walked in silence with their eyes on the path.

At camp, they managed a two-word conversation before retreating from the day.

"Bed?"

"Bed."

Valentina went to her camper. Green to his shed.

He fell into his bed, muddy clothes and all. Exhaustion wrestled with misery and, eventually, his mind surrendered to dreamless sleep.

He woke in the early afternoon and felt shockingly whole.

He groaned, stretched, and touched his face. The sensation didn't summon a bolt of pain.

That's better.

He sat on the edge of his bed, feeling wonderfully neutral and promising himself never to take feeling simply fine for granted again.

All the moisture was gone from his mouth and he worked his tongue, trying to coax it back. He sat up and rubbed the grit from his eyes.

Catskill was sleeping somewhere full of inhuman pressure and quiet and the effortless normalcy of that knowledge made Green shake his head in disbelief.

"There's a monster inside my mind. And we're family."

His stove had gone dark and he held his palm above the ashes to check for heat. There was still enough warmth there that he knew leaving a log to smolder would return the fire to life by evening. He was beginning to know such things. He placed a log in the fluffy gray ashes, then went out to find his teacher.

She was in the library tree.

Green heard voices as he entered the hatch.

Valentina sat in front of an open laptop. She was video chatting with someone. It was like spotting a microwave in a Renaissance painting of biblical martyrdom.

He hadn't thought she was a Luddite exactly. He just hadn't expected her to own a computer.

She was wrapped in a thick coat, though it must have been nearly seventy-five degrees in the room, the electric heaters purring away near the trunk.

She motioned for him to pull up a seat.

The woman on the screen was ancient, a dried apple dollface offset by a colorful pile of shawls. Her left eye was missing. In its place, a stone the color of a tropical lagoon gleamed conspicuously.

"My apprentice. Green," Valentina said.

The old woman gave a shallow bow.

"Hello, young man. You've found yourself quite a teacher."

Her smile deepened the lines of her face. The map of her wrinkles suggested a face that was fond of smiling.

"In a sense, Mr. Green has already met you," Valentina said.

"Oh? How's that?"

"I've started him on your journal."

Green leaned forward in his chair.

"Clara?"

A tingle of excitement.

Both women nodded. Clara beamed.

"I'm flattered," Clara said. "How far in are you?"

"Well, you just learned that Herkimer is . . ."

"An asshole," Clara supplied.

Green laughed and Valentina frowned.

"Ah, yes. My old instructor has some antiquated ideas about cursing," Clara said. "Though, she just cheats and curses in Russian or old Italian or whatever language she assumes her company doesn't know."

Clara winked her one eye and Valentina shook her head.

"I was filling in Clara on our night's work," Valentina said.

"I have some context to add," Green said.

He told them about touching Catskill's memories and the wolf's view of the fawn as an outsider to reality. It was surreal to tell such an impossible story to an audience that simply listened closely and took it all in stride. Clara and Valentina reacted with calm interest as if Green had just retold the week's weather forecast.

"Interesting," Clara said. "Many assumed that the Appalachians had a territory guardian, it being an ancient transitional place, but no such creature had been confirmed. Until now. How fascinating."

"Territory guardian?"

"Creatures that act as reality's immune system, you might say. Like the orbital kingfisher that hunts the West Coast or the omni-crab down in the Florida Keys. These are organisms that live on the borders of what is real and are very protective of those borders. The simple fact of the guardian's interest supports Valentina's theory."

Green looked to Valentina for clarification.

"That the fawn is an invasive species, not just to this area, but to this reality, and the Hole in Nothing is the creature's link to the outside," she said.

He nodded. He didn't need to suppose things about Catskill's viewpoint. He knew.

"Alright. Yeah. It fits with Catskill's understanding, that the fawn is an invader," Green said.

"There is also the fact that, based on the pattern of attacks, the fawn seems place-bound to the area surrounding the hole," Valentina said. "That suggests that the rift is more than just the fawn's point of entry."

"Right, you told me that hypothesis before, but we're still left with the important question. How do we make it leave? I know Catskill's mother defeated and banished it in the past, but I don't know how. He doesn't know. And if Catskill can't catch it or chase it away, then neither can we."

"Note, Clara. Green has shifted from 'it' to 'he' as his pronoun of choice for the horned wolf since his encounter last night."

Clara tapped her chin.

"'Scuse me. Kindly don't talk about me like I'm not here. Also, what about my point? If Catskill can't catch it or force it out, what hope do we have? There's nothing we can do to it that Catskill couldn't have managed."

"You're thinking too simply, Mr. Green," Valentina said. "You're thinking of physicality, of strength and speed. Yet, the fawn isn't a rogue mountain lion. It is not a part of our reality. It is operating under a different set of rules. As such, we may not need to force the fawn to do anything, nor physically catch it in order to remove the threat. As we discussed, the fawn and the hole may well be codependent phenomena. That is our current working theory. The fawn's continued existence here is likely reliant on the hole's presence and, unlike the fawn, the hole cannot evade us."

Green ran fingers through his hair and shut his eyes, trying to digest the information.

"Look, kid," Clara said. "Think of that fawn's enduring existence in our world like a string of unearthly, paradoxical Christmas lights. That Hole in Nothing is the extension cord connecting those lethal lights to some sort of unfathomable power outlet beyond the bounds of our universe. You close the hole, the cord is cut. Pop. Out go the lights."

Green sighed.

"I wonder how hard it would be to get my old job back," he said.

Clara chuckled.

"It gets easier," she said. "The point is, that thing only gets to remain here because it is maintaining some kind of unbroken connection with an elsewhere place where its existence makes sense.

Otherwise, our reality would have spit it back out through a variety of methods. Your wolf is one of those methods."

"Hang on, this is all well and good, but if I'm remembering correctly, the one reliable tactic we know of for closing these rifts involves a suicidal trip through that doorway, right? Did Valentina tell you what that thing did to the stuff we tossed through? The slime? The sparks? All the times nothing at all came back?"

Valentina frowned. She huddled down into her coat, despite the thrumming heaters.

"Ms. Rodriguez is well aware," Valentina said. "Again, we have not quite exhausted all our options."

"Just for a lark, let's start with the ideal-case scenario," Clara said. "How is this solved if everything goes just exactly how we would like?"

"The fawn chooses to leave and the rift closes behind it," Valentina said.

"I'm guessing that is what happened with Catskill's mother," Green said. "Catskill is terrifying and his mother was, apparently, an order of magnitude more terrifying. I bet she gave it plenty of good reasons to leave."

"And your new friend hasn't been able to do the same?"

A strange, bitter indignance ran through him and he had to shake off a rising anger.

"No. Not yet. He thinks of it as a stalemate."

"Do you know how long ago the mother forced it out?"

"Not really. I saw the memory. But Catskill thinks of saber-toothed tigers as recent residents, so it's hard for me to get a sense of timescale while in his head."

"Hmm. Well, Valentina has tried flowing water and matter stitching to close the hole," Clara said. "She tried willing it shut, too, but I've suggested some ways to make another attempt more efficacious."

Valentina nodded, but looked doubtful.

"That will be our best bet at present," Clara added. "She can attempt to employ willpower from much nearer the doorway. I'm guessing proximity is a factor. And, Val, try that poultice recipe I sent. It smells like low tide but the Kelleys swore by it for enhancing their intention focus while doing metaphysical work."

Green looked to his teacher. She looked paler than usual and her tired eyes made him wonder if she had stayed awake while the spore-log toxin ran its course.

"Not our best bet," Valentina said. "Though certainly our preferred method."

Clara furrowed her brow.

"This isn't the Lake Itasca Mist-Arch, Val. I don't think closing this one from within is a real option. Not with any expectation of survival, even for you."

"You wouldn't actually consider going into that thing, right?" Green asked.

"I'm going to remind the two of you that this isn't an academic question. Lives are at stake. Perhaps more. We have a responsibility to solve this. Remember, despite the popular modern self-deception, we are not separate from nature. We are also part of this world's defenses."

"We know, Teacher," Clara said. "Let's just put potentially deadly plans a little further down our list of strategies for now, eh?"

Green imagined stepping into the coroner's van and lifting the white sheet. He imagined a different reality in which a group of college kids were driving away from Kinkaid Cabins, a little hungover and smelling of campfire smoke. He imagined Kyle Cartwright, at home with his family, cooking dinner and daydreaming of his next fishing trip. He imagined the day he fell in front of the bus, but this time he left work and, on a whim, took a taxi home.

We don't always know when our plans are potentially deadly.

"Hell, if it comes to going inside, I could go," Clara said. "I have fewer years to sacrifice, after all. I am getting awfully tired of endless doctor visits and feeling mule kicked every time the weather changes."

"And you suspect an unknowable void outside reality will be a more comfortable place to spend your remaining time? Ridiculous," Valentina said. "The value of a life is not measured in potential longevity. Also, if you will recall, I taught both of your sons and I won't be telling the twins that I used their mother's life to plug up a cosmic rathole."

Clara snorted a laugh.

"Hear that, Green? Valentina doesn't need to curse because you can hear the implied curses whenever she wants you to. It's an art form."

"Yes, well, Ms. Rodriguez." Valentina emphasized the formality. "Thank you so much for lending us your expertise."

Clara clapped her bent brown hands together.

"There it is again! Hear it?"

"I can," Green said. "And thank you for the journal. It . . . has been more than helpful."

"Aw. You're welcome. Don't you forget to do the same for up-and-comers when you get on your feet. Record it all. Herkimer got that part right at least. It's lonely, isn't it? Being one of us strange animals. Gotta let each other know that there are kindred spirits out there."

Green smiled.

"Goodbye, Clara," Valentina said. "We'll be in touch."

Clara winked again and the screen went dark.

Valentina lifted a trembling hand and closed the laptop. Green wondered if the effects of the spore-log were holding on longer for his teacher.

"I didn't think we had internet access here," he said.

"We don't."

"Ah . . . Right."

Valentina stared past Green, her expression grim and distant.

"Seriously, you aren't actually considering stepping through that hole, are you?"

Of course she is.

"As I said, it may well come to that. Such an act may be survivable. Human choice is a powerful force. I am rather willful and may fare better than a stone or scrap of firewood."

"We'll find a solution. We have an ally in Catskill now. That could change things."

"It could, but observe."

Valentina pointed to her lips and blew out a long breath.

Green saw pale condensation even in the warm room.

"I am afraid the fawn did to me what it failed to do to you."

Fear slid a knife between Green's ribs.

His teacher's trembling and her tired eyes were not the work of the spore-log. He studied her face more closely. There was a slight blue tinge to her lips that made him think of a visit to Mr. Reynard's hospice room.

"The cold has taken root in me and, like the birds we collected, it is not subsiding. I believe it is intensifying. I am struggling to form a rationale for how I am still alive. It's interesting."

"That's . . . terrible. Does Clara know?"

"Not yet."

"Don't I remember a speech or two about transparency and community?"

Valentina glared.

"I will follow up with Ms. Rodriguez once our plan of action solidifies. I didn't want to worry her before it was necessary."

"How do we fix this?"

She studied her own trembling fingers.

"This cold is the glass fawn's influence. When the fawn goes, I expect its influence will go with it."

Green stood and walked to the window. It was as if he had just noticed the ticking of a time bomb tucked beneath the floorboards. He looked out across the camp, desperate to think of something Valentina could have missed, knowing it was impossible. She had been a cryptonaturalist since before his great-great-grandfather was born. He didn't even know the word "cryptonaturalist" a month earlier.

"How long do we have?"

Valentina laughed without mirth.

"I don't know, Mr. Green. This has never happened before. Based on pure intuition, I would guess I can endure a day or two. Perhaps less. I feel as though I am underwater and am looking about wondering why I have yet to drown, with no compelling explanations coming to mind."

"A day or two! What do we do?"

"We stay calm. We think. We research. We do the best we can with what we have."

Green paced back and forth.

"I'm more sure of it than ever. I'm bad luck."

"Nonsense. You have been a help already. I consider myself fortunate to be alive after such an encounter. More fortunate still that I have some time to undo what has been done. Others on this mountain have not enjoyed such second chances."

"And if the strategies Clara suggested don't work?"

"Then, Mr. Green, you will wish me luck, we will say our goodbyes, and I will step through the doorway between the pines."

CHAPTER 15

Temple of the King

Valentina sent Green to his customary chair to read. As she spoke, her visible breath wordlessly made the same point again and again. *Time is running out.*

"There's gotta be something I can do to help you."

"My plan for this afternoon is to research the poultice Clara mentioned, craft it, then cross-reference a dozen journals on the subject of willing closed gaps in reality. Few of the entries are in English. All of them are above your level of experience as a cryptonaturalist. Mr. Green, sit and continue your own studies."

There was a tremor in her voice and her breath was forming ice crystals in her eyelashes.

His thoughts reached toward Catskill.

Dreamless dark and the weight of mountains.

No help there.

He touched the acorn in his pocket, imagining a mythic bird scolding him from a street sign.

No help there either.

He looked at the floor and felt his own warmth draining away.

"If you think of something I can do to help . . ."

She dismissed him with a look, then went to gather her research materials.

Green tried to continue reading Clara's journal, the image of the living person fusing with the image he had conjured from the written word. It was no good. His teacher's every breath, every creak of her chair, felt like sand slipping through the hourglass. He took to wandering the room and pretending to read the spines of books.

He was back in Mr. Reynard's hospice room, except this time Green's friend wasn't resting peacefully, soothed by sedatives. He was fighting for his life against an enemy Green couldn't see or touch. He was fighting alone.

"Go rest," Valentina said without looking up from her reading.

Even shivering, even dying, she found it easier to shoo Green out of the way while she engineered stratagems for escaping the deep winter that was stealing her life away.

He didn't have the heart to argue. He retreated to his shed where his spiraling worries could wear patterns in the walls of his skull without disturbing his teacher.

His phone buzzed against his hip, a rare spark of cell service bringing a text notification. He kept it in his pocket out of pure habit, but he was beginning to forget it was there. When was the last time he'd charged it?

No doubt an exciting new MLM or real estate scam.

He'd check it later.

He sat on his cot watching serpent tongues of flame flickering in the stove as the pallid afternoon lost ground to evening. The footsteps of coming night were a funeral march. Night brought the cold, it brought the glass fawn, it brought one of Valentina's last chances to banish the creature that was killing her.

Is this her last chance?

How many chances did the old cryptonaturalist have already over the last five centuries?

How many do-overs does one person get?

His fingers found the acorn and he jerked his hand away. Just then, he hated the small brown everything that thrummed in his pocket like a second heartbeat.

What is it?

The moment of my death?

A payment for a meal?

A practical joke from an inscrutable crow?

He had spent just over a week as a new immigrant in the mirror world of cryptonature. What did that experience buy him? What plan could he offer to someone who counted lifetimes like seasons of a half-remembered childhood?

A tap on the door.

"Come in."

Dancer ducked inside like a parent stooping into their child's blanket fort.

"Well, look at you," she said. "Snug as a bug in the sort of place a bug would consider snug."

"Hey, Dancer. Good timing."

"Yeah?"

"Yeah. I was feeling a little too sorry for myself. Good time for a visitor."

"Sorry for yourself? Doesn't seem like the sorta night for that, fella. Beautiful autumn evening in the mountains and all. And heck, if greeting cards were scratch 'n' sniff, half of them would smell like this room. Pine and woodsmoke. Plus, this."

She pulled out her customary lumberjack-plaid thermos of sassafras tea and offered Green a cup from her pocket.

"Maybe I could start a scratch 'n' sniff greeting card company," she said. "Happy quinceañera. Enjoy some Mountain Smells."

Green's traditions were young in this new life, but one of them was that he didn't refuse Dancer's tea. He took it and breathed the steam. Not quite root beer. Not quite lemon. Something earthy with notes of oak and autumn.

"You sure you aren't a cryptid, Dancer? You make life out here seem a little too easy sometimes."

"Heh. If I was, I wouldn't tell you, would I? Gotta make you work for it."

Green glanced around his tiny living space.

"I'd invite you to sit, but I don't have any chairs. What has you out roaming?"

"No worries. Can't stay. I just wanted to check on the status of our looming danger. I already chatted with your boss about that. Made my rounds and all the members of our little community here are on high alert."

"You talked to Valentina? How'd she look?"

"Not great. I suppose you knew that. The whole thing still sounds a touch precarious. And I got the distinct impression she was shooing me, know what I mean?"

"I do. That was part of what I was feeling sorry about."

"Understandable. Funny thing about empathy, huh? Part wings, part iron anchor. The duality of all worthwhile things, am I right?"

"Uh, hard to say."

"Heh. Well, I'll ask you the same thing I asked ol' Val. Any way I can pitch in?"

He raised his cup.

"You already helped."

He took a long sip. Dancer smirked a crooked smirk.

"Medicinal. Don't I know it," she said.

"Honestly, I just wish there was more I could do for Valentina. I'm not much help."

Dancer shrugged away the comment.

"Nah. Hogwash. That lady is weird as rain when the sun shines, but she's also as practical as a door hinge. You wouldn't be staying at her camp if she didn't think you were helpful. Just be on hand. Sometimes that's the most helpful thing of all. Being nearby. I'm sure she's up there in the Perch concocting a genius plan as we speak."

"The Perch?"

"Her tree house. I like to think of it as the Perch. On account of all the crows up there. That's my little nickname for it."

"The crows?"

"Yeah, the crows. There's always crows up on the roof of that place. I think they roost up there. Geez, man, I know you haven't lived in the woods long but crows ain't exactly migrating warblers. I don't know how you overlook crows. Personally, I love those birds. Whip-smart and elegant as evening wear."

Gears clicked inside Green's skull.

He drained his cup and handed it back to Dancer.

"I gotta go. You've given me an idea."

"Makes sense. I've often thought of myself as a classic muse type."

She sat the empty cup back down on his little side table and grinned.

"Don't forget to come by and return that cup. Safe travels, Green."

Tradition.

She ducked out the door and took long strides into the dusk.

Crows.

He hadn't seen a single crow in Valentina's camp. Not once. Dancer was seeing a piece of nature he wasn't. Not a rag moth. Not a horned wolf. Not something teetering on the line between real and imagined.

Plain old crows.

Unless they weren't plain old crows.

Unless something was actively preventing him from seeing them.

It was obvious, like the moment you realized the sunglasses you misplaced were still up on top of your head.

The memory replayed, Catskill at his side, the impossible bird perched on the No Parking sign. It croaked deep and dark as the small hours of the night.

If you must call upon our court at this early date, find us in the wilds.

Unlikely. In plain sight. At the temple tree, above the place of memories. Yet, we would rather you did not. We have fulfilled our part.

Those words had seemed like gibberish. Then, they hadn't seemed relevant as the spore-log rattled his bones. They seemed like a riddle for another time, especially as Valentina spoke frozen words about time running short.

At the temple tree, above the place of memories.

Why was I drawn to this mountain? To this camp?

He thought of Valentina's few rules, the only prohibitions she mentioned when offering an apprenticeship.

You will not open locked doors. You will not enter my living quarters uninvited. You will not fiddle with any equipment you don't understand. You will not visit the roof of the library.

Green set his jaw.

He entered the hatch and earned an *I thought I dismissed you* look from his teacher.

"Just passing through," he said.

He climbed the rope ladder and opened the narrow hatch to the roof. Bits of twig and dry leaves rained down and itched in his collar as he pulled himself up onto the ridged metal roofing.

"Mr. Green! Stop! Get down from there!"

He ignored her.

The roof was grimed with lichens and littered with debris. High above, the silhouettes of several crows perched on the upper branches like outriders of full dark. He hadn't seen them from the ground.

The Crow King's words echoed in his mind.

Yet, we would rather you did not. We have fulfilled our part. And dealings with you are always rather complicated.

He slammed the hatch and stood on it, clinging to a branch for balance on the slick pitched roof. Below him, he felt the vibration of Valentina pounding on the hatchway. Her muffled words drifted up, but he couldn't understand them.

"Okay. I know you're here," he said. "Show yourself."

For a long moment, the words hung in the air.

Nothing happened.

He was a man in a tree scolding the sky.

Then, it all changed.

A falling oak leaf froze in place near Green's cheek and déjà vu hit him like the first fat drops of a downpour. All around him, the world was locked in sudden stillness.

The Crow King spoke.

"Not the most polite request for an audience we have ever received. We were not expecting you yet."

The bird was cawing, a deep, hoarse sound that pounded the air like a hammer, but there were words in the sound, words translated by something that slept beneath the mountains, beneath Green's own psyche.

Electric blue eyes in a silver-black head studied Green from entirely too nearby. A beak like a pewter pickax hovered inches from his upturned face.

There was the deeper shadow hanging above the crow's head, a patch of fully ripened dusk in the shape of a seven-pointed star.

With an effort of will, Green pushed aside his fear and spoke.

"Well, I live forty feet from this spot now, so it seemed neighborly to stop by."

The crow puffed out his throat feathers. He made a gurgling, croaking sound that Green understood as laughter.

"Sleep comes hard on an empty stomach. A flight to the moon is longer than you think. Spring always has two false starts. And . . . even here in your infancy, you are still you. Why should we expect any different?"

The croaking laugh came again.

A dozen more crows, unaffected by the frozen landscape, glided in to perch in the branches above and watch the conversation. One crow used a swooping bluebird, frozen mid-flight, as a platform to gain a better view of the scene. The crows all laughed along with their king.

"My infancy?"

"A private joke, human. For now, at least, your memory flows to you from a single direction. Ours flows from many. Do not concern yourself overmuch. There is dignity in each of our allotted measures of strength and struggle."

As he spoke, the king grew. Once the size of a man, the giant bird now sidestepped along his perch to make room for a body the size of a tiger.

"I know you said you'd rather I didn't visit, but I really need help. I have so many questions. And my friend . . . my teacher . . . is dying."

The king cocked his head, studying Green with one eye, then the other.

"Our preferences are our own affair. You need not carry them for us. Yes, we know about Valentina and your fight against the outsider. Indeed, such things are among the reasons we honored your request."

The crow looked down at the hatch beneath Green's feet.

"Please. I don't understand. I have so many questions. Can you help us?"

The Crow King was now too large for his branch. He stepped down onto the mottled sheet metal roof. The surface made a soft popping sound as it accepted the ten-foot-tall bird's weight.

"We sympathize. We hold you and your teacher in great esteem."

"Then, please, do something. Like you did when you saved me from the bus."

The king stood motionless.

"That is . . . one interpretation."

"I saw you. In the memory. You chose to save me. You gave me this magic acorn or whatever the hell it is. I still don't even know what it is doing to me."

"Chose? Yes, we were able to pluck that moment because someone chose you. But it wasn't us. The meal was to our liking, the trading of a token obeyed our own ancient custom, but the choice was entirely yours. Otherwise, we could not have accessed a thing as private and personal as your death."

"I chose? What does that mean?"

"Indeed. You chose. At least twice. We heard you choose beneath the bus. And, more to the point, a much older version of you, forward in your future, but backward in a twin of this world's past, asked us directly to be present on the street that day. We repaid one of the favors we owed to past and future you. In this dimension and in others. Your cheerful facility with paradox has always been superlative among your kind. Perhaps your chief talent."

This is meaningless.

Frustration lit a fire behind Green's eyes. He had the urge to swat a nearby crow from its perch, but he forced himself to swallow his anger.

"That doesn't make any sense. I asked you to be there? What do you mean? My future, but the world's past? I don't understand."

The Crow King paused, seeming to consider his words.

"You will, old friend. Soon, you will."

There was an odd tenderness in the bird's tone.

"We wish we had liberty to tell you more. Yet, for your sanity's sake, for the sake of what you still must accomplish for our mother, even you must experience some things in their conventional order."

"I just want to know what you've done to me!"

"You give us too much of the credit. Your own crafting of meaning shapes your path far more than we could. The truth of that acorn in your pocket holds to that same foundational principle."

Green pulled out the acorn and looked at it.

It was unchanged. A common acorn.

"Is that some kind of riddle? Can't you just tell it to me simply?"

The king looked up into the branches.

"The strangest human we know visits a royal pan-dimensional manifestation of collective history-spanning crow intelligence while battling an incursion from beyond reality . . . and he asks us for simplicity."

The birds above all croaked with hoarse laughter.

The Crow King turned to look out at the surrounding forest, stooping his massive frame low beneath the uppermost branches. He paused to wipe his three-foot beak against the central trunk, a motion like a barber stropping a straight razor. As Green watched, the king continued to grow. The huge corvid turned his attention back to his guest.

Green deflated with a sigh. It was all too much.

"Could you at least try to explain?"

"We are trying. Know that simply being here is costly to us. The body of a life is as much made of choices as matter and energy. Are we expected to explain your own choices to you? Who can decide for a creature to be different? To be strange among his peers? To mean something more than stuff stretched across space and time? Who chooses?"

"Catskill called me 'not-man.' What did you do to me?"

"The guardian's senses delve deeper than simple substance. He doesn't just smell the seed. He smells the tree to come."

It was like standing at a locked door, sensing something vitally important was there, just out of reach.

The crow looked down at him and chittered softly, as if in thought. The creature seemed to make a decision.

"Hmm. Perhaps . . . A demonstration. A brief lesson. Come. Be quick. Lend us your acorn," the king said.

The king's cawing voice had grown deeper and louder. Green could feel the vibrations shivering along his collarbones. The words brought with them a smell of decay mixed with the cloying sweetness of overripe fruit.

With nervous care, he held the acorn up on his open palm.

A storm-colored blur darted at Green's hand and the tiny nut was pinched in the crow's kayak-size beak. The king twitched his great head and sent the acorn flying over the edge of the roof, falling to the ground below.

"Wait! No!"

The Crow King didn't answer Green's protests. The giant bird tilted forward, spread wings the size of billboards, and soundlessly followed the acorn down, untouched by the frozen landscape.

Green let go his hold on the branch, stepped to the edge to look over, slipped, and fell off the roof.

He sucked in a breath of surprise as his hip impacted one of the motionless oak leaves, frozen in the act of falling. It crinkled like dry paper, but held his weight. Clutching at empty air, he teetered on the leaf, rolled, and fell to the side before colliding with another leaf like a punch to the stomach. Then to the ribs. Then to his left armpit before he fell the last six feet to the ground.

"Ow."

He stood, brushed the dirt from his jeans, and looked up at the Crow King.

The bird's growth rate had increased. Now, the king's eye was level with the library roofline.

Green fought to regain his breath and composure while looking up at the tyrannosaurus-size crow.

"My acorn. Where is it? I need it back!"

The Crow King pointed his beak to the sky. He cawed three earth-shaking caws. The shock waves sent Green stumbling away, pressing palms to his ears and squeezing shut his eyes.

When he looked up the king towered as tall as the oak. Somehow, the Crow King was both a giant bird and something else. Green had flashes of seven silver beaks radiating outward from a central dark-feathered hub and wings that stretched along directional planes that weren't.

The seven-pointed star above the creature's head was now a massive window looking out on a darkling sky where tattered clouds scudded across the face of a great yellow moon. The king was both a dark pinnacle and a limitless crossroads.

The image made Green's stomach turn and the edges of his vision began to darken.

The feeling made a wolf stir in his sleep. A borrowed growl rattled through his senses and the vision of the Crow King resolved back into simply an impossibly giant bird.

The king's three caws had changed the landscape, calling in other seasons of the year.

Now, along with the falling autumn leaves, the trees were dotted with green buds, verdant growth, and insects paused mid-flutter. Islands of snow lay alongside blooming trillium and trout lilies. Acorns were scattered in profusion among the dandelions and the mirror gleam of iced-over puddles.

"Your acorn is here," boomed the voice of the Crow King. "Retrieve it."

Green had a sinking feeling even before he surveyed the piles of acorns.

There's no way.

He looked down at a dozen acorns scattered near the toe of his right boot.

Kneeling, he prodded the innocuous little things with his fingertips. A few were of uncommon size. Several seemed to have insect damage. One was missing its cap. Fully half of them looked like they could have been *his* acorn.

"This is impossible. Tell me you know which one it is."

The Crow King's voice was like an avalanche.

"You called the acorn magic, did you not? If it is so singular and special, so heavy with significance, then select it."

"I can't!"

He grabbed one of the acorns and stood, holding it up to the colossal monarch.

"This looks just like the one I had. Just like most of the ones I can see from here. Is this it?"

"That is not for us to say."

"Of course it is! How am I supposed to know?"

The Crow King gave another harsh, rolling laugh that sounded like a passing freight train.

"Don't laugh! This is life-and-death!"

The dark feathered mountain settled.

"We apologize. We are not used to seeing you struggle so. We remember you as one who cheerfully baffles others."

Green grimaced and felt tears coming into his eyes.

"Perhaps a test," the Crow King suggested. "Place it in your pocket and see if it feels like your acorn."

It seemed utterly pointless, but he also couldn't think of a better option. So, he placed the acorn in its customary place.

He rested his palm over the lump, feeling the shape of the acorn through the denim. It felt correct. The tightness in his throat began to ease.

"Well?" the Crow King asked. "A result?"

"It . . . feels right."

"There you are."

"But . . . was this the same one you tossed from the roof?"

"It's the one in your pocket, isn't it?"

Another corvid laugh like thunder.

"Seriously. Is this the same acorn?"

"Consider the lesson. Stop trying to give away your power. Make the choice. Believe in the choice. You used the word 'magic.' Human, we will tell you this. The magic of this world is more reliant on meaning than objective reality. Fact may be a found thing, but meaning is a crafted thing. It requires your participation, your choice. If you require that acorn to be magic, then you must make it so."

Green rubbed his eyes and shook his head.

Above the king, thousands of crows flew in a great spiral radiating outward from their lord. The Crow King looked up at his court, then back to Green. A blue fire flared to life in each of his nostrils, sending a rising braid of dark smoke up into the coming evening.

"We cannot remain here much longer. Not while remembering our manners."

Green suddenly felt very small and very conspicuous.

The king tilted his head and looked down at Valentina's library.

"For your teacher and for our future friendship, we will say more than we might wish."

Green felt something odd in the pit of his stomach, like he was in an elevator that couldn't quite decide on a speed or a direction. Gravity was misbehaving.

Stretching high over the treetops, the king spoke up into the chaos of dark wings above him. The number of crows had multiplied many thousandfold. Looking at the shifting sea of ebon wings above the king, Green couldn't imagine that many crows existed in the world. At least, not this world alone.

"It is not always in our power to decide what a thing is . . . But what a thing means? That power may often be claimed."

The Crow King stood erect and fully extended profound wings that flooded the sky with perfect, starless dark.

"When the time comes, make the choice. Be the choice. Craft the magic you need. A beacon. An anchor. A wellspring of courage. Trust yourself in the crafting."

There was a moment of total darkness.

The king's voice faded into a distance that was somehow more than physical. His final words seemed to come from within Green's skull.

"If you find yourself struggling on the doorstep, remember, desire may move us as sure as blood and bone and wing."

Then, he was back on the library roof.

The oak leaf at his shoulder finished falling, spinning down to land on the hatchway beneath his feet.

"Mr. Green!"

Valentina's muted voice came through the hatch.

High above, a half dozen crows croaked with laughter.

There was no handle on the topside of the roof hatch, but it didn't matter. Valentina threw it open the moment he stepped aside. She was red-faced and her heavy breath puffed white like a steam engine.

"Get. In. Here."

He frowned and followed her in. The hatch fell shut behind him.

"You wanted to help and now you are actively antagonizing me? Did you forget the few rules by which I asked you to abide?"

She leaned on the back of a chair. Her breathing had become more labored.

"No. I thought . . . I thought I had discovered something useful."

She glowered.

"And did you?"

Green sighed.

"Not really. Maybe? It's hard to say."

"Do you have any idea what you risked going up there?"

"I mean, I kind of riled up the Crow King, if that's what you're asking."

Valentina raised her brows and shook her head.

"You are . . . a remarkable . . . infuriating individual. Do you know that?"

"If it helps, he said he likes your style. I mean, that was the general sense of it, I think."

Valentina knuckled frost from her lashes.

"Mr. Green, if you knew half of what I knew about that creature . . ."

"Well, I don't know. I don't know because you didn't tell me. You were awfully quick to lecture me on openness yesterday. Can't help notice you didn't mention the giant crow living above your camp when I told you my story of falling in front of the bus, ya know, the story with a giant crow in it? Remember?"

She sighed.

"I was bound by certain promises. And, odd as it may sound, the entity you met above the library was not at the top of my list of suspects for the time-bending black bird you described. That creature typically disdains direct intervention."

She motioned for him to sit and joined him. Green told her of his experience with Catskill and his previous encounter with the Crow King newly deciphered with the wolf's help.

Valentina looked at the ceiling, then back at her apprentice.

She looked exhausted.

"That crow . . . That creature is monumentally dangerous. Elementally dangerous. I have had dealings with it in the past and we have something of a formal arrangement now. It is . . . one of the protections of the camp I mentioned earlier."

She shook her head.

"You should be reading journals and going on tiny outings to study glass mice and shadow flies. Not this."

"I'm . . . sorry? I guess?"

"You know," she said, "there is an old, long-debunked theory that supposed cryptonaturalists create the cryptids they observe, that their interest manifests the reality. It's the 'spontaneous generation' of antiquated cryptozoology theories. It's absurd and yet you make me revisit it. You are an engine of coincidence."

"Uh, point of fact, it's *your* roof. And that bird is *your* pal."

"Bird? Pal? Think again, Mr. Green. The Crow King is a bird the way Everest is a rock and troubling alliances do not pals make. You should remember that."

Valentina looked terrible. Her face was waxen and she kept raising trembling fingers to rub the frost from her eyes.

"Do we have a plan for tonight?"

"Yes. I am afraid we do. Can you feel your connection with the wolf?"

He reached his thoughts toward Catskill and found him awake and eating something bent like a question mark, stitched into the stone of a cave wall. The mountain guardian was excavating his prey with stone-crushing thrusts of his horned muzzle.

Green winced.

"He's . . . eating breakfast, but Catskill will be available to help when we need him. The fawn is not on the mountain yet."

Valentina's frozen sigh hung in the air like a ghost.

"I won't tell you not to trust that creature, in fact I would suspect it may be incapable of breaking its explicit oaths, perhaps even of uttering falsehoods, but you should avoid the mistake of prescribing human thoughts and motivations to it. It is not your pal. It is not your pet nor your assistant."

"I think he can help us. How could that be a bad thing?"

"Still 'he,' is it? Fine. He, then. I am simply trying to warn you of a common pitfall related to inexperience with cryptids. Many hidden life-forms possess uncanny intelligence and the ability to communicate with humans. It can be rather intoxicating. It leads some young cryptonaturalists to fall into what is sometimes called the 'imaginary friend fallacy.' A whimsical name for a too-often lethal misunderstanding of cryptonature. Catskill is not human. In fact, he is more than just not human. He is also not mortal in the conventional sense. In my experience, removing a mundane life-cycle creates an entirely different mental framework for actions and priorities."

You would know.

"Didn't you recently tell me that immortality isn't a thing in nature?"

"I'm not suggesting he's eternal. I'm suggesting his kind of mortality is so entirely different from ours that his moral and epistemological frameworks are beyond our capacity to grasp."

"Okay, I can acknowledge whatever that's supposed to mean, but right now I appreciate there being someone else on the team who can get closer than a hundred yards to the glass fawn without . . ."

Dying

". . . being injured."

"Listen to your word choice. 'Someone.' Be mindful. That's all I'm asking."

"Understood, but my point stands. If the fawn comes for us while you're willing shut the hole, we're going to need Catskill's help."

Plus, if I was wrong about this acorn in my pocket, I might not survive another encounter long enough to say, "I told you so."

"About that. I prepared the poultice and have concluded my supplemental research on rifts in time-space. I am as prepared as I can be to make another attempt to will the hole shut. As Clara said, proximity may be a factor. I need to get closer . . . without inadvertently going through."

Valentina's shivering intensified while she spoke.

"Did you learn anything about ending the fawn's effect on you? Short of kicking it out of our universe, I mean."

"I'm afraid not. It is difficult to know how the fawn continues to exert a hold on me. I could try to momentarily leave this dimension through a number of means, but that carries its own raft of potentially deadly consequences. Too risky when I cannot guarantee the result."

"Yikes. Okay."

"I would try simple geographical distance, but I am in no condition for a crawler ride."

"You mentioned them before. Do I get to know what they are yet?"

Valentina waved a hand like Green was asking a tediously simple question.

"They are subterranean creatures that can bend space and will barter passage with humans they trust. It is an efficient, if unpleasant, way to travel the world and there is a crawler tunnel node below this very camp. It is a large part of the reason I chose to base myself in this location."

Green thought of the tiny locked shed with the orange door he hadn't been given access to and pictured a ladder leading down and down into the dark.

"What if I went with you? Could I help?"

"Absolutely not. Do not break my rules again, Mr. Green. Crawlers aren't a Greyhound bus. You acclimate them to your presence and intent slowly to earn their trust. A surprised crawler is vicious and unpredictable. In fact, when they recognized my scent and not yours, I fear they would assume you were the payment I offered for passage. As I said, concerning your associate Catskill, do not make human assumptions in dealings with cryptids."

She couldn't understand. Catskill was not a business partner. Catskill was family. He was not making assumptions. There was no need to assume. He and Catskill had lived each other's lives. What deeper understanding was there?

"I know your stance on cars, but what about a more traditional mode of transportation? We could walk to my Prius this minute and be six hundred miles away by morning."

"No. Crawler rides and dimension sliding have the virtue of letting me go far and return in the space of a few hours. The solution cannot be to shirk all responsibility and abandon the mountain to the glass fawn. There is no one else here who can do what we can. I can bear this misery long enough to do what needs done. We must focus on the disease, not the symptoms."

Valentina coughed frozen vapor into the air.

"Alright, so where does that leave us?"

Her eyes trailed down to Green's hip.

"Mr. Green, look at your hand."

He was grasping a fistful of denim with the acorn in its center.

"I think you should unburden yourself of that object. You know as much as you are going to know about it. Give it to the earth."

He released his grip with an effort and crossed his arms.

"I'll deal with it eventually. I really think we need to focus on you right now. You can't keep this up. You look . . . rough."

"No, I can't keep this up."

A resignation that looked an awful lot like doom settled on her face.

"God. You're gonna go through that thing tonight?"

"I certainly do not relish the plan. But we work with what we have. The fawn will be on the hunt again any moment. My hesitation may mean another victim. If the choice is between falling off a cliff or into blackberry thorns, you choose the thorns."

A hole in reality that might turn you into a fine mist is nothing like blackberry thorns.

"Wait, look, we still have time. It's not fully dark yet. It's still only . . ."

He pulled his phone from his pocket to check the time, a habit from an old life.

The text notification he ignored earlier was on the screen.

It was from Alf.

Hey, bro. Station closed tonight. Technical difficulties. Moths are involved. Don't ask. We're camping at the Hole tonight. Like ya said. Gotta guard it from the tourists. Solidarity, brother. Be sociable. Come drink a beer. Bring that six-pack you owe me.

Green's skin crawled.

"What is it?" Valentina asked.

Green texted back.

No. Don't go there. I'll explain later.

A red exclamation mark appeared next to the text.

Message not sent. No service.

"Shit."

He clenched his teeth and looked up into the gray, bloodless face of his teacher.

"I think we need to go now."

CHAPTER 16

CAMPFIRE STORIES

GREEN PACED THE GRAVEL LANE WHILE VALENTINA MADE final preparations, then together, they set out for the Hole in Nothing. Valentina's steps were halting and every second breath came with an audible sound of effort. On past hikes, he marveled at the silence of her footfalls. Now, she shuffled and stumbled through the fallen leaves.

"Can I at least carry your pack?"

She grunted a negative.

All of Green's instincts told him to stop walking deeper into the dark woods. They needed light and warmth. He wanted to give her his coat. He wanted to stop and make a fire. He wanted to find a road and hitchhike back to a heated room. Again and again these urges slapped him across the face and he had to answer each one, *It wouldn't do any good.*

He hated that answer.

He no longer feared the horned wolf. He no longer needed to wonder if the fawn was nearby. Catskill knew, so he knew. Yet, as his mentor fought for her life, he felt more naked and vulnerable than ever.

Valentina was the one who knew what she was doing. Now, she could barely stay upright.

He clutched his senseless acorn and, while he resented the impulse, he didn't pull his hand away. Any comfort was a treasure in the dark woods. Maybe it was his original acorn. Maybe it was a practical joke from a mythic crow. Maybe it didn't matter.

Valentina spoke like the creak of an old screen door.

"Can you communicate with Catskill? Any sign of the glass fawn?"

"Yeah. Not nearby."

He didn't have to think questions at the wolf and wait for an answer. The answers were just there, sitting on a shelf in plain view. A front porch had been added onto his consciousness and it was always a glance away.

"The fawn is near Hickory. There's a covered bridge with a flag mural and . . . I see a grain elevator? I think? Tall cylinder thing with a conveyor belt."

She nodded and brushed more ice from her eyelashes.

"I know the place. North of town."

"Catskill is circling. Trying to keep the fawn from moving toward town. Trying to contain it without provoking it to blur away. I was thinking of asking him to come guard us, but . . ."

"But he is doing more good where he is. I agree."

She coughed and stumbled, clutching at a splintered poplar stump before spilling into the leaves. Green gave her a hand back to her feet. Her skin was colder than a corpse.

As they walked, he noticed her pulling a hand from her pocket and stealing glances at her fingertips. It looked like she was afraid of what she might see, the dark crescents of oncoming frostbite.

He checked his phone. The sleek black rectangle was already beginning to feel unfamiliar in his hand. It was metamorphosizing into a totem of a bygone religion.

No service.

No texts.

Still no way to warn off Alf and Jerome.

I'm as much help to them as I am to Valentina.

If the cold was good for anything, perhaps it would keep Alf and his friends from visiting the Hole in Nothing tonight.

Yeah, right.

He hadn't known Alf long, but he couldn't picture him saying, "It's a bit cold, bro, let's just not go." They were already planning to get drunk in a pitch-dark wilderness next to a tear in reality. What was a little chill in the air compared to that?

"When we get there . . . you're going to use that poultice Clara suggested, right? Use willpower to shut it?"

Valentina coughed and shook her head.

"Yes, but I need you to prepare yourself for the other eventuality. Ultimately, Mr. Green, closing the hole from inside is our surest method. I have come to terms with that likelihood and you should too."

Valentina pulled a wad of linked keys the size of an apple from her pocket and handed them to Green. They were cold as ice and heavy. Then she produced a folded paper and handed it over as well.

"Here. These were part of today's preparations. All the keys to the camp, above and below ground. The paper has instructions and a written statement for you to broadcast should I not return, as well as several contacts who may be interested in taking you on as an apprentice."

Her teeth chattered on the last word.

"You have the keys, but *do not* explore. Your visit to the roof could have gone much worse. Do not go up there again. You cannot rely on the crow's continued civility. Stick to the structures you know. Again, do not visit the crawler tunnels. I do not expect I need to say such things, but I'm saying them for my own peace of mind. Understood?"

"Understood."

Green looked at his teacher.

Her lips were like day-old bruises and an unhealthy shadow was beginning to bloom on the tip of her nose. He thought of the girl under the sheet at Kinkaid Cabins, the dark stains he had mistaken for Catskill's touch.

"You don't think you'll be coming back from this, do you?"

"Hope for the best, prepare for the worst, Mr. Green."

"That's it? You really are just going to . . . what did you say to Clara? Plug the rathole with your life?"

She looked angry, then tired.

She turned and kept shuffling down the trail, speaking to the dark woods ahead.

"We are out of time. If I did not believe it was worth doing, I would not be doing it. Principles, Mr. Green. Our principles must be more than self-preservation."

He thought of the lives that had been lost. He thought of the lives that still may be lost. He did not argue. He followed.

It was too cold for insect song. The mountain was the whine and knock of trees fretting in the wind and the chatter of desiccated leaves.

She shrugged her coat up and tucked her chin into the collar. It made her look like a toddler in an oversized hand-me-down.

"Still, it's true that I have never risked getting closer than a meter to the hole. Getting closer may well be the key. The poultice recipe Clara provided also has a promising track record. We shall see. One way or another, it will be intriguing to find out. Whatever happens, do not fail to record your observations to share with our colleagues."

She pulled up her chin and smiled at Green. Even with blue lips, it was a genuine smile.

"You are easily the toughest person I've ever met," he said.

She gave a shaky half bow.

"I am old. I am a field scientist. I am a teacher. I am a woman. And, I think it's fair at this point to say, I am Appalachian as well. It is a rather tough combination."

Her voice was thin. Her shoulders shivered. Her breathing was labored. But there was still that wicked fairy fire in her eyes.

Valentina Blackwood.

He didn't know how much of that name was original to her. He didn't know how she was still alive. He didn't know even a fraction of her story, but something told him he knew the parts that counted and he was in absolute awe of her.

She returned her attention to the dark path and he followed suit.

Between the dark and Valentina's gait, their progress was slow.

He visited Catskill in his thoughts.

The wolf was always moving, always questing with the same certainty of purpose.

Cornfields.

Pinewoods.

A weedy lot full of huge spools of wire and telephone poles stacked like cordwood.

Racing across the brush-choked foothills with hummingbird speed and agility.

No distraction.

No fatigue.

Green couldn't keep his mind on Catskill long without losing his footing and veering off the path. Being in the wolf's thoughts for even a second left him feeling disconnected from his own limbs, and when he returned to himself he felt small and slow, painfully slow.

He checked his phone again and again. Nothing and nothing.

They reached the hole near 10 P.M.

"That's not good," Green said as firelight came into view, an orange glow fifty yards down the trail.

As they approached, they heard laughter and voices. A guitar strummed. The empty jangle of a tossed beer can tinkled through the trees.

"Mr. Green, you speak with the children. I will begin the work."

Maybe it was the cold. Maybe the fawn's influence grew after nightfall, but she looked like she'd aged twenty years on the walk. Her shuffle had become a limp. The firelight filtering through the trees revealed the dark stains of frostbite clearly visible on her nose, chin, and cheekbones.

He failed to hide the shock on his face.

"I can imagine how I look. I am losing feeling. We need to hurry."

Green walked forward into the firelight. He cleared his throat as he went, hoping to avoid scaring the people sitting around the campfire. It was no good. The guitar had drowned out their footfalls and the ring of light made the night beyond into a blank black wall.

Jerome fell off his log with a full body flinch that brought a discordant yelp from his guitar. Alf stood and stumbled backward. A young woman swimming in an oversized purple hoodie let out a cry and flicked out a folding knife.

Jerome groaned on the ground, the first real sound Green had ever heard him utter.

"Man, Green, you gotta warn somebody before you lurk outta the woods like that," Alf said.

Jerome set his guitar aside in the leaves and began gathering up the playing cards that had spilled from his coat pocket when he fell.

"Sorry. I tried," Green said.

"I didn't think you'd got my text. Where's my six-pack?"

"I did, I just couldn't answer. Zero service. No beer today, Alf. We're here to work on that . . . business I mentioned earlier."

"We?"

Valentina walked directly toward the Hole in Nothing.

Alf flinched back again when he saw her.

"Shit, bro. Anybody else with you?"

Green shook his head and waved to Jerome and the stranger.

"Hi, I'm Green," he said.

The girl in the hoodie stowed her knife, wrapped an arm around her knees, and half hid behind a curtain of hair dyed gunmetal gray.

"Casper," she said, raising a finger in greeting. Tattoos of wildflowers peeked out from the cuff of her sleeve.

"Oh, thanks for your work on my car."

She dipped her head.

Jerome held up his deck of cards, tilting his arm back and forth like a metronome. Green nodded to him.

Really? Now? Fine.

"Yeah, I got one."

King of clubs.

Jerome flipped over the top card. An ace of hearts.

Green shook his head.

"Sorry."

Jerome stuffed the deck back into his pocket and pulled his guitar onto his lap.

Alf produced an old flip phone and pointed it at Green.

"Gotta drop that smartphone and get one of these, bro. This place doesn't like smart things. Believe me."

His words were slurred.

"And even my texts only get through like half the time out here. Like a message in a bottle. Whoosh. Splash. Tossed into the sea. Hey, what's your friend doing?"

Valentina was shrugging out of her pack in the shadow of the crossed pines.

"She is . . . getting to work."

"Cool. Well, welcome and all that. Pull up a log. You know Jerome. You met Casper. You got some drinking to do to catch up with us."

"Listen, Alf, I've been trying to text you all day. You guys really shouldn't be out here tonight."

"No? Why's that? Don't tell me the moths are involved."

Alf took a pull from a bottle and frowned.

"Alf. Look. This is serious. All those deaths."

Alf swayed on his feet. His expression darkened.

"The deaths? Yeah? What about them?"

"Well, that's why. They're all . . . I mean, those people were all killed by the same thing."

Alf's eyes widened. He tottered back and forth.

"I told you," Casper said to his back.

Jerome looked around at the dark trees.

"Woof. Bro. Well, that ain't good news. Didn't sound like attacks to me. Jerome's cousin, chick named Duke, plays D&D on Tuesdays with a guy who has been installing a new HVAC system at the sheriff's office. He said those campers didn't OD. Said they all froze to death. So, something is, what, freezing people?"

Word gets around fast, apparently.

"Alf, has it been cold enough to freeze people to death?"

"How should I know? I've mostly been an indoor cat lately, smokin' and watchin' streams with Jerome."

Valentina stepped forward into the firelight. Clara's poultice gleamed wetly in two thick lines, above and below her eyes. The effect was something halfway between a zombie and a raccoon. She reached forward and placed the back of her hand against Alf's cheek. He gasped and recoiled from her frigid skin.

"Listen to Mr. Green. You are in danger. This is not a night to wander the woods."

"Shit, lady! You okay?"

Valentina ignored him and limped up to the fire. Her fingers looked stained with wine and seemed to be curled into involuntary claws. She leaned into the heat.

"Sorry, Alf, but you need to listen. You guys need to get going. Get home."

"Okay, okay," Alf said. "Heard, chef."

He took another pull from his drink and glanced back at his friends.

"So, what do you want us to do though?"

"Like I said. Get back home. Get indoors. Someplace with lots of light and sound, if possible. We have business here, but you guys should get to safety."

"Right, bro, the thing is. We were gonna camp here tonight. It's a legit hike to get home. Like . . . hours. And on top of that . . . In answer to your previous question about my drinking, yes, I may be a little bit too drunk to get home."

"I didn't ask about your drinking."

"Touché, Mr. Detective. Well played, bro."

Jerome was fingering chords without strumming, making buzzing phantom music as he moved his fingers on the fretboard.

Casper stood and walked over. She seemed more sober than her friends.

"I live three hours away," she said. "We spent the afternoon getting here. At least here we have the fire. That's something, isn't it? Like, better than walking through dark woods until two A.M., I mean?"

Green thought of the victims at Kinkaid Cabins, the blond girl in the mint green coat. They were sitting around a fire too. Maybe somebody was playing a guitar. It didn't do them much good.

At the same time, a long walk through the woods sounded like the least safe thing in the world when the fawn was actively pursuing sparks of life to snuff. Here, at least, he could warn them to run if the fawn approached. He would know because Catskill would know. Yet, they were also sitting in the heart of the fawn's territory. If Valentina and Clara were correct, they were camping alongside the mechanism that maintained the fawn's foothold in reality, the mechanism Valentina was about to attack.

He looked to his teacher.

Her resting expression had become a wince. The pale wisps of her frozen breath vanished into the campfire smoke.

"I believe you are correct in thinking the walk home may be the greater danger," Valentina said. "The decision, of course, is yours."

Alf hooked a thumb at the fire.

"Well, we got light. Jerome's got sound covered. I plan to be out cold in a tent in the next couple hours. I'm gonna stick to that plan. Brother, I've made all sorts of bad decisions and these mountains keep letting me live anyway."

Casper studied the rising sparks.

The little bubble of firelight created a dome of smoky, shifting branches beyond which the stars were muted glimmers.

"Yeah," she said. "Me, too, I guess. What is it, anyway? Some kind of monster?"

"Not a monster," Green said. "An animal. But it's dangerous and we're trying to figure out how to keep everyone safe."

He wasn't sure that logic applied to something from outside their universe, but Valentina met his eyes and gave him the slightest of nods.

Jerome began playing again, a low and slow version of "Folsom Prison Blues."

To Green's surprise, the young man sang as he played. He had a good voice, deep and resonant.

Alf sighed.

"Shit, bro. Old man music. He loves the sad old man music. Gotta say, though, it kinda fits the vibe. For once."

"Alf, did you make the brochure for this place? The one I saw in the station?"

"That I did."

"And for Candle-Fly too?"

"I made most of those flyers."

"Why?"

Alf took another drink and tilted his head from side to side.

"Because the best things don't give a shit about advertising. It's a favor. Or a hobby. Or, hell, I don't know, man. You gotta do something, right? You ever worked at a gas station?"

"Do you actually work at that gas station?"

"Not on paper, but yeah."

Valentina moved toward the barricade and Green watched her go.

"What made you think this place was worth visiting? It's dangerous."

"Have you seen it?"

"We came here a few days ago. I told you that."

"Nah, man, like I said, not during the day. Go look."

Alf rose and set his beer on the log, spilling it immediately. Foam cascaded. He turned and went to the barricade. Green followed.

"See? Hang on. You're too damn tall, bro. Bend down."

Alf was swaying on his feet, standing next to Valentina. The Hole in Nothing was a patch of dark between the crossed trees. There was nothing to see.

Green walked over and took a knee. He leaned over the barricade and put his cheek on the rough bark of the top branch. Then he saw.

The weather and the firelight made the sky above him a drab, dim nothing. The sky viewed through the hole was different. There, in the crook where the two leaning trees met, a wedge of sky was visible over the horizon. It was like a picture of deep space, black marbled with veins of blue and violet. The stars were vivid, dusted across the darkness like spilled crystals.

Valentina hunched down as well, staring up at the pie slice of cosmos.

"Lovely," she said.

Green looked back to Alf.

He was smiling, his arms spread wide.

"See? Kinda seems like a stupid flyer is the least I can do, don't it?"

"I . . . see your point."

Alf turned his face up to the sky.

"Quelle surprise. He sees my point. And if you haven't figured it out yet, bro, those flyers are mostly for me. Like, reminders. Shit, I'm not supposed to be there. The flyers ain't supposed to be there. The room with that rack ain't supposed to be there."

Alf broke off in drunken laughter.

"The damn moths ain't supposed to be there."

He spun around in slow circles, eyes on the treetops, turning like a carousel. A branch caught his foot and he spilled onto the ground, laughing as he fell. He stood and walked back to the fire, picking leaves from his hair.

Green looked back to the vivid sky beyond the crossed pines.

Valentina's breath was a strained wheezing in his ear. Up close, he could smell the poultice, a mixed scent of old fish and clay.

"Any idea why it looks like that?" he asked.

Her tired eyes looked distant.

"I knew that sky. It is the sky of a different time. Before electric lights blanketed so much of this country and world."

"Why would the rift show us that?"

Valentina shook her head.

"I don't know. Time distortion, perhaps."

Green gave his mind over to the storybook stars.

Behind teacher and apprentice, the friends at the fire found their voices again.

The wind flowed down the mountainside.

Leaves spun and slid across the forest floor with a rattle and hiss.

Jerome played on. Alf had a loud one-sided conversation with Casper. Valentina studied the ghost of a sky from another lifetime.

Green stood in the midst of them all feeling a deep longing, a childhood longing, an aching certainty that if he only knew more, he could protect himself from his mistakes, he could be useful and meaningful and correct. He had already stepped through an improbable gate and found himself in a new kind of life. He was just beginning to understand his own new place in the world. Now, he just wished he could preserve it. He was tired of strange thresholds and new worlds.

Catskill's thoughts were there in the dark beyond the firelight and the dark behind his own nascent instincts.

He saw the fawn through the wolf's eyes, moonlight in the shape of a deer, slipping between the trees of a distant ridge. It had once carried with it a spell of eerie beauty. That spell was thin and powerless now that Green had witnessed the alien creature's innate wrongness up close, had witnessed the consequences of its presence.

One way or another, this has to end.

CHAPTER 17

CLARA'S BROADCAST

This is Clara Rodriguez broadcasting on Crypto-Naturalist frequency 11-58-1.

I'm speaking on behalf of Valentina Blackwood.

Perhaps she is listening now, but I doubt it. I expect that she is on her way to do something possibly kind and certainly dangerous.

Many of you listening to this know Valentina well. Hell, many of us have lived and studied with that menacing old creature.

"Here's your toast. We might be eaten alive today. Grab your galoshes."

If she gets you when you're young, she lives in your head forever.

I know she lives in mine.

Well, I'm not young anymore and I've been thinking about old Val.

I was trying to recall a single time I've heard her ask for real help and I came up empty. Now, we've all heard her share opportunity, calls to study, or announcements about singular events, but that's not asking for help. Not really. She shares the crop, but not the sowing or the harvest work.

We spoke earlier today, and again this evening. She asked me to do this broadcast.

Alright, not this broadcast exactly.

She asked me to share warnings.

Firstly, observing the decay of a rag moth's body should not be considered safe. Details are foggy, but Val's new apprentice is not a vanilla human and his observations can't be fully trusted as evidence of safety.

She knows how to pick 'em, doesn't she?

I met the young man. He seems sweet.

Similarly and secondly, the glass fawn is a lethal danger and simply getting within a hundred meters or so of the creature is likely fatal.

So, naturally, she did exactly that.

She made light of it when I spoke to her, because of course she did. Of course.

My guess is that she needs help and that she'd likely scold us for showing up to offer it.

I'm in my ninth decade now and I think I've finally reached an age where I don't particularly give a damn if Valentina scolds me. Better late than never.

Look here, if you're able to go, go.

I doubt there is anything to be done tonight, but I know there are more than a few of you who could be there by tomorrow morning. She'd never ask you to, but I am asking.

Valentina may, at this moment, be walking through a dimension gate with no way to know if she'll come out the other side whole or at all.

Honestly, I expect she won't. This rift is a nasty piece of business.

Recent evidence suggests the glass fawn is from outside our reality. Not from the shadow place. Not a threshold gap. Not from one of the braided timelines, a mirror world, or the long hallway. I'm talkin' a full outsider. Val and I believe that enduring hole on that mountain of hers is what's allowing the creature to remain. So, she's going to shut it, whatever the cost.

When . . . if . . . the worst happens, that green apprentice of hers will be left wandering alone in the woods. He'll need us.

I won't call her plans foolish. Nobody can do the risk-to-reward calculus on that course of action but she herself. That kind, weird old bat knows her business better than we do.

But if she does step through . . . and if she does come back injured or changed . . . I want her to see faces from the community she helped build, even if she just rolls her eyes at each and every one of you.

There's a crawler node on that mountain. "Stone jaw," in crawler tongue.

And I know many of you have your own methods of expedited travel.

Use them.

If she's angry, blame me. What's she gonna do about it?

We don't want that apprentice of hers to try anything drastic, especially if he panics. I can only guess what she has tucked away in that camp of hers.

That fella is terribly fresh and maybe a little cursed with outsize talent.

Well.

Who am I to judge someone else as strange, eh?

Now, that's enough chin-waggin' from me.

If you've got prayer or something like it, send it Valentina's way. She can be irked by my requests all she wants after she's back home safe and whole. Knock on wood.

If you're hearing this later, Val, and you think me stubborn and cantankerous, well just ask yourself who my role model might be.

I love you all. Spare a thought for your elder tonight and I don't mean me.

Clara Rodriguez, signing off.

CHAPTER 18

STEPPING THROUGH

VALENTINA STOOD DANGEROUSLY CLOSE TO THE HOLE IN Nothing. She was making her final attempt to will shut the rift, to heal reality and cast out the fawn by severing its tether to the outside. It was her last chance to avoid stepping through.

The teenagers sitting fireside fell silent, watching Green and Valentina poised like statues on the wrong side of the barrier.

Long minutes passed. Green hovered his hand just behind her collar. She was swaying like a reed and he worried that she could pass out at any moment. He tried to add his own will and hope to her efforts, desperately wishing to protect his new friend and guide.

Somewhere, a barred owl hooted his territorial "who cooks for you" call.

A log popped in the fire.

He stayed tense, his eyes on Valentina's shoulders, ready to snag her when she fell.

Nothing.

Nothing.

Nothing.

A gust of cold wind whipped through the trees, parting Valentina's hair and showing a paper-white line of scalp. Green shifted his weight from foot to foot.

He risked a check on Catskill.

He saw the fawn rolling down the side of a steep ravine like a luminous pearl. The wolf raced behind, down a near-vertical surface. Both creatures were unaffected by the landscape, but Green's stomach turned as he pulled his thoughts away.

When his mind stepped back up to the window of his own eyes, Valentina was looking at him.

Her face was drawn and haggard.

"It's not working. I'm going to get my pack. I may need it if I arrive somewhere unexpected. It's time I step through and close it."

His throat tightened.

"Wait, let me try. I haven't tried yet. Give me some of that poultice."

"Mr. Green, look at me. It wouldn't do any good. I have had practice with this sort of thing and I am getting nowhere. Your job here is to monitor the fawn."

"What if we tried together, side by side?"

She shook her head.

"My vision is beginning to tunnel. Even if closing the hole merely deposits me back here, whole and free of the fawn's influence, I may have already waited too long to survive these injuries."

"And if you experience one of that thing's more extreme effects?"

"Then it won't matter, but within the scope of what I can control, I will prepare for the more hopeful outcome."

Green couldn't help imagining his teacher transformed into a plume of greasy smoke or sun-bleached bones clattering to the ground as she stepped through.

Even then, what if it doesn't work? What if she sacrifices herself for nothing and the hole stays open, and the fawn stays and kills again?

"I am going to get my pack. In order to will the hole shut from inside, I need to be conscious. I told you to prepare yourself for this."

"I'm just asking if we've tried everything."

"No, of course we haven't, but I am dying. Others may be dying. And . . . it's more than that."

"What do you mean more?"

"I mean that wolf in your head is this ecosystem's primary immune response to an invader like the fawn. Like a white blood cell attacking a bacterium. And that response is failing. There is a reason that the glass fawn has only been seen a handful of times. Whenever it squirms its way into our universe, nature rejects its presence. That rejection is breaking down here."

"If Catskill had more time, maybe he could break the stalemate."

"He doesn't. Neither do I."

She wrapped herself into a hug and stood shivering in the dark.

"The world looks resilient to humans because we live fast, distracted lives. We do not feel the planet spinning beneath our feet. We do not have much firsthand experience with systemic fragility. Many of the cataclysms we know of are locked safely behind the glass of the fossil record. Stone seems solid and the seas appear immutable. It is an illusion. Yes, the Earth is resilient, but ecosystems? Ecosystems are a green film above a thin layer of soil. So many species, including us, hang in the sky like hot-air balloons. A simple fire. A sheet of nylon separating the warm air from the cool, producing lift. We think nothing will disturb these systems because we do not remember them being disturbed. We have been in the basket of the balloon all our lives."

Green looked at her death's mask face and wondered if these would be his last, defining memories of his brief mentor.

"I know that ecosystems can be fragile. I'm talking about you. I'm talking about not exhausting all the options available to us."

"And I'm trying to get you to understand that the glass fawn isn't just an individual threat, nor is it a slow accumulation of greenhouse gases. It is not arctic ice melt or a warming sea. We work in the realm of ecologies built on the backs of single organisms. What is the glass fawn in terms of that framework? A thing from outside our reality that tore a hole in the world to get in."

"You're saying Catskill is failing to stop a dangerous trespasser. I get it."

A strange, territorial anger flashed across Green's mind like heat lightning.

Valentina started limping toward her pack.

"No, I don't think he is failing to chase a fox away from a chicken coop. I think he is failing to turn away a dagger sinking toward the heart of life in these mountains. And it is quite possible I am thinking too small. Nature does not let the glass fawn stay in our world. Not anywhere. Biology doesn't tend to produce globally observable needless behaviors."

Dread, certain as the mountain, dug a well in Green's core and dropped stone after stone into its echoing depths.

Plunk.

Plunk.

Plunk.

"If we just had a little more time."

"Mr. Green, every breath hurts now. I have endured and spoken and explained this much to reflect my very high opinion of you and your potential, but this needs to be over and done."

She dragged her pack close to the warming fire.

There was nothing left to say. He bit back empty protests and nodded at his teacher. He looked up and saw that Alf, Jerome, and Casper were all staring at them, listening to their conversation.

Alf stood, unsteady, clutching a bottle in both hands.

"I'm . . . I'm real sorry."

Valentina turned to him.

"So am I."

She stood in the firelight and reached trembling, frostbitten hands toward the flames. Jerome set aside his guitar, stood, and wordlessly lifted her pack. Casper helped her feed stiff, unresponsive arms through the straps.

"Perhaps I am on my way to stand beneath that antique sky once more. Perhaps even a reunion with old friends. Stranger things have happened. I never tested the anomaly with a living animal. Its effect on me may not mimic a pine log. It's impossible to know."

She opened her mouth to speak, then closed it. Then started again.

"Mr. Green, I cannot honestly say that I expect we will meet again, but I can honestly say I hope we do."

He forced on a smile, then a landslide of terror hit him like a wave of shattered stone.

It's coming.

It's coming.

It's coming.

Catskill burst through the door of Green's mind. There was a fleeting image of the fawn blurring across the landscape, stretching to the horizon like spilled watercolors, outstripping its own afterimage. Then the light all collapsed into the distance and it was gone. Terribly, utterly gone.

Green staggered and fell to his knees, returning to himself just as his teeth cracked together.

A breath later, and he was back and shaping warnings on his tongue.

It felt impossible that it was already too late.

It was already too late.

The fawn was there.

It was just there, stepping from the shadows into the ring of firelight.

A bad punch line.

A tragedy so complete and absurd it was comedy.

Valentina stood by the fire. Alf and his friends hung about in their loose circle. Green swayed on his knees.

Then, they fell.

Valentina, Alf, Jerome, and Casper tumbled to the dirt with obscene little thuds.

Each of them convulsed on the ground like toppled windup toys and the fawn wasn't even looking at them. It didn't even pay them the respect of its active attention.

It was looking at Green.

Green didn't have a chance to stand before the buzzing disk in the center of the fawn's head drew his eyes and left him bodiless in the white wastes of an alien blizzard.

He passed long, weightless hours in that featureless nowhere, feeling paradoxically bereft of physical form and somehow soiled. A senseless feeling of urgency gnawed at him, but there was nowhere to stand and analyze it. There was no solid ground. There was no geometry, no motion, no breaths to measure out the time. And if there was a job to do, any job at all, it must be to unmake the galling, hateful thoughts that stained the pale, smooth blankness. The perfect forever. The pristine oblivion. The unbroken winter.

Something shook the world and Green's consciousness flickered back into his skull just as clods of earth rained down, knocking the fire into a column of sparks and dimming the light.

Catskill erupted from the soil, given speed like thought by the mountains that were his breath and blood.

Green surfaced from a thousand years of deep, frigid water and gasped in a breath.

The wolf was at his side.

Taking hold of a lupine shoulder that rippled like liquid stone, Green hauled himself to his feet.

His mouth tasted like burning plastic. He spat. There was a kick inside his chest as his heart remembered to beat. Then, the horned wolf and Green growled as one.

The fawn didn't move and already Green could feel too many fingers tapping at his windowpanes, reaching for his mind.

"Hold its thoughts," Green said.

Catskill took a step forward, the shadows rolling back from his head, a dark flower blooming into a skull. His jaw dropped open in a toothy, wolfish grin, a jagged mountain range of darkness rising on his back like a map of the young Appalachian range a billion years before the first mammal huddled in its den.

The fawn reared back on its hind legs like a ram about to charge, then just stood in defiance of gravity. A bent, luminous figure full of arrhythmic, pulsing motion. Within its head, the too-perfect disk awoke between the dark spots that weren't quite eyes. The disk shivered and spun, an organ that excreted corruption.

Green felt the oil of the fawn's thoughts slide from his mind as Catskill began his mental assault.

There was a moment of odd, frozen peace.

He looked at the monstrous wolf standing at his shoulder, the creature who had made his first nights in the mountains a terror, now his brother and his strength.

He looked at the fawn, the first cryptid he had seen at Candle-Fly Camp, the form he thought ghostly and beautiful, an avatar of the ephemeral beauty and mystery of existence.

He looked to Alf and his friends. They were shivering violently, face down among the dirt and cinders. He thought of Mr. Reynard beneath his thin blanket. He thought of the dark, sightless eyes of half-buried songbirds. How long could they have left to live? Seconds?

Beyond the firelight, there was something wrong with the trees. They were slipping. Losing focus. A profound elsewhere was exerting a new kind of gravity on the little clearing. Reality was breaking.

He looked to his teacher. She was on her back, teetering on her pack like an overturned tortoise, but her dark-rimmed eyes were fully awake and focused on Green.

A terrible clarity touched a single cold finger to his brow and he had the urge to scream.

He did not scream.

Words came to him.

A croaking voice that seemed to fall into his thoughts from somewhere in the dark sky.

Make the choice.

He tugged on a crooked smile.

Already ice was crystallizing in his beard, spreading like lichen on stone.

He reached for the acorn, pulling it from his pocket. Bringing it up to eye level, he spoke to the little nut.

"Magic. Because I say so."

Catskill spoke within his mind. There was pain in the words.

Holding difficult . . . it is stronger now.

Green nodded to Valentina. She watched him, her face a frozen mask of pain. He held the acorn up in the space between them and repeated the Crow King's words.

"A beacon. An anchor. A wellspring of courage."

He spoke the words, his choice, his meaning, into the acorn and did his best to believe his own voice.

Hold slipping . . .

He walked to his teacher and placed the acorn in her coat pocket.

"Plant it."

Something drew his eyes down and down beneath his feet, a watchfulness he could feel, something too distant and dark to conjure any images in his head. There were words down there, too, a voice like Catskill's but different.

Protect my pup, mountain-kin.

Green thought his response down deep into the world.

He turned and walked to the fawn.

There was his teacher's way.

The math of the situation. Knowledge. Close the hole to remove the threat.

There was Catskill's way.

Attack the invader bodily. Strength. Let it feel the jaws of the mountain.

There was Green's way.

A childhood memory surfaced, scooping up a small brown spider in a juice cup. Carrying the tiny creature from the kitchen to his mother's tomato plants on the back porch. Returning it to a world of leaves and dappled sunlight.

"So. Let's get you back home."

He stepped up to the glass fawn.

A nosebleed began tapping a drip-drop rhythm on the front of Green's jacket.

From so nearby, it was too painful to look directly at the creature, so he focused on the blurring treetops at the edge of the clearing.

Holding his breath, he leaned forward and bundled the fawn into his arms. He lifted. The deer's substance seeped through his clothing. It stuck to his skin like dry ice and the disk in its head picked at his sinews, trying to untie the knot of his body.

"Hold harder."

Catskill let out a roar and Green felt his body knitting back together.

One of the fawn's limbs went boneless and wrapped laterally around his forearm like ivy.

He walked to the Hole in Nothing carrying the fawn.

The hole had grown, swallowing the crossed pines. As he watched, the makeshift barrier tilted and vanished into the hungry nothing. A murmuration of dark birds erupted from the far side of the void with a clap of thunder.

It was impossible.

It was simple.

He walked to the edge of the growing emptiness, turning to look back at the chaos of the clearing.

It began to snow in his thoughts and he knew Catskill was losing his fight.

"What a strange, beautiful world," he said.

Somewhere, an unlikely cricket chirped in defiance of the cold.

Green shut his eyes, set his intention, and stepped through the Hole in Nothing.

The doorstep was not a place.

Green was falling in every direction at once. Expanding. Losing cohesion. He had no recognizable senses because he had no sense organs. The organizing principles that allowed a body to be a body were back on the other side of the door, the door he had just willed shut.

Yet, somehow, he did have awareness.

Brains were not brains in that liminal gap of fractured, kaleidoscopic potentialities, but he still had thought.

There was pain, but the sensation was like an item listed on a written inventory. Impersonal. Important only in that it was still his to claim.

Within the cacophony of his unbound mind, unrestrained by linear time or finite nerve cells, concepts roiling like a spherical sea hovering in deep space, one idea called loudest for Green's attention.

I am not alone.

The glass fawn was no longer a fawn. No longer squeezed into shape within the narrow, prescriptive confines of reality, it blossomed into a borderless, fecund meadowland of long, finger-rich hands, into the concepts of grasping and beckoning.

Even in that place with no direction, he knew those fleshy thickets were reaching out from something.

He sent his awareness running down those many-jointed fingers, rivulets of his mind tracing the thing to its source, raindrops seeking for groundwater.

What he found was a vast, lightless disk of emptiness that pricked his understanding by embodying absence while still having teeth to chew.

It hated its own manifested fawn-thing as it hated Green as it hated all diversity of form and perspective. It hated its imprisoning compulsion to exist and to hate.

There was no direction, and still he could feel himself being dragged toward that hungry, grasping thing. He had no body, but it was touching him all the same. Greed and disdain, a galling, violent aversion for all things, bled from the fawn-place like a sustained scream.

Green wanted to resist.

He thought of resistance.

It was like stomping the brakes while the car slid across ice toward oncoming traffic.

Resist with what? Push against what?

The gnawing outsider was like a black hole at the center of a questing galaxy of needful mouths and Green was just a pebble tossed into its gravity well.

Maybe it won't even hurt. At least not forever.

There was a sound in that place with no sound.

A sound like the distant caw of a crow.

What had the king told him?

Desire may move us as sure as blood and bone . . .

He called for the memory and it surfaced from the liquid cluster of his experiences like a breaching whale.

Magic and meaning. Desire and choice.

He had made his choice, the choice to save his friends.

I made other choices.

The acorn.

He sent his awareness streaming out in all directions.

Somewhere, away from the thing clutching him, there was a green speck like a shining emerald. His beacon. His anchor. His acorn.

Yet, how could it matter? Green was just Green. The thing that would devour him was a timeless elemental force strong enough to threaten his entire universe.

His mind began speaking with the voices of others, those he carried with him.

The Crow King spoke.

You think it is bigger than you? There is no size where you are. Meaning, old friend. Your meaning is as strong as you choose.

Valentina spoke.

Mr. Green, you are a cryptonaturalist. If you're quite finished with your observations, there is work to be done.

Catskill spoke.

Crush the unreal thing. You are the mountain's kin. The mountain calls you home.

Dancer walked out of the dark, took off her hat, scratched her scalp, and looked around.

Huh. Pretty weird, bud. I'm not leaving one of my hats in this place, but I'll keep one warm for ya.

She tossed him an empty cup.

I'm trusting you to return that.

Even without hands, he caught it. The metal was cool on his fingers. It smelled like sassafras.

He turned toward home.

As he began to slip away from the biting disk, the soundless sensation of the fawn's scream intensified.

Green tried to will peace into all that endless winter of agonized hunger.

Yet, he knew he couldn't make that choice for the outsider.

He could choose only for himself.

CHAPTER 19

REMEMBRANCES

<u>*V. Blackwood: Journal 516, PG 64*</u>

It has taken me two months to write this entry. As a best practice, I prefer to write these accounts when the event is fresher in my memory. Still, I needed the time I needed.

I suspect no one who reads this will have met my apprentice, Mr. Green. I myself knew him a terribly short time and that time was marked by a string of tragedies. I have detailed those events in previous entries.

A tragic loss is like a lightning strike. In the moment, it is too fast to process with anything beyond instinctual reaction. It is too bright and sudden and absolute. It is a flash and then an emptiness. The real tragedy comes home to us as thunder, rumbling across the distance, that terrible roar of expanding air that shakes the world. The crack. The flash. These are just the birth of a new sorrow. The aftermath is what haunts and harms most acutely. That thunder can roll on for a lifetime. Sometimes, more than one.

I shall say that it speaks well of Mr. Green that the first rumble which followed his loss was, most of all, the rumble of kindness.

There was an outcry of grief from those few here who knew him.

There was a deluge of support from the cryptonaturalist community.

Seven colleagues responded to Ms. Rodriguez's thoughtful and presumptuous broadcast asking for help on my behalf. They arrived early the next morning.

They were:

Juniper Gray
Max Dean
Laksha Patel
Angela Hall
Cat Stone
Jake Threepwood
Willow Armstrong

It was a large gathering by cryptonaturalist standards, though I was hardly in any condition to receive them. They were well-meaning and I was not hospitable. Max Dean broke the lock on my crawler tunnel shed when he arrived from Chicago and Jake Threepwood infuriated me by being both far too ill to travel and utterly unwilling to explain how he got here, but all of that aside, it was still good to see them. In retrospect, if not in the moment.

My injuries were grim. The past two months have been a painful process of sloughing skin and endless wound care. My face, hands, and feet are still a patchwork of raw pink and something resembling reptile molt. Still, I am sensible enough to feel fortunate. My body is healing faster and more completely than I had any right to expect. The Tree of Swans continues to shape my physiology in unpredictable ways. Though on the morning I limped back into camp with the aid of three teenagers, I was not ready to feel fortunate.

The end of the glass fawn's influence made healing possible. Yet, in the short term, the victory seemed primarily to make space for physical and emotional agony. The dead remained dead. The lost remained lost. Injuries were still injuries. Even so, our world continued intact, and I thought it a miracle that the young people who accompanied me sustained only superficial damage. Their psychological burdens may be a different matter.

Ms. Dancer was kind enough to summon an ambulance and deal with questions. I shunned medical care and the complications that would have accompanied it, but I paid a high price of pain and doubt for that decision.

The community members who arrived did the circuitous things people do to show support for a person in a time of suffering and mourning. They cleaned. They made too much food. They endured strained silences to keep me in close proximity to warm bodies.

At some point in my long life, I acquired the ability to shut down sadness when I chose.

At some point later, I acquired the wisdom to realize that sadness has its place and purpose.

What is there to say about Mr. Green?

What is there to say about his actions?

He sacrificed himself to save others. To save me. To save a knot of locals he barely knew and an untold number of strangers he would never meet.

His principles were stronger than his instinct for self-preservation. He picked up the glass fawn, stepped through the Hole in Nothing, and was gone.

The hole vanished with him. Nothing reemerged.

The horned wolf, Catskill, he called it, howled like the north wind, like a wounded thing, and leapt off into the night. I felt the earth tremble at that sound. Imagining what such a creature does in its grief is beyond me. I will not guess.

Perhaps Green lives on in some unknowable way. If I had anticipated events, I could have better prepared him.

Useless thoughts.

Clara and I still suspect that, eventually, his atoms must return to this dimension, though that process may take a decade or it may take a thou-

sand years of slow osmosis through the walls of our reality. Yet, with the hole closed, even that small comfort may only be wishful thinking. I doubt we can begin to conceptualize the number of variables involved.

It is also possible his remains have already returned, nourishing the cycle of living things, a part of the wholeness of nature. Such thoughts carry a kind of comfort for me. Would they have comforted him, I wonder?

My worst fear is that, in carrying the fawn through the hole, Green could have been fully torn away from our version of reality, where we may take for granted such comforts as change or sleep or even our cycles of life and death. I try not to dwell on that fear.

I find myself cherishing a sentimental hope that, if nothing else, his dust returns to these mountains. I want him to be a part of this landscape, this beautiful place that he should have absorbed into his heart over slow years of learning. I want that old wolf who guards this region to know that his human ally has come home to rest.

Fanciful thinking, I know. Something about him encourages that sort of whimsicality. It is difficult to put my finger on precisely why.

I honored Mr. Green's final request, planting his acorn in the center of his campsite. I caged it off from questing squirrels and I can scarcely walk past without checking on its safety.

I paid Ms. Dancer to keep his camp unoccupied, more of a symbolic gesture than a real practical necessity. Now, his hateful vehicle can sit there in peace, no doubt becoming a nesting place for mice now and wasps in the spring. Already, the car has gained a respectable coating of leaves and twigs. Someone tucked a king of clubs playing card beneath one windshield wiper. I cannot guess why.

Ms. Dancer was eager to learn the significance of the caged acorn and I answered her questions. On one frosty morning a few days ago, I caught her sipping from her thermos and talking to it. I believe she was complimenting the sunrise.

I looked in on Alf and Jerome at the Count and Countess gas station last week. How I do loathe that awful place. They were surprisingly well and cheerful. They both had visible discoloration on the tips of their noses, ears, and fingers that I expect will take many months of healing, though I don't think they will scar. I am told the young woman Casper had similar injuries. I did not express to them my thought that it is surpassingly strange any of them survived their encounter with the fawn.

Naturally, our conversation turned to Mr. Green and the quiet young man, Jerome, asked if I thought it was odd to miss someone you barely knew.

I told him, "No."

I do not think it odd at all.

I offered Alf and Jerome the same comfort I offer to myself, the knowledge that Mr. Green achieved precisely what he set out to do. He left his old life far, far behind. He found something meaningful in the woods. He did something worth doing with his time here.

You might assume that losses like this are easier after centuries of living and countless such wounds on my heart.

I wish it were so.

V. Blackwood: Journal 516, PG 101

It is March 12th and the heavy snows of this winter have melted from all but the most shaded hollows. The mountains are muddy and disheveled. Here, a hanging limb broken in the January ice storm. There, a temporary stream of snowmelt carving a trench in the soft topsoil along Moss Man's Row.

There is a fresh smell in the air and the pregnant quiet of a deep breath before a song. The sap is rising. We are at the tail end of maple syrup season and many heavy buckets have visited the sugar shacks and the low, boiling fires. The woods are waking up.

Now it's maple sap. Soon it will be spring beauties. Jack-in-the-pulpit. May apples. The whole green cacophony that feels impossible in early March and inexorable by mid-April.

One awakening is particularly pleasant to me this morning.

The acorn I planted at Mr. Green's campsite has germinated.

I checked the cage just after dawn and there it was, a scruffy sprout that will be a spread of small oak leaves in a few weeks. That little banner of growth suggests that the seedling's taproot is already sunk deep. It is good. I may trim back the surrounding canopy to ensure plenty of sun.

Come autumn, it will be a foot tall.

Twenty autumns later, perhaps forty feet.

Today, it is a small thing, a token thing. It feels like a large victory.

I pointed the seedling out to Ms. Dancer and she fussed over it as if I had shown her pictures of a new baby. She may always be counted upon for enthusiasm. I suggested that if she insisted on watering it with sassafras tea, that it should at least be cooled first.

"Of course I cool it first," she said.

When the snows were a white vastness that grants even our simple, human eyes something akin to real night vision, I thought I saw the horned wolf pacing around Mr. Green's campsite. I suspect it allowed me to see it, though I cannot guess its purpose. There were no tracks the next morning.

Some of my colleagues have asked if I will turn toward a special emphasis on studying the horned wolf, a new and largely unknown cryptid, no doubt an important strand in the web of global cryptoecology. It is certainly a rich avenue of inquiry.

The answer is no.

That line of study strikes me as simultaneously impolite and rather unlikely to yield much new data. I have roved above and below these mountains for more than a century and had never heard so much as a rumor of the horned wolf prior to Mr. Green's arrival. There are many worthy aspects of nature that simply will not humor methodical observation. I have made peace with this.

However, I often tell the askers that I am considering such a study, if only to fend off other researchers for now. Not that the wolf needs my protection. If it does not want to be found, I have complete faith that it will be so.

How humbling is nature? How many lives could you spend studying a single tree and still feel yourself a neophyte in the school of its character? What a gift it is to know that the ship of our curiosity will never run aground in the seas of Earth's mysteries.

V. Blackwood: Journal 516, PG 165

There are many dates that loom large in my mind. Scores of births and deaths. Scores of victories and defeats. Things as trivial as the first time I saw a movie—June 22nd, 1922. Things as distasteful as the first time I was shot—December 13th, 1754.

I was beginning to think most of the dates on the calendar had become significant for one or more noteworthy memories, but October 3rd was not one of them until last year.

A year ago to the day of this writing.

It is a cliché, but it is hard to believe he has been gone a year.

I thank time for numbing pain. I curse time for numbing pain. In all my years of life, I have not decided if the human brain is meant to manufacture contradiction or if contradiction is merely the by-product from other vital processes. The results are the same.

Tonight, I have invited Ms. Dancer to the cabin to share cheese on toast with me in remembrance of the lost. I will drink wine. I will indulge in maudlin frivolity. I will not write about it here.

I have business to attend to before this evening.

There is always more to do and somehow we must honor the parts of us that deserve to mourn the past while also honoring our drive to build a worthy future. Somewhere between those opposing weather fronts is the storm of my present thoughts.

I must return to work.

Today is for the future.

Tonight is for the past.

The present takes care of itself.

CHAPTER 20

STRANGER IN THE WOODS

GREEN STUMBLED BACK INTO REALITY AND FELL NOSE-first into October loam.

He clutched one of Dancer's tin cups to his belly and it knocked the wind from him as he hit the ground. The cup bent beneath his bulk.

This time, he had chosen to put his cheek on the asphalt as the bus rushed to meet him. He did it with open eyes. The fear of entering the rift still vibrated in his limbs.

Stepping through the hole, Green held firm to two intentions. They lingered on like woodsmoke in his beard.

Close the hole. Let the fawn find home and peace.

Already, his recollection of his time on the outside doorstep faded to static, unable to hold together as a narrative and take root in a real, living brain.

His mind papered over the vanishing memory, tying his present to the moment he carried the outsider from the world. He lay still, feeling the absence of the fawn in his arms like a warm cup of coffee on a cold morning.

He understood that he had made the journey home. That was enough.

Is this home?

The ground was cold, but already he was warmer than a moment before.

He filled his lungs with the scent of the forest floor, pipe tobacco and compost, pine and rain, then he rolled to his back.

There was the sky he'd seen through the Hole in Nothing, a glossy field of too many stars. The night sky Green had known most of his life was a faint twinkle through smoked glass, not this jeweler's display of vibrant gems.

What has it done to me? Where am I?

He sat up.

Catskill was no longer turning up the contrast on woodland night. Now, it was truly dark.

A sinking realization hit him. He hadn't worn his pack through the hole. He had no supplies. No food. No fire.

A fragment of poetry fell from the trees and landed in his lap.

> *Sometimes I grow weary of the days, with all their fits and starts.*
> *I want to climb some old gray mountain, slowly, taking*
> *the rest of my lifetime to do it . . .*

He rubbed his eyes and combed fingers through his beard, raining leaf litter on his chest. He stuffed Dancer's now-bent cup into his coat pocket.

Green grappled with an odd, claustrophobic feeling, as if he were a new captain tasked with piloting a body and he found the vessel's quarters too tight for comfort. He focused on taking slow, deep breaths. The sensation passed.

Automatically, he reached for the acorn. Its absence felt like a missing tooth.

He settled for pulling out his cell.

No service.

He considered turning on the flashlight function, but decided it would be better to let his eyes adjust.

Pocketing his phone, he sensed a warm glow nearby and searched for it. The mountainside was uniformly dark, but there was a glimmer in his awareness that had no relationship to sight. Steadying himself, he concentrated on the radiant idea. He found it within, standing near the place Catskill's mind had recently occupied. There was an image of a huge, spreading oak standing tall in a pillar of golden sun. At the tree's base, deep within the wood, he could see an acorn ringed in emerald brilliance. It wasn't there with him in the dark woods. It was elsewhere, a beacon on a distant horizon, a recent addition to his internal landscape.

That's new.

A skitter drew his attention back to the world of tangible things.

A fat squirrel the size of a cat scuffled out of the trees and sat in the nearby dark like a charcoal drawing. A bulge in its cheek distorted the silhouette of its pointed face. Gimlet eyes considered Green.

"Hello," Green said. "I could use the company."

The squirrel opened its jaw wide and the bulge rolled into the black O of its mouth, white as a pearl before the dark limbal rings rose up like a sunrise revealing the orb to be an eye. The eye looked very human. It flitted up and down, taking in the prone man.

"Hey, I know you. A cyclops squirrel."

A mouth opened in the squirrel's belly and it spoke in a rich rolling baritone.

"Hark ye, groundling, do not bury yourself like a nut here, your hull to be cracked in winter's jaws, lest the squirrel queen pluck you up and punish your fraud. Look not upon her. See not her whiskers. Perceive not the arching fountain of her tail."

The taste of ash settled on Green's tongue.

The taste I remember. The talking is new. Sure. Why not?

He clapped his hands together and chuckled.

The squirrel scurried back a foot.

"I may not have my pack, but I can't leave you creatures behind. That's a comfort, I guess."

Getting to his feet, he stretched stiff limbs, twisted at the waist to crack his back, and smiled down at the squirrel. He didn't feel like Catskill was translating. He didn't feel like the squirrel was actually speaking with human language. It didn't seem to matter.

What has the hole done to me?

"Harm me not," the squirrel said. "I am in service to the hidden queen of be-leafed halls."

"Uh-huh. I wouldn't harm you, friend. I'm happy to meet you."

The squirrel cocked its head.

"Is there a town nearby? Where can I find more humans?"

The squirrel scratched beneath its belly-mouth and looked skyward with all three of its eyes.

"Hmm? A riddle? The mill is nearest."

"Not a riddle. Just need directions."

"I see. As you wish. Walk downslope to the river. Shun the ford. Keep the close bank. Follow it north to the mill. Your pace is unknowable, but perhaps you shall reach it before the dawn."

"Thank you, my friend."

"I . . . that is . . . you are . . . quite welcome."

Green nodded, swallowed the bitter taste, stuffed his hands in his pockets, and walked down the dark slope. The world was dim, but the moon and stars made walking possible. The squirrel called after him.

"You shall not see the squirrel queen, yes? You shall forget that I spoke of her?"

Green waved a hand.

"Already forgotten."

"As well you should," the squirrel muttered to itself and raced up a nearby tree to disappear among the latticework of branches.

If not for the past few months, the interaction with the squirrel would have felt like a conclusive departure from reality. Now, it seemed strangely natural. And yet, something was off. Green frowned up at the vivid sky and wondered what his mentor would say.

"Data. Go and find out."

He had no sense of the geography of the area, but "downslope" was an easy enough direction to follow. The mountain felt like the mountain he had walked with Valentina, but the sky told him his journey home was not over yet.

He made an intentional effort to reach toward Catskill in his thoughts and found a profound stillness. Not quite nothing, but not the connection he'd had ten minutes earlier. The landscape didn't seem as dark as before he reached for the wolf. There was something there, something that waited near the strange, distant oak he could sense, but not reach. He could tug on that thread once he had seen to his immediate survival.

He walked through uncertain woods and heard the chiming of little metal gears in his mind. Mr. Reynard sat at a table in the corner of Green's thoughts, working on a picture of a clockwork osprey clutching a clockwork fish in its minute-hand talons. He looked content, just sitting by to keep him company.

In the mental image, Green reclined in a hospital bed, watching his friend work.

"Hey, neighbor. Are you a part of this world?" Green asked.

Mr. Reynard winked, but did not answer.

A cloud shadow fell on the window and Green's imagination was seated on the cot in the cabin.

Valentina entered with toast, smiling her wicked witch smile. Dancer ducked in behind her.

A comforting, monstrous wolf with a great bare skull like a weathered hunk of driftwood sat beside the cot and an oak seedling in an indigo pot decorated the rag moth's table.

I am alive and I am moving forward.

He found the river as night began to fade from the eastern sky. Soon after, he found the mill. The look of the place, coupled with the antique brilliance of the departing stars, shed new light on the situation. Green's heart pounded.

I may be in the right where. But this is not the right when.

Summoning courage, he knocked on the door and met a stone-faced couple who visibly muscled aside their suspicions to offer the strangely dressed newcomer kindness.

They had biscuits.

They had coffee.

They had news of the year.

1894.

He did not vomit when they told him, but it was a close thing.

The Crow King's words came to him.

Forward in your future, but backward in a twin of this world's past . . .

What had Valentina told him about the man who traveled back six minutes? No paradoxes. No changing the future. No meeting yourself. A pocket timeline.

He tried to focus on gratitude. He was back in the world. Perhaps it was too much to expect precision on a return trip from outside reality.

I did pretty well, give or take a hundred years.

Seated at the millers' table, weathering incredulous looks, Green chewed his food mechanically and tried to keep his emotions from his face. Against all odds, he had managed to survive. He had gained a home and lost it. He was more absolutely alone than ever before. Even without the universe's rejection of paradox, he knew nobody in the nineteenth century.

Nobody?

When breakfast was had and talk turned to harnessing the horses and driving the exhausted stranger to Hickory, Green was biting back on a flood of questions, but one slipped through his teeth.

"Do you know anyone by the name of Valentina Blackwood?"

CHAPTER 21

A CHANGE ON THE WIND

IN THE AUTUMN OF THE PRESENT, A YEAR AFTER GREEN went through the Hole in Nothing, a mile beneath the forest, Catskill smelled a shift in the world. It was an air thing. A tree matter. A ripple from far, far above.

May it wait until the spring?

He posed the question to the mountain.

The responding silence said *no*.

He licked at nothing in frustration.

An under-saint was on the move, assembling itself, roaming near the borders of the lower webworks. It was flirting with the idea of entering Catskill's territory to hunt for warm blood. He could feel the compressed sediment of the creature's mind growing a fault line, building up tension. A quake was imminent.

Perhaps it was not a proper wish, but he wanted it to come. He was grateful for the wholesomeness of the task. His duty was clear. It was deliciously straightforward.

The surface call bit his snout, the idea of leaving his cat and mouse game with the giant blasphemy, climbing back up to the bedrock, the sandstone, the aquifers that smelled of air and seas, the too-soft clay and soil.

The year had been odd.

Last autumn gripped his thoughts with unusual ferocity, constantly drawing his mind away from the *now,* which was the seat of his power.

The outsider. The glass fawn. The not-man Green. Sudden kin. Here and gone like bloodroot in April.

It was a unique victory and a unique defeat.

And somehow, impossibly distant, he could still feel his lost packmate. The feeling came and went. Each time, he reached for the sensation, offering a piece of himself, but couldn't quite hold it steady. In a way, the uncertainty of it was more galling than an outright loss.

Far above, autumn had returned to the mountains. He had hoped to stay down deep for the whole season. Let the surface have its seasons. He did not need them.

In winter and spring, he visited Green's old den. He spoke to Green's seedling oak. The tiny tree wore his scent. He brought good earth to her roots and gave her his blessing. Now, he wanted to hunt, to be washed clean of memory by the weight of the mountains, to be a stranger to the sky until the snows fell again.

The dark precipice at the deepest point of his universe called to him whenever his mind turned toward mourning. That call was dangerous. He wanted to drink in the silence of stone and let it heal him.

It didn't matter what he wanted.

Most of all, like his mother before him, he wanted to serve the mountains.

He felt the under-saint's tendrils lazily brushing the stone beneath his paws. He had angled for the perfect ambush for a month.

A careful trap. Wasted.

He growled and felt the saint convulse and slip back into smoke and hideous potential, retreating into abstraction like a groundhog diving for its burrow.

It would return. It had something to prove.

Let it try.

The wolf bared his teeth, then swung the plane of his perception vertically, beginning the journey skyward, running through stone that welcomed his passing.

During his ascent, he tried to focus on the new smell.

What was the change he sensed?

The mountain distrusted unexpected shifts.

So did he.

Yet, the scent did not register as anger.

Not hunger.

Not panic.

Not an invader.

Not an injury.

It was the vibration of an approaching . . . what?

A parallel world. A mirror place. A point of intersection thinning to permeability.

It was a prickle on his skin, the mountain's skin.

Such sensations could presage an unwelcome coming. A threat to solve.

A flux worm or the Fickle Seamstress.

So why did this feel different?

Up through the stone, the hollows, the stacked slate, the clear water, the root thickets, the living soil.

He rose from the earth into the heartwood of autumn, crisp and electric. The world of air and light stood on the border of sleep, where stubborn wakefulness feels the fullness of its power. Creatures that rejected the dormancy of the cold, the dead months, walked the world like orphans left behind by the living warmth.

The sun was setting and the wind swam with a million spent leaves on their pilgrimage back to becoming soil. Catskill stood and raised his muzzle, the red horizon muddying the pale bone of his skull. The smell was clearer here.

A change.

An arrival.

Something was coming, then it was there.

Recognition sprouted ears on his head and stood them at attention.

A latch clicked in the wolf's mind and he tensed.

He was not alone.

A voice spoke inside him.

A voice familiar, yet different.

CHAPTER 22

GONE BUT NOT FORGOTTEN

VALENTINA AND DANCER SAT BESIDE THE CABIN HEARTH toasting bread on long forks and drinking cheap wine from tin mugs.

Valentina pointed.

"That is too close. You are going to burn it."

"Ah, my word, do forgive me if I'm not used to toasting my bread in this very modern, normal, and typical way you've chosen. Gosh, maybe if I had remembered to bring my own long bread fork, I'd be having more luck . . . you absolute wing nut."

Valentina smirked.

"Glass houses, Ms. Dancer."

Dancer raised her mug to her host and Valentina clinked her own against it.

"Is this a funeral, Val? I mean, is this funerary bread I'm toasting? Is that why we're drinking wine? Wine seems like a church drink to me."

Valentina watched the fire. She had told Dancer the story of Green and the fawn a year earlier, but the story did not answer this question.

"I suppose," she said. "Perhaps it should be. He is more absent than if he were simply dead."

"Hell's bells, Val. If you're gonna say stuff like that, you really need to let me switch to whiskey. I brought some."

Valentina pointed at the fire and Dancer saw that her bread had charred black.

"Aw, crackers."

She drew out the fork, examined the smoking wreckage, and tossed the slice into the embers.

"You know, if those solar panels of yours aren't powerful enough to operate a toaster, we can run electric out here. I'm sure I've offered before."

Valentina handed her a new slice of bread.

"I have all the electricity I need, thank you. Toast it slowly."

Dancer grimaced through a sip of wine and skewered her new slice.

"I get that wine was all they had in Bible times or whatnot, but, not unlike toasters, the technology has improved in ways that might surprise you."

She crossed her legs, propped her toasting fork on the toe of one boot, and positioned her bread too near the fire again.

"Green was nice, wasn't he?" Dancer said. "The sort of nice that seems like it isn't taking much effort to perform."

"He was."

"'Course, he was scared witless half the time I knew him."

"He was that, too, yes."

"That makes the 'nice' part all the more special, don't it?"

Valentina nodded.

"But, good gravy, I almost clapped him in a headlock and marched him straight back to civilization after he came near freezing to death on his first night car camping. Then again, I might have acquitted myself similarly if he had met me back in whatever city he was from."

She shuddered at the thought.

"God forbid," she added.

"Mr. Green managed things that people in my profession may strive their whole careers to achieve, and he did them accidentally."

Dancer laughed.

"Yep. That sounds right. You gotta hand it to him though. He owned his haphazardness. Like, you ever meet somebody that you just know gets out of bed each morning trying to win something when what they really need is to learn something?"

"I think that describes a great many people, yes."

"Well, he wasn't that."

"No, he was not."

Valentina was silent for a moment.

"I still cannot believe how often he wore that hat you gave him."

Dancer scoffed.

"Jealousy does not become one of your age and wisdom. I can scarcely believe that a woman who possesses such an august collection of bread-toasting forks fails to recognize elegant headwear when she sees it."

The cabin door was propped open. Wind sent a trio of oak leaves scraping along the packed-earth floor. The air was October chill and smoke, wine and toasting bread.

A small interruption in the breeze tingled the back of Valentina's neck and she turned to the door.

There, at the knife-edge of sight, the horned wolf waited, white skull hanging in the dark distance.

Valentina stood.

She looked at Dancer, then back to the door.

The wolf was gone.

"Val? What is it?"

A crow cawed somewhere high in the branches.

Valentina's eyes were sparkling.

She walked to the wall and retrieved another camp chair. She unfolded it and placed it fireside between her own seat and Dancer's.

"You expecting somebody?"

Dancer threw an arm over the back of her chair and looked out into the night.

Valentina held up a hand for silence.

Then, he stepped inside.

Dancer gasped.

Green paused, smiled, and touched the brim of his hat.

He looked scuffed and sun-ripened, but not much older. His beard was wild. His eyes were deep shadow and moss.

Valentina shook her head.

"I cannot believe you did it," she said. "Did you find another doorway?"

"Oh, I wouldn't put it quite like that," Green said.

His voice was different, a mix of accents she couldn't place. He walked forward, setting Dancer's bent and weathered cup on the rag moth's table.

"How did you manage it? Where have you been for the last year?"

Green stroked his beard.

"A year, eh?"

Valentina narrowed her eyes.

He ran his hand across the tabletop. She watched the motion. A woven bracelet of blooming, multicolored flowers shining like stained glass hung at his wrist, tinkling against the wood. The design was familiar, a protection against southern bramble leeches.

"Mr. Green. How?"

His expression grew distant.

"Well, a century and a fair amount of help from new and old friends didn't hurt," he said. "But, as usual, nature did most of the work."

He took off his hat and moved as if to hang it on an invisible hook.

The hat hovered, then swung across the room with a hornet's buzz before perching on the top corner of a metal shelving unit.

She watched him, struggling with a rare loss for words.

Green cocked his head. Something seemed to draw his attention through the wall, up toward the boughs of the library oak. He smiled and nodded a greeting.

Returning his focus to the cabin, he looked around him like a man stepping into a storybook. Dancer continued staring, open-mouthed as he settled into his camp chair and reached for a toasting fork.

Finally, Valentina found her voice.

"A century?" she asked.

Green grinned at his old teacher.

"Bit of a detour. I took the long way back."

ACKNOWLEDGMENTS

Thank you to my wife, Leslie, for your endless support, advice, and creativity. Having a partner who *gets it* has been a foundational strength of my writing life and I am so grateful.

Thank you to my agent, Rach Crawford, for all your work sharpening this book and finding a wonderful home for it.

Thank you to my editor, Julian Pavia, for your brilliant insights and our many fruitful conversations about the attitudes of crow monarchs and the fickle nature of return trips from outside reality.

Thanks to the entire team at Ballantine Books for making my weird story sparkle. It's a humbling, exhilarating experience to work with such an amazing group of professionals.

Thank you to the big, odd, generous online community of poetry fans and podcast listeners who have been supporting and encouraging my work over the years. From my strange little indie podcast to my often-unconventional poetry, your enthusiastic responses have been a constant, affirming reminder that creative vulnerability, whimsy, and connection are worth the effort. Thanks for being strange animals with me.

ABOUT THE AUTHOR

Jarod K. Anderson is a strange mix of fantasy nerd, nature writer, podcaster, poet, and erstwhile academic. He once accidentally picked up a rattlesnake and has slept in the branches of a maple tree more than most writers. He created and voices *TheCryptoNaturalist,* a podcast about real love for imaginary nature, and he regularly shares his poems and prose on social media. He has published three books of poetry as well as the memoir *Something in the Woods Loves You,* about his lifelong struggle with depression and the healing power of the natural world. He has an MA in early modern English literature and insists he's more fun than that makes him sound. He lives with his wife and son in a little white house tucked between a park and a cemetery.

jarodkanderson.com
Instagram: @cryptonaturalist
Instagram: @jarodkanderson
Bluesky: @jarodkanderson.bsky.social
Facebook.com/Cryptonaturalist
Facebook.com/JarodKAnderson
patreon.com/c/Cryptonaturalist
substack.com/@jarodkanderson

ABOUT THE TYPE

This book was set in Garamond, a typeface originally designed by the Parisian type cutter Claude Garamond (c. 1500–61). This version of Garamond was modeled on a 1592 specimen sheet from the Egenolff-Berner foundry, which was produced from types assumed to have been brought to Frankfurt by the punch cutter Jacques Sabon (c. 1520–80).

Claude Garamond's distinguished romans and italics first appeared in *Opera Ciceronis* in 1543–44. The Garamond types are clear, open, and elegant.